Also by Caleb Wygal

Mytle Beach Mystery Novels

The Brass Key (Short Story Prequel)

Death on the Boardwalk

Death Washes Ashore

Death on the Golden Mile

Death on the Causeway

Death at Tidal Creek

Death on the Back Nine

Lucas Caine Novels

Moment of Impact

A Murder in Concord

Blackbeard's Lost Treasure

The Search for the Fountain of Youth

MYRTLE BEACH BURNS

A MYRTLE BEACH MYSTERY

CALEB WYGAL

Visit the author's website at www.CalebWygal.com

Published by Franklin/Kerr Press
1040 Dale Earnhardt Blvd. #185
Kannapolis, North Carolina 28083
www.FranklinKerr.com

Edited by Lisa Borne Graves
Cover art and design by Mibl Art

Interior design by Jordon Greene
Author photo by Small Seed Photography/Jennifer McGowen

Printed in the United States of America

FIRST EDITION
Large Print ISBN 979-8-3304-1009-5

Fiction: Cozy Mystery
Fiction: Amateur Sleuth
Fiction: Southern Fiction

For Myrtle Beach,

Which sparks inspiration like the never-ending waves lapping against its golden beaches.

CHAPTER ONE

STATIC CRACKLED IN LUCIEN'S headset, but the voices came through loud and clear. One voice was gruff. The second smooth.

Voice 1: **Look, kid. I know I don't always come off seeming like the nicest guy, but I like you. You've been a real help to the department.**

Voice 2: **Appreciate it.**

The voices paused. Rhythmic bumps sounded of tires going over a bridge. Lucien watched a GPS display, particularly the yellow dot in the middle crossing over the bridge spanning the Farrow Parkway exit on a second screen.

Voice 1: **I know you're still held up on what happened with your wife.**

Lucien cursed under his breath. Despite the surly tone of the man's voice and knowledge of his borderline illegal activities, Lucien knew the speaker to be kind. For his sake, Lucien hoped the man didn't step over the line.

Voice 2: **I can't help it. I was almost at a point where I moved on with my life, and then Gomez told me her suspicions. After that, that's all I can think about. I** must **know.**

Voice 1: **I understand.** [heavy breathing] **Let me tell you.**

“Don’t do it,” Lucien whispered, but the voice had no way of hearing his warning. In fact, the speaker didn’t know this conversation was being listened to.

Voice 2: **What?**

Voice 1: **I knew what had happened to you even before we met on that first case.**

Voice 2: **You did?**

Voice 1: **I did. I was supposed to be with Banner that night but had a prior engagement I was unable to break. He kept a tight lid on what had happened, but Gina and I discussed it after his passing.**

Voice 2: **And then we happened to cross paths after I stumbled into**

your investigation of Paige Whitaker's death.

Lucien despised the second voice and the person behind it. Clark. He hated that name. If not for the event he just mentioned, everything would have proceeded according to plan. Now his meddling might ruin it all, but there was still a chance Moody could play right and keep his mouth shut.

Voice 1/Moody: **Correct. It was clear to me that you were still haunted by your wife's death, even before Gina told you about her suspicions.**

The road noise ended as Moody parked his vehicle. The GPS showed that they were outside Clark's home. He'd attached a tracking device to the Jeep. Lucien had the power to detonate the bug and set the fuel ablaze if it came to it. Boom! The thought of doing so with Clark in the car was satisfying.

The door on the police-issued Ford Explorer chimed as the doors opened and then closed. Lucien knew this wasn't the end of the conversation since two doors meant both men exited. There wasn't a camera aimed at that part of Clark's house. If they both went inside, that was a different matter. Like the drive from the police station to Clark's, Lucien could hear but not see.

It didn't matter. It would be enough.

Voice 2/Clark: [faint outside the car] **If you walk me to my door, I'm not giving you a kiss goodnight.**

Smart aleck. Lucien hated Clark's sense of humor. The voices faded. Lucien moved the cursor to a different tab and clicked for the microphone feed that had been planted between cracks in the siding on the front edge of Clark's porch roof. It was invisible to the naked eye.

The feed caught Moody's next words mid-sentence.

Moody: **. . . ship of that house on the Waterway? The one beside that kooky doctor?**

Clark: **You mean the rental?**

Moody: **Yeah. That one.**

Clark: **I did. I couldn't find the name of the person who owns it. Only some anonymous holding company.**

Lucien's blood rushed.

Moody: **What was the name?**

Clark: **Summit Capital Holdings.**

The boss wouldn't like this. The cat was out of the bag.

Moody: **I thought so.**

The detective had better stop talking if he knows what's good for him, Lucien thought, already dreading the phone call he would have to make at the end of Clark and Moody's conversation.

Clark: **I went on the Horry County records search website that you gave me. I punched in the address, and that's what came up. It didn't allow me to dig any deeper into the company.**

Whew! Dodged a bullet there.

Moody: **Going to need you to follow up on the company. Go to the Register**

of Deeds at the county courthouse in Conway.

Clark: **Why? The case is over. Besides, Chief Miller took me off the case.**

Chief Miller was a joke. Nothing more than a pawn in the greater game of chess being played among a tight-knit group of the Myrtle Beach elite.

Moody and Clark discussed the rental house in question. Neither knew its secrets, but for some reason the detective wasn't dropping it. He would if he knew what was good for him. And Clark. Clark mentioned Lucien regarding finding out who printed the steamy pictures they'd found in that idiot Zach's pool house.

Like I'm going to do that, Lucien thought.

Then Moody said the words that sealed his fate: **Look, Clark. There's something I need to tell you. About your wife.**

Clark: **What is it?**

Moody: **I can't tell you tonight.**

Clark: [In a harsh whisper. The microphone was that high tech.] **Then when? Is it about the night of her death?**

[Both whispering now]

Moody: **Not quite. There was a reason I wanted you to hang with me on this case, but I don't want to say more than that right now.**

Clark: **Then when?**

Moody: **Tomorrow. Noon. Remember the place you met Gina and I when**

you had the OceanScapes murder figured out?

Clark: **Yeah. At the Ba—**

Moody: **Don't say the name. I know what you were going to say. Be there. Get Gina there. She needs to hear this too if I'm right.**

It didn't matter if Clark said the full name or not. Lucien knew exactly where they were talking about. It might be more difficult to plant listening devices there before Gina met with Clark. If Gina met with Clark.

Clark: **What if you are?**

Moody: **Then this city might burn to the ground.**

Lucien laughed out loud. That's the truth. The good thing for Lucien, the

boss, and other interested parties was that he was pretty sure the meeting between Moody, Gomez, and Clark would never happen. At least not with all three present.

When the conversation ended, Lucien hit a button on the computer keyboard and pulled out his cell phone.

He punched in a phone number that wasn't saved on his device and never would be. He had it memorized and would delete any record of the call having been made after hanging up. It was late, but Lucien was sure that the boss would be up.

"What do you got?" the voice asked when it answered.

Lucien took a deep breath. "It's Moody. He's gone rogue."

CHAPTER TWO

MOODY GRUNTED AS HE put the Explorer in gear and pulled away from Clark's residence. He'd let his emotions cloud his judgment and knew the clock was ticking.

He called the same phone number Lucien had called. The person on the other end had just ended their brief call with Lucien. Moody had no clue.

Without preamble, Moody said, "He came across Summit Capital Holdings."

Moody figured the person would be angry. The voice on the other end asked without a trace of emotion, “What did you tell him?”

“Nothing.” What Moody said wasn’t a lie, but he didn’t want the person on the other end of the line to know he’d urged Clark to go to the courthouse to ask questions. “They bought the house at the back of Swaying Palms. I’d asked him to find out who owned it. I had no clue it was your people. I swear. I wouldn’t have asked him to do it had I known about it. It was supposed to have been busy work.”

The person didn’t speak as Moody covered the distance on 544 from Prestwick Golf Course to Chick-fil-A. The person knew Moody wasn’t telling the entire truth, but Moody didn’t know about Lucien’s involvement. Everything was compartmentalized. Moody's dishonesty would be dealt with.

"Nothing you would have known."

Moody bit the inside of his lip and asked the question he needed to ask that might lead to the city burning down. Figuratively. Maybe. "Can Summit Capital be traced back to you?"

"Doubtful. If some computer geek at the NSA did some digging, perhaps. If they did, my name isn't attached as ownership, but it could lead to some very uncomfortable questions."

There it was. Moody felt something bordering on elation. He wouldn't touch it. He valued his life, but that didn't mean he wouldn't put Gina and Clark on it. He'd already determined that after meeting with them at the Bar-B-Cue

House, he and Marge would hop on a plane bound for the tropics and stay out of town until the dust settled.

Marge was a unit secretary at the police department and Moody's wife of thirty-four years. They kept packed suitcases in their closets in case they needed to bolt. That time was coming in less than twelve hours.

The person groaned. "Look, I'm not going to sleep tonight. I made up a new batch of what you like, the stuff that helps you sleep. Want some?"

Moody twisted his lip. He would have a hard time sleeping after today and worrying about tomorrow. "Yeah. That's the good stuff. I need some rest. Drop some by if you'd like."

"I'll drop the package off by your front door. Don't want to disturb your missus."

"No, Marge wouldn't appreciate that."

Moody didn't know why the person referred to it as "the package," but the person had their reasons which Moody wouldn't question. The detective knew he was crossing the line and playing a dangerous game.

"It'll be waiting for you."

"Thanks."

The voice said, "Good. Go home and get that rest. Thanks for letting me know about Clark."

The call ended.

Moody went home, retrieved the "package," kissed his wife, and brewed a cup of calming tea for his nerves. He drank his tea and fell asleep, grateful that he had lived to see another day.

It was the last one he would ever see. He never woke up.

CHAPTER THREE

12:37 PM | Bar-B-Cue House | Surfside Beach

I stared at Gina Gomez in disbelief. My body went numb. Moody dead? I'd seen him twelve hours ago. He was alive, surly, and well. Like always. My lips trembled. Moisture pooled in both of my eyes.

Tears welled in hers. The water reflected the sun streaming through the Bar-B-Cue House windows. She looked at me and didn't know what to say. I didn't either.

The waitress approached our table and saw Gina's face, then looked at me. I held up a hand letting her know to give us a few minutes. She nodded and walked across the dining room to check on guests at another table.

Our booth was in the back corner of the restaurant. No one was seated near us. Aromas of pulled pork and brisket drifted through the air. Rock music from the 60s, 70s, and 80s played through overhead speakers. Jim Morrison sang an old The Doors tune. More cars pulled into the lot. The restaurant was starting to get busy.

This wasn't the place to talk about this.

I reached across the table and grabbed her hand. She looked up at me in surprise as I broke her from her thoughts.

“Come on,” I said. “Let’s get out of here.”

Without a word, she climbed out of the booth. Our fingers remained interlocked all the way out of the restaurant to the side of my Jeep. We’d come back and get her car later. I opened the passenger door. Our hands parted. She enveloped me in a deep hug. The fabric on the shoulder of my shirt grew damp with her tears.

After a long time, she released the embrace and quietly thanked me, by kissing my cheek, before I helped her climb into the Jeep.

I went around to the other side, took a deep breath, looked at the sky, felt the side of my face where her lips had touched it, and opened the driver's side door.

This was, in many ways, unreal.

***

We wound through several side streets in the direction of the ocean. The radio droned at low volume. Gomez didn't say a word. She trusted me.

Without speaking, she reached over and grasped my right hand from the steering wheel and pulled it over to lay between us. A swarm of emotions raced inside of me. To me, us holding hands wasn't a display of affection. It was more of a way to signal comfort for her.

Andrea, the woman I had been seeing, might disagree, but right now, I had bigger things to worry about.

I signaled to make a right-hand turn onto Cedar Drive. A green car passed before I made the move. Patchy clouds hung in a light blue sky. As I navigated the turns, I tried to frame what happened to Moody in my mind. At this point, I didn't know any details of how he died, only that he was gone.

He drove me home last night after wrapping up the paperwork at the police station concerning the murder of Zach Lawson.

Moody said there was a reason he wanted me to hang with him on that case. I didn't know that during the investigation. He revealed that last night outside my house. The only thing I figured was that Moody must have known something about Zach that tied into Autumn's death. She died three years ago while at her desk at the city courthouse from what seemed like natural causes. Thanks to Gomez, I'd come to learn that Autumn might have been murdered instead. There were no visible marks on her body, leading me to believe that she was poisoned somehow. I had her cremated and spread her ashes out in international waters. There could be no exhumation to determine if foul play was involved.

The thing that nagged at me, until now, was that Moody had wanted me on the case because of the victim. But it was me searching for the owners of a rental house, behind where Zach was killed, and finding it belonged to a group called Summit Capital Holdings that got Moody's hackles up. The last thing he told me to do was to go to the courthouse in Conway and try to learn more about who owned that house. Had he heard of them?

He left my house last night saying there was something he needed to check. That's why he wanted to meet Gomez and me at the Bar-B-Cue House. I hardly slept last night thinking about what that information could be. It had to have something to do with Autumn.

A year after Gomez revealed her suspicions to me about Autumn's death, it seemed like progress was on the horizon, but all leads came to a screeching halt upon learning about Moody's death. Whatever he knew died with him.

Surfside Beach had paid parking this time of year for non-residents. I had a Surfside Beach address, but it lay in an unincorporated zone outside of the city limits. Even though I drove a golf cart to the beach from my home, I still had to pay to park in my own town.

However, there were a few places I went where I didn't have to pay. Like here. I parked the Jeep on a narrow strip of grass beside a tall white fence just off N. Ocean Boulevard in between a huge SUV and a golf cart.

I reached in the backseat and pulled out a beach towel that I kept there in case I had the sudden urge to go to the beach and get wet. Like now, but without the wet part. After helping Gomez from the car, I led her hand-in-hand across the street, up a beach patrol access ramp between two beach houses, and down onto the beach.

Sunlight glittered on turquoise waves. A brother and sister flew kites near the sand dunes. Brightly colored beach houses stretched to our right until they reached the Surfside Beach Pier and continued to what felt like infinity. The Holiday Inn Oceanfront was on our left, next to the Ocean Lakes Campground. Tourists and locals had their spots picked out along the beach with various colored umbrellas, chairs, and towels. A Jimmy Buffett tune played from someone's small Bluetooth speaker. Seagulls squawked. Women holding bags prospected for shells along the water's edge. People of all ages played in the warm waves.

The chamber of commerce couldn't have asked for a more postcard-perfect day.

The sights, sounds, and smells of happiness played all around us as our world had just come crumbling down.

CHAPTER FOUR

I FOUND A SPOT in the sand away from everyone but with an open view of the ocean and spread out the long beach towel for both of us to sit. Gomez sat and drew her knees up to her chin and wrapped her arms around her shins. I'd grabbed a wad of tissues from the glove box just in case.

Once she was settled, I sat beside her—not quite close enough where our legs touched, but close enough that the scent of her freshly washed hair permeated the air. It carried the fragrance of mint and pomegranate. I resisted the urge to grab a handful of strands and take a big whiff. I loved the smell of shampoo on a woman's hair after a shower.

I wasn't going to rush her into talking about Moody. She needed time to process it all, as did I. Minutes passed as we sat on the towel in the sand. I don't know how long we sat there, but long enough that people came and went from the beach. One woman passed us twice in her search for shells. The ocean crept closer to us. The tide was coming in.

Then she was ready. She cleared her throat. "Marge says they think it was a heart attack."

Hair stood up on the back of my neck.

Gomez said, "He'd been having problems with his heart. Had a minor heart attack a while back and had been going to the doctor about it since then."

Moody had been away at a heart doctor appointment the day I solved the murder of Connor West. He'd compared the health of his heart to an '81 Yugo. There weren't many of them left on the road. A stray memory passed through my head at the thought of that case. It had been Moody who had sent me the initial text, summoning me to the state park at—he claimed—Gomez's request. That did not turn out to be the case. I'd asked myself for months after why he'd done that. Was it because he'd met me, and having a clue as to what really happened to Autumn, he wanted to have me around with the purpose to have me eventually figure it out?

As I'd learned this past weekend, the gruff Moody had a soft side. I would miss him.

"Seems right," I said. A wave crashed in front of us that sent a pair of seagulls into flight. "Except it doesn't."

"What do you mean?" she sniffled.

I counted off each name on my fingers. "Moody, Ed Banner, Autumn. What do they all have in common?"

"They all died of heart attacks."

"In the normal course of nature, one might say it's a mere coincidence. You know my thoughts on coincidences in a mystery."

"There are none."

"Right. This time, a heart attack suggests a pattern. Patterns can be traced. Do you believe in coincidences?"

"Nope," Gomez said, "I'm trained not to."

"Do you think that's a coincidence?"

A short silence, then, "No."

"Me neither. They're all connected."

"What are you saying?"

I looked at her. She looked at me.

I said, "Someone killed them all."

Her eyes searched mine. Slowly, her head bobbed up and down. "I agree."

"What can we do about it?"

"I need to talk to Marge."

"And do what?"

"Push for an autopsy."

“Think she would go for it?”

“I hope. She’s a stern, stubborn woman.”

“Sounds like the type of woman who could’ve kept Moody in line all those years.”

“She was. He had a bit of a mean streak to him that I had to keep reined in.” She smiled softly as if recalling one of those moments.

“I can see that.”

She snorted. “I know you never saw it, but he was quite sarcastic when we caught suspects in a lie.”

I reflected on this past weekend when Moody and I investigated Zach Lawson’s murder. A few snippets of our conversations made me smile. “I caught some of it.”

“I need to go see her anyway. Offer my condolences in person and see if there’s anything I can do.”

“Want me to come?”

She gazed at the ocean, lost in thought. A wave crashed to our right, sending some poor dad head over heels into the water. His kids pointed and laughed.

“No,” she said at length. “This is between us women. Our bond.”

“Is there enough to open an investigation?”

“Let’s see if we can get an autopsy first and go from there.”

“What if his wife doesn’t go for it?”

“Then there would be nothing official to be done.”

"What about unofficial?"

She stared at the breaking waves in front of us and said, "Then you and I will have to team up."

CHAPTER FIVE

MY HEART POUNDED AS the sunlight glittered on the ocean. It seemed like everything was coming to a head. Tony Bruno's admonition to "trust no one" echoed around my skull. Trust no one, that is, except for the woman beside me.

That voice in the back of my head also said I could trust Andrea, Bo, Mom, Dad, and the people who worked for me. Wait. Could I trust all of my employees? For sure, Karen and Margaret were on my side. They'd been at the store since it opened when Autumn helped run the show. They were two of the most dedicated and trustworthy people I'd ever met. What about the young woman who I'd tabbed to run the second bookstore location in Garden City, Winona? Surely, she had nothing to do with this. Or did she? Humphrey was a bumbling oaf who had problems tying his shoes. I didn't think he had the brainpower to be that deceitful. That might be the angle they wanted me to believe, though.

Then again, maybe they were not involved at all. This entire situation was having me jumping at shadows. If Moody was killed to keep him from telling me something about Autumn's death, that meant my life could be in danger as well.

I didn't know what I would do if someone threatened me with physical violence. I didn't know how to shoot a gun, nor did I own any. I've never thrown a punch in my life. Could I do it if needed? Watching fight scenes in movies was one thing, but I had the feeling that real life action like that was much more dangerous than they let on. The explosion that threw me fifteen feet through the air and broke my ribs while trying to track down Brian McConnell gave me a dose of reality. It was only yesterday, which seemed like an eternity ago, when a gun was fired at me on the docks at the Dunes Marina. The splinters the bullet caused to plume when it struck the wooden piling I had been hiding behind at the time were still vibrant in my mind.

Gomez broke into my thoughts. “I need to go speak to Marge.”

“Okay.” I hadn’t made a move to get up. I had other things on my mind. Questions that needed to be answered before proceeding. “Would it be possible to get his cell phone or cell phone records?”

“Moody’s? If there’s an official investigation and we have a warrant. Unless Marge volunteers them to us.”

“Do you think she would?”

She shrugged. “I’ll try to talk her into it.”

“We need to find out if he spoke to anyone after leaving my place last night.”

“I’ll ask her if she knows or just let me take a peek at his phone.”

“Please try.”

“I will. Clark, what are you going to do?”

I traced a trail in the sand with a finger. “Fulfill Moody’s last request to me. It’s the least I can do.”

***

I dropped her off at her car where she gave me a hug across the seat, telling me to be careful. Then I ran through the drive-thru at the Bar-B-Cue House. We didn’t eat lunch, and I’d already smelled the meat smoking. It was an involuntary response to a set of stimuli. My former Psychology 101 professor would be proud I remembered Pavlov and his studies.

With a pulled pork sandwich in hand, I headed up a congested 544 towards

Conway. I'd pass Brooks Stadium and my alma mater, Coastal Carolina, along the way. I didn't take notice of any scenery. My thoughts were on Moody and Autumn. It occurred to me that I should reach out to my parents and Andrea and tell them about his death, but I was in no mood to answer what might be difficult questions. Later.

Traffic backed up going over the long bridge spanning the Waccamaw River into Conway. Downtown Conway looked like many other small-town downtowns built in the early part of the 20th century with brick buildings, churches, banks, sidewalks, and quaint shops and eateries. The Trestle Restaurant was a local favorite, although it had been years since I'd been there.

I hooked a left onto 3rd Avenue, and another left on Elm past the Crafty Rooster to 2nd Avenue and the Horry County Courthouse. It was an imposing courthouse in a cluster of government buildings. I followed signs pointing to various parking lots for the different departments until I found a cramped lot for the Register of Deeds. The temperature inland here was warmer than what it was when Gomez and I sat in the sand earlier, but I could tell cooler weather was ahead.

I navigated my way into and through the building until I reached the Office of the Register of Deeds. A woman with thick, curly hair and glasses stood behind a plexiglass fronted desk. The name on the tag hanging around her neck identified her as Karen Polhemus. A tall Mc-

Donald's cup sat by her left hand on the desk. She must have just come back from lunch. It seemed like there's been a Karen around every corner of my life in the past year.

"Hi. How can I help you?" She showed more enthusiasm than I would expect from a civil servant.

"Yes," I said and removed the sticky note from my pocket containing the address for the rental property that was near Zach's body at Swaying Palms. "I'm trying to learn more about the group who owns a home in Myrtle Beach."

"What type of home? Single family, apartment, townhome?"

"Single family."

“Easy.” She reached beside her and pulled a business card from a stack and reached it under an opening in the plexiglass. “We keep all that information conveniently online. Here’s the web address where you can look at all the properties in Horry County.”

Two other windows were open in the office. Each had a line. We were on the right side of the room. One person stood in line behind me. I didn’t think this office would be this busy on a Monday afternoon. Karen craned her neck to look at the person behind me before straightening it. She was eager to help the next person. “Will that be all?”

I slid the card back across the desk to her and forced a smile. “Actually, I’ve already been on that website and found who owns the property."

She arched an eyebrow. "Then why are you here...if you don't mind me asking?"

"Because I want to learn more about who owns the place." I felt like I'd already explained this. Maybe Karen had a faulty memory. "I clicked their name, but no other information popped up."

She asked the obvious question. "Did you try a Google search?"

"Of course. I couldn't find anything."

She nibbled on her bottom lip. "Hmm. That's quite a pickle. What's the address?"

I read it off to her and she entered it into her computer. While keeping her eyes on the screen, she said, "I see Summit

Capital Holdings as the registered owner. Is that who you found?"

"It is."

"But you couldn't go any farther. Hmm." She tapped a finger on the side of the keyboard in thought. She shifted to the side to get a better view of the person in line behind me. "Excuse me? Can you please use one of the other lines? This is going to take a few minutes."

The woman let out a disgusted grunt and did as she was told.

"Sorry," Karen said. "Give me a minute."

Her fingers moved so fast on the keyboard that it might vaporize. She clicked the mouse several times and the printer under her desk whirred. She said, "Summit Capital Holdings is apparently one of these anonymous corporations like a phantom landlord—it owns all those properties, but good luck trying to trace it back. It's the real estate version of a ghost in the corporate world."

"That's what I was hoping it wasn't."

"I'm sorry I don't have better news for you."

She reached under her desk and pulled out a stack of four sheets of paper. "What I was able to do was print off each property they own. The top sheet is a list of their holdings in Horry County. The next two are all the places we have records of with their name on them in South Carolina, Horry County included. Sorry I couldn't separate them better. The last one has all the information I have on Summit Capital. They're registered in Antigua."

She reached the papers across to me, and I accepted them like they were made of gold.

"Thank you so much," I said.

"Don't mention it," Karen said and leaned forward. "I wasn't supposed to do that, but I recognized you. I love mysteries, including your book, and I figure if you were here trying to find out who owns this place, then you must be trying to solve a case."

I held the papers to my chest. "The biggest case of my life."

I thanked Karen again and she gave me her business card in case I needed anything else and said, “Let me know when your next book comes out.”

I tucked it in my back pocket. It never hurts to have connections. I handed her mine in case she learned anything more.

Two more people had gotten in line behind me, so I ducked into the hallway with the papers in hand. I placed my back against the wall in an out of the way spot and scanned the first sheet. The one with the Horry County properties. It contained ten or so holdings. Several of the addresses were on streets I didn’t recognize. A few were scattered on Kings Highway. Others were around the Carolina Forest area. Three were located on Ocean Boulevard.

I recognized one address immediately. My blood ran cold.

CHAPTER SIX

Before I processed that specific address being on the list, something caused me to look up as a woman passed by. I don't know if it was the motion, her perfume, or my intuition, but if I hadn't, I would have missed out on a golden opportunity. "Judge Whitley?"

She stopped in mid-step to turn in my direction. I had the sense that she'd seen me standing there and was trying to rush past without me seeing or recognizing her.

“Clark Thomas,” she said in an efficient tone. She didn’t possess a Southern or Northern accent. It was clipped. Educated. Washed away by Ivy League classes perhaps. “Long time no see.”

Now wasn’t the time for me to remind her that I’d sent her several emails after learning of Gomez's suspicions about Autumn’s death because I didn’t want to get off on the wrong foot. Autumn clerked for Judge Whitley at the time of her death. I’d combed court records to see if there were any cases on the docket around the time of her death that might have led to someone sending her the threatening text messages and then finding a way to murder her. Whitley’s courtroom dealt with mostly traffic and boating violations. Nothing on the agenda had stood out, and I'd tried to contact her.

My emails had gone unanswered.

Now here she was, standing in front of me. She was short, stocky, and wore unremarkable straight brown hair to her shoulders. She had on a green blouse over navy dress slacks and a comfortable pair of dark shoes.

"Yes," I said. "I don't think we've seen each other since Autumn's memorial service."

"That's it. Nice seeing you again. I hate to run, but I had to come down here to take care of something for the Historic Commission. Take care." She searched my face and hesitated her departure. "Your eyes are red, and your face is puffy. Are you okay?"

I didn't want to admit to this life-hardened woman that I had shed a few tears on the way here. Nor did I want to tell her what happened to Moody because I was suspicious of her silence.

"Yeah," I said. She was obviously in a hurry, but I wasn't going to let her get away that easily. I peeled off the wall and matched her hurried stride after she took my answer as a reason to escape. What she said made a lightbulb turn on in my crowded brain. "Wait. Did you say Historic Commission?"

"Yes. The Historic Commission for Myrtle Beach. I've been the chairman of the board for eight years. I grew up here and helping safeguard our city and its heritage is very rewarding. It's a passion of mine."

"That's right. I remember now."

When I had been a member of the Myrtle Beach Downtown Development Corporation, anytime we'd make plans that involved changing anything, we had to consult with the Historic Commission. I had been a minor member and didn't do much more than voice my opinions. I had little active involvement. It's just as well that I had gotten kicked out after I was busted for breaking and entering at the OceanScapes Resort. Because I hadn't taken a big role in matters, I never had to deal with the Historic Commission, and in turn, Judge Whitley. For those with dissenting opinions on how the corporation should operate, my lack of involvement meant that they couldn't have pointed a finger at Judge Whitley for giving me preferential treatment. She had been my wife's boss after all.

Her role was something that I'd forgotten about after Autumn's death and my leaving the corporation. Since then, they have moved forward with a new Arts and Innovation District initiative to make over downtown Myrtle Beach. The groundwork was already being laid. My good friend, Marilyn, was still a member and had shown me the plans. They were ambitious, no doubt, but with the local university involved, once they were implemented, they would highlight an area of Myrtle Beach that saw little traffic despite being a stone's throw away from the Boardwalk.

The plan involved reinvigorating Main Street at 9th Avenue, a retail hub at the historic Downtown Core, a vibrant civil park, a cultural hub with a children's museum and integration with the Chapin Library. A new, fancy hotel had opened there within the past two years, rising above downtown. There would also be a central civic complex which would include the recently remodeled and expanded City Hall, workforce housing, an art museum, and theater and art spaces to boot. The commission's hope was to create a myriad of life, work, and play opportunities to attract multigenerational visitors and residents alike.

Judge Whitley played a vital role in preserving the history of Myrtle Beach while opening the pathway to the future.

Our chance meeting had an awkward feel to it, but I had to take advantage of this rare opportunity.

She started to continue her travels when I said, “Can I ask you a question right quick? I know you’re in a hurry, but this shouldn’t take long. It’s about Autumn.”

The judge’s shoulders fell sympathetically. She glanced at her smart watch and calculated. “Yes. Of course. What would you like to know?”

I directed her to the side, out of the way. “Do you recall anything shady happening in your courtroom around the time of Autumn’s death?”

Her forehead wrinkled. “There’s always something shady going on in my courtroom. That’s the nature of the people who stand in front of me. Why?”

I searched her eyes for any hint of deception or dodginess. I detected none. I repeated those five words Gomez said to me that changed my life. "I think she was murdered."

Whitley pressed her lips together and closed her eyes. When she reopened them, she looked in both directions before whispering, "What makes you think that?"

Suddenly, the pressing matter she was here to attend to wasn't as pressing. "I've spoken to one of the detectives who came to your office to investigate the night she died and found threatening text messages on her phone from the night before."

Her chin worked back and forth. "Yes, I had gone home early that day and left

Autumn with a pile of paperwork. We had been so busy that day. I felt bad about it at the time, and infinitely worse about it every day since then. My son had an awards ceremony at his school that afternoon that I'd wanted to attend. I had promised to let Autumn have a half day the next day to make up for it since the docket was clear. Earlier that week, she'd put a bug in my ear that she'd like to break off early one day if possible. She'd said something had come up that she'd wanted to surprise you with."

I immediately knew what that surprise had been. "Did she tell you what it was about?"

"No. She said she'd tell me after."

"She was pregnant." I pursed my lips, breathed out, and pressed on. "I suspect that's the news she wanted to tell me about."

Whitley put a hand up to the side of her face. Her eyes grew glossy. "Oh, my goodness. How did you find out?"

An emptiness entered my being at the joy of fatherhood being snatched away from me before I could learn the news from Autumn. "Her mom told me after her death."

"Oh, so she'd confided in her."

"She did." I would never know if we would have had a boy or a girl. I could imagine having a girl like Libby, but not knowing had kept me up late at night wondering what sort of father I would have been. Hopefully, I would've been the best dad.

Thankfully, Whitley had vast experience of keeping the topic of conversation focused through her years on the bench. She steered us back to the matter at hand. "To answer your question, I can't think of any cases that week where someone would have wanted to kill her over. She didn't interact often with the defendants on trial. And why not come after me, who has the power to punish a crime? How do you think she was killed?"

"The only thing we can figure is that she was poisoned somehow. I didn't have an autopsy performed because the signs of a heart attack were apparent."

Whitley said. "Autumn had that heart condition. You would have figured her death was from that."

"I did. That's what the doctor said when it happened."

"You had her cremated, right?"

"I did. There aren't any remains to exhume to run tests on."

"That's unfortunately a stalemate. I don't know what to tell you."

Whitley glanced at her watch again. My time was running out. She was such a difficult person to reach that I wasn't sure if I'd get another chance to speak to her. I could go sit in her courtroom and hope she noticed me, but as the judge, she entered and left the chamber through a door behind the bench. Her office was located out of reach from the public.

"Who has access to your office?"

Her jaw worked back and forth as she formulated a list. It was a trait I noticed in her.

“Let’s see. My staff. Attorneys. Building personnel.”

“So, an extensive list.”

“Yes, especially when you factor in the variety of lawyers who come and go.”

“Are there cameras back there?”

“No. We have three as mandated by the state. One on the main door, the front portion of the courtroom, and on the gallery of spectators.”

“Got it.” It wasn’t a dead end but made the task of narrowing down who might have done it almost impossible without the police’s reach.

She placed a hand on my arm. “Look, I’ll give you my number. If there’s anything you can think of that I can help with, let me know.”

“Thank you.”

We exchanged quick text messages so we would have each other’s contact information. She gave me a curt nod and continued her quest.

She rounded the corner and disappeared. Had I missed something? I wasn’t a CIA human lie detector, but it almost seemed like she hadn’t told me everything. Even though she had promised to help if I had other questions, Tony Bruno’s words of caution again echoed inside my head. “Trust no one.”

CHAPTER SEVEN

I RETURNED TO MY Jeep but didn't start the vehicle. I sat there and stared through the windshield. The brief conversation with Judge Whitley was much too short. I wished she wasn't in such a hurry. Now I had her phone number. I'd let our chance meeting rest a day and then ask her out to coffee. I didn't want to come across as too eager. Something told me to play it cool with her. Besides, I had a lot on my plate at the moment. Not the least being the printouts from Courthouse Karen.

There was one specific address on the list Karen had given me that stood out. It made no sense. I would talk to Gomez about it, but she was going to be tied up dealing with the aftermath of Moody's death. The person to whom the address belonged to also made me cautious in talking to Gomez first about it.

My friend Chris came to mind as someone to go to. I'd wrongly accused him of murder the first time I investigated a case. Being the good chap he is, the two of us became friends and quasi-business partners. He played an integral role in helping me expand to two bookstores and hadn't asked for a dime in doing so. He'd also been alongside me at the ill-fated dinner party on the Golden Mile when John Allen Howard was murdered. Chris had helped me in the crazy aftermath. He possessed a keen analytical mind.

Bo, my brother, might also be someone to bring into the loop. He might be self-absorbed, but his mind worked on another level. He had been a key contributor in the early days of Uber and cashed out into a too-early retirement. It was "too early" because he made millions upon leaving the rideshare company but frittered his money away over the following two years. As of last night, he'd taken up residence at my parents' house.

After starting the engine, I scanned the addresses on the sheet owned by Summit Capital. There was only one troubling address I recognized, but a few others might be near downtown.

Before putting the Jeep in gear, I checked my email on my phone. There were two from Kevin. He worked for Lucien in the forensics department at the MBPD. Apparently, he didn't get the memo that Chief Miller had taken me off the murder investigation involving the slimy real-estate mogul, Zach Lawson.

Kevin had CC'ed me on an email meant for Lucien, Police Chief Sue Miller, and Detectives Moody and Gomez after the case was solved. I figured he was just doing his job and being thorough. The subject line read: **RE: Burner Phones Found in Zach's Pool House**.

After Moody and I had conducted our initial interview with Zach's wife, Paxton, we gained access to their pool house where Zach had taken up residence after their fight. He had planned on divorcing Paxton, and we found divorce papers on the coffee table in the pool house he had yet to deliver to his wife.

Among other odds and ends, Moody discovered three cheap burner phones in Zach's dresser. He'd bagged them up and sent them to the lab.

Now Kevin was sending us the results. I clicked on the email out of pure human curiosity. The case was over. My part was done. The phones should have been meaningless at this point.

"Should have been" being the key phrase. Kevin's findings boggled my mind.

None of the cell phones had ever been used. They were bought, likely with cash to make them untraceable, from

Walmart. He knew their origin from their IMEI numbers. Since they hadn't been used, there were no text messages or call logs for Kevin to forward. The only information he had to convey was the phone models (all Nokia C110s) and attached phone numbers. Since the phones were bought at the same time, the numbers were sequential.

(843) 555-2311

(843) 555-2313

(843) 555-2314

My heart absolutely stopped. There was a missing number in the sequence. It was a number I knew by heart. It was:
(843) 555-2312

The phone number used to send Autumn the threatening text messages the night before her death.

CHAPTER EIGHT

START OF TEXT MESSAGES

He went to the courthouse. Not the city courthouse, but the county one.

Did he go to the Register of Deeds?

Yes. Don't know what he learned, but the clerk gave him a printout.

What was it?

Unknown.

I'll find out.

That's not the worst of it.

What is?

He had a chance encounter with Whitley.

That's what I had hoped to prevent. What did they discuss?

They were in a busy hallway. The microphone was in his pocket. Couldn't hear much. He asked about Autumn's last days.

Was my name mentioned?

No. The judge is too smart for that.

Good. BTW, you're #2 now. Can you handle it?

I'm your man.

Good. Make him think twice about meddling anymore.

Understood.

Keep listening to everything he says. This is top priority. You'll be compensated properly. Let me know if he speaks to Whitley again.

If he does?

I'll take care of him the same way I took care of the others.

END OF TEXT MESSAGES

CHAPTER NINE

I SENT A TEXT message to Gomez:

We need to talk. I learned something but don't know what it means.

Next, I sent Bo a message asking if he was at Mom and Dad's. He responded almost immediately:

Yes.

The trip from Conway back to Surfside Beach passed in a blur, as did the last two hours. It already seemed like yesterday when we'd learned that

Moody was dead. In the span of the 120 minutes that had followed, my life was flip-turned upside down. North was South and East was West. Nothing made sense, and I needed to talk to someone about it.

I tried ringing Chris first, but the call went to his voicemail. I hung up without leaving a message.

Gomez hadn't responded by the time I pulled into Mom and Dad's driveway. Mom came to the door after I rang the bell. It must have been the expression on my face or my body language. She knew the physical signals when her children were put out.

"What is it?" she asked, her brow furrowing in concern.

I didn't answer right away. She wrapped her hands around my waist. Her head came up to my shoulder.

"Whatever it is," she said, "you can tell me."

I couldn't tell her everything. Not at this moment. I needed to make sense of the address and who it belonged to before revealing that in case that could put her in danger. The rest—Moody, the mystery phone number, the conversation with Whitley—came out before I took off my shoes.

She popped another pod of Paul Newman's coffee into her Keurig and hand-delivered a steaming mug to me on the couch. Dad was watching a muted, closed-captioned Braves matinee game on the big screen that dominated their wall. He'd recently replaced his 55" curved TV with an 85" monster flatscreen after explaining that 55" inches was no longer an acceptable size in this day and age." I mentally translated the reason for the change as really saying, "Because he's getting older, his eyes are getting worse, and he has more money than he knows what to do with."

I didn't have a television above 42" but, then again, watching the tube wasn't a big part of my everyday life.

Their living room, dining room, and kitchen were all on one big open floor plan. Each room flowed into the other. The dining room table sat across a gap behind the sofa. Bo had taken up residence at it, with his laptop plugged into a nearby outlet. His fingers danced across the keyboard as he kept half an eye on the game and the other half on his computer screen.

Mom sat down beside Dad on the loveseat, while I sat on the opposite end of the adjacent sofa. Bo was behind me.

“Now, tell me all about it,” Mom said, cradling a red mug in her hands. “Detective Moody died?”

Dad’s eyes became unglued from the TV. “What? Didn’t you just see him last night?”

“I did.”

He sighed. “It happens fast,” he said from experience. He’d served two combat tours during the Vietnam War and had several friends alongside him who had been killed in the line of combat.

“What happened to him?” Mom asked.

The corners of my mouth took an involuntary downward turn. “He died in his sleep. They think it was a heart attack.”

Mom placed a hand on the side of her face. “That’s tragic. How old was he?”

“I’m not sure,” I said, “but I know he was getting close to retirement. Early sixties maybe.”

“Such a shame,” she said.

“It is.” I took a drink of coffee and felt the warmth course through my body. “He had heart problems. Had a heart attack a couple years ago.”

“I’ve seen that among people I grew up with,” Mom said. “Your father and I have several former classmates who died that way. When the first heart attack hits, you're always afraid that the next could be the last."

"Right." I set the mug down on the coffee table and leaned forward. "Here's the thing. He died of a heart attack. A heart attack killed Autumn, and the detective who investigated her death died of one as well."

"Are you suggesting they're connected?" Dad asked, the Braves game forgotten.

Mom has been a voracious reader of mystery novels since her youth. She's read every Agatha Christie, Sherlock Holmes, Ngaio Marsh, and Dorothy Sayers novel many times over. She no longer reads physical copies of books but reads on her tablet instead. Mom had donated almost all her mystery books to Autumn and me when we opened Myrtle Beach Reads. She basically started our Mystery section. She'd read so many fictional murders that she has helped advise me when I've investigated real ones. She knows the patterns.

"That's too big of a coincidence to ignore," Mom said. "All three deaths occur in the same way to people who share a connection?"

"The connection might seem obvious, but there's another connection that I haven't seen or figured out yet," I said. "But I'm getting closer. There's more."

"Like what?" Dad asked.

"You remember the messages someone sent Autumn the night before her death?" I asked.

“Of course,” Mom answered. “They came from some unlisted number.”

“Correct,” I said, lifting the mug to my lips and sipping. “I’ve asked myself over and over why she didn’t come to me. Why didn’t she tell me about them? Knowing the little bit that I know now? I think she was too scared to involve me.”

Upon saying that, I looked at Mom and Dad. I now considered my life in danger. Moody had told me to sleep with a baseball bat under my bed last night. I didn’t sleep at home at all. I came here and crashed in their guest bedroom upstairs. I just told them my suspicions. They were now in danger. I had to protect them. I had to run, but not until I tried to make sense of what I’d learned this afternoon.

But, what if I didn't make it? They killed three people—including my wife—and would never get justice. It was why I could not walk away from any of these cases. The victims had families with unanswered questions, never had closure, never able to move forward, move on, like me. I had to tell them more.

"I discovered who the number belonged to," I said.

Mom and dad's jaws collectively dropped. Bo stood up from his seat at the table and put his hands on the back of the couch. He was now fully engaged.

"Who was it?" Bo asked.

"Zach Lawson."

"You've gotta be kidding me," he replied.

"I wish I were." I sat back and crossed my legs. "Moody and I found three burner phones in Zach's pool house. The forensics technician who processed the phones included me on an email with his findings about the phones' numbers. The phones had never been used, so there were no call or message logs to recover. Their numbers went sequentially, except there was one missing."

"The number who texted Autumn," Mom deduced.

"Correct," I said.

"You mean the guy who did that was the same guy you brushed up against in the clubhouse and then investigated his murder?" Bo asked with a higher octave in his voice.

"Seems like it," I said.

"Was he the one who murdered Autumn?" Dad asked.

I spread my hands. "It's pointing in that direction."

CHAPTER TEN

But wait, there's more, as the saying goes. I hadn't figured out how or why Zach could have done it or the other murders. I relayed this to my family.

"Would it be helpful," Bo asked, "if you knew whether or not Zach had been near the courthouse that day?"

"It absolutely would," I answered. "If we figure that out, we might be able to place him in the same part of the building where Autumn died."

Bo grabbed a half empty beer bottle from the table then came back to behind the couch, standing over me. "Why didn't you tell me about the phone number?"

I squinted. "Because we rarely talked before this weekend. Besides, I'm not sure what it would have mattered."

"Ay-yi-yi." He ran a hand over his face. "Clark, do you not know what I did for Uber?"

When Bo began working for this startup tech company in Silicon Valley, he had described it as a rideshare service. With me not knowing much about coding or programming or even what the word "ridesharing" meant at the time, I just accepted that it was another project my older brother was working on four thousand miles away on the West Coast. I had my own set of problems while trying to get my bookstore off the ground.

“No, I don’t,” I answered.

He ran a finger over the condensation on the side of his bottle. “I designed the module connecting the GPS coordinates of the drivers to our system.”

“I never understood that,” Mom said.

“Me neither,” Dad agreed.

Bo and I shared a look that signaled how we both knew Mom and Dad weren’t exactly up on modern technology.

I said, “Okay. I’m not sure why that matters.”

He smirked like he always did when he used to have to take his little brother by the hand and lead him across the street when we were kids. Me being the little brother.

"Because," he said, "when I did that, I helped design a sophisticated tracking system to collect GPS and acceleration data during trips. That data was then transmitted to our servers for processing and long-term storage. It helped us analyze our drivers' driving expertise. It also helped us alert the authorities when the need arose. The system allowed us to weed out bad drivers, ensuring that our riders were guaranteed their safety."

"Okay," I repeated, drawing out the word.

He laughed. "You don't get it. Let me spell it out for you then. I may be able to get the information you sought when you turned the telephone into the police without having the actual telephone."

Electricity shot through my veins while considering the implications. Why hadn't I thought to ask Bo? He had helped me with the social media help I had needed before. He was more tech savvy than me, but him being capable of this kind of feat was beyond what I had thought he was able to do.

I asked, "What would you need?"

"Come around here." He sat at the table in front of his computer and took a long pull from the bottle, finishing what was left. He set the empty vessel back on the table.

I got up from the couch and walked around, pulling a chair over to sit next to him.

He turned the screen in my direction. "Simple. All I need is a good computer."

Bo explained that he wouldn't be able to trace any routes taken if the person using the phone was in transit. The phone had to be connected to an app, like Uber, to trace actively. As the messages were sent to Autumn three years ago, that wasn't possible. "But, what I can find," Bo explained, "is where any calls or messages were sent from."

"Like what city?"

He shook his head, chuckling. "You don't get it."

I chuckled. "No, I don't. This is over my head."

"The nuts and bolts of it are over most people's heads. Let me put it this way: If the phone was used at an outside table at a restaurant, I can tell you exactly what seat the person was sitting in."

"Wow." I let out a low whistle. "That exact?"

"Yup. I narrow it down to which cell phone towers picked up the signal which then triangulates down to within inches of where the cell phone was being held."

"That's amazing."

"This is child's play compared to some of the things I saw while working in Silicon Valley and training with the CIA."

Bo spent three years in Langley, training and working as an intelligence analyst for the NSA before moving to Silicon Valley. He'd told me when he quit and moved across the country that he'd seen and heard things that would haunt him forever while at the Pentagon. He took his computer expertise with him to do something less traumatizing.

"I bet."

"Give me a sec." He clicked on the touchpad. A window appeared on the screen filled with graphs, numbers, and code I didn't understand in the top part. The bottom section was a Google Map zoomed in our current location in Surfside Beach. "What's the phone number?"

I gave it to him. "I don't know what you can find. The number has been disconnected."

Bo nodded. "Meaning Zach probably tossed the phone off the end of a pier to get rid of the evidence."

"Yeah, or something like that."

After my limited interactions with Zach, it made full sense that he was the person who sent those messages to Autumn. From the time I'd first read them, it seemed like the sender was someone with a big head and position who looked down on lesser mortals.

Mom and Dad had gotten up and crowded around behind us. Dad put his hand on the table to keep himself steady. Mom put her hands on Bo's shoulders.

As he punched the number into a search box, he asked, "How long has the number been out of use?"

"Beats me," I said. "I discovered it and tried calling it about a year ago only to find it had been disconnected. That could have happened long before I did that."

"I imagine Zach destroyed the phone after Autumn's death," Mom said.

"About three years, then," Bo said.

"Will your program still work?" I asked.

"Let's see," he said and stabbed the ENTER key.

The map blinked and then expanded. It was slow moving, but as the data assimilated, blue pins appeared, one by one, on the map clustered around Zach's home on the Golden Mile. A table appeared below the map. As each blue pin appeared, another line of data would be added to the table, starting with the oldest on record. It gave the GPS coordinates, time, and date of each pin. I hoped it would show the phone number Zach had tried to call.

He hadn't used the phone much. Besides the pins around his home, some popped up at a location off Robert Grissom Parkway in the middle of Myrtle Beach. The map widened to indicate a pin at a place in Conway. I was just there. Zach had likely visited the Register of Deeds while conducting business. With the timestamp information, I might be able to figure out what exactly he was doing there. This was helpful.

There were only around fifteen different times the phone had been used in total. The date of each new point grew closer to March 23rd of that year. The day Autumn died.

Then the map did something we weren't expecting. On March 22nd, the map widened by a significant margin.

A feeling of foreboding came over me. My mouth went dry as I grasped for words. "That's not good."

“No,” Mom agreed, not taking her eyes off the screen. “That’s evidence, right?”

No one answered her question. It was more rhetorical. We all knew what the contents on Bo’s screen meant.

“Looks like the last time the phone was used,” Bo said, “was the night before Autumn’s death. The problem isn’t when the messages were sent, but it was where they were sent from.”

I stared closely at the map, trying to see the name. Bo was right. His program narrowed the phone’s location down to a couple feet. In this case, exactness didn’t help. It didn’t matter.

Zach had sent the messages to Autumn from a house almost two thousand miles away in Bridgetown, Barbados.

***

A full minute passed without any of us commenting. We tried to grasp the meaning of this.

"Hold on," I said, pulling out my phone. "I took a screenshot of the messages he sent to Autumn and saved them in a sticky note."

It didn't take long to find the picture of the messages. My stomach churned while reading them for the thousandth time, but the first since I had discovered who'd sent them. The image showed the time at which message was sent and received. I compared that with the entries on Bo's screen.

"One moment." I squinted to get a clearer view of the data.

"What is it?" Bo asked.

"Not all of the entries listed here coincided with the messages sent to Autumn."

"How so?" Mom said.

I looked from my phone to the screen and back again to be sure. "There were two messages sent before these and one after."

"Oh my," Mom said. "Zach must have been communicating with someone else."

I nodded and stared at the screen. The question was, with who?

CHAPTER ELEVEN

MY PHONE BUZZED. IT was Gomez returning my text: **Miller told me to go home for a few days and mourn. Spoke to Moody's wife. We do need to talk. Where are you?**

It made sense that Chief Miller would give Gomez some sort of bereavement leave, even though she and Moody weren't family. They had been partners for nearly three years, investigating crimes and spending long hours together. His death had already affected her emotionally. I saw that while sitting on the beach with her earlier.

It affected me too. The many questions that surfaced after learning Autumn's death may not have been from natural causes were being answered. Moody had tasked me with investigating Summit Capital Holdings. He may have known more about them than he let on. Why else would he have me go to the Register of Deeds?

My family had stopped talking when they saw me reading Gomez's text.

"What is it?" Mom asked.

"It's Gomez," I said. "She said we need to talk."

"Well, what are you waiting for? Go," Mom urged.

Numbly, I pushed the chair back and got to my feet. Dad clasped a thick hand on my arm. “Promise me you’ll be careful.”

I looked him in the eye. “I won’t do anything stupid.”

“That’s not a promise,” he said.

“I know.”

“Clark,” Mom said. “We know how important this is for you. For us and her parents too. I understand this has gotten bigger than just her death. There’s apparently more to it.”

“Seems so,” I said.

“Here’s all I’ll say about it,” Mom said. “Nothing will ever bring Autumn back. You were the perfect pair. You can take comfort in knowing something.”

“What’s that?”

"That there is life beyond Autumn."

My heart caught in my throat.

Mom rubbed my arm. "You have the hope of a bright future once all this is taken care of. I know you need to put this to rest before you can move on, but you're almost there. This feels like we're in the climax of some great story. Do you feel it?"

Mom had vocalized all the thoughts and hopes I'd had in this entire process. There would never be a point where I put my life with Autumn in a box high upon a shelf and forget about it. She would always be a part of who I am, but I recognized that life moves on whether we like it or not. In a soft voice, I said, "I do. Thank you."

I looked at Bo and pointed at his computer screen. “Can you send me that data?”

“Sure thing.”

“Thanks.” The skills that he used to find where Zach’s burner phone had been used raised an idea. I said to him, “Have you thought about offering services like this to private investigators? I’m sure there’s a market.”

He rubbed a hand on his chin. “Hmm. I could use a job.”

***

I thanked Bo for his help and went upstairs to grab my duffle bag and toiletries. Mom and Dad gave me big hugs and more words of caution before I tossed my gear in the back of the Jeep. I told them I didn't want to put them in harm's way by staying another night, and that I would be in touch.

After I backed out of the driveway and drove along the street exiting Ocean Commons, I called Gomez. When the phone rang, it occurred to me that I left my parents' house without a destination in mind. She didn't answer, and the phone went to voicemail. I didn't leave one, but the phone pinged a second later with a message from her saying she couldn't talk, but to meet her at my bookstore on Ocean Boulevard.

The question I pondered was whether to tell Gomez about a specific address I'd discovered on the printout from the Register of Deeds without confronting the person who I had thought owned it first. I was going to tell her about the phone numbers and Zach's involvement. If she told me in her message that we needed to talk, what had she learned?

Something told me that I might not be getting any sleep anytime soon. As of this moment, I didn't know where I would be sleeping next. If I didn't want to endanger my brother and parents, then I surely didn't want to do that to Andrea and Libby. Speaking of which, I needed to speak to Andrea. We were supposed to have dinner together tonight, but that seemed unlikely at this point.

My mind was abuzz, and tremors ran through my fingers that I couldn't control as I clasped the steering wheel. With all that had happened today and yesterday, I was a wreck.

It was about to get worse.

Much worse.

CHAPTER TWELVE

I DROVE UP OCEAN Boulevard to the Shops on the Boardwalk shopping center where Myrtle Beach Reads was located. It was in a brightly painted strip containing four businesses. My bookstore, Andrea's Coastal Décor, and a souvenir t-shirt shop owned by ancient, cheetah-print yoga pants-wearing, chain-smoking Theresa who didn't hide the fact that she had the hots for me—despite being old enough to be my grandmother. That might be stretching it, but the years of constant cigarette use did not give her a youthful glow. The fourth business, an ice cream parlor, was on the opposite end of the building. The aroma of their baking waffle cones was my kryptonite.

When I drove past the front of the shops, before making a right onto 4th Avenue and into an employee-only parking lot on Flagg Street, the signs on the promenade to both Theresa's I Heart MB Tees shop and the ice cream shop had been taken down. It caused me to wonder if the owner of the building had asked them to do it. Neither of their signs had been exactly pleasing to the eye.

My phone pinged at some point along my journey here. I checked my notifications to find an email from Mayor Rosen's secretary, summoning me to his office at City Hall on Thursday to receive a commendation and the one-dollar fee we had shook hands on to investigate the murder of Zach Lawson. Knowing what I know now, I wished I hadn't pressed palms with him. It seemed like a quick turnaround from solving the case to receiving the award, but by now, it was beginning to become commonplace.

I walked around to the front of the building from the back, careful to avoid the back steps of my store where I'd discovered Paige Whitaker's body. The memory of that made me shudder. That day started all of this, my involvement with helping solve cases. It was what had led to learning Autumn had been murdered. I would not regret the danger I was in now if it led to answers of the most important murder I had to solve.

A bell chimed above the entrance to the bookstore as I entered. The store was busy with tourists and locals browsing the shelves. I stepped around a new Classic Books display Margaret had set up at the front of the store to show off several leatherbound, gold-embossed masterpieces of literature. The likes of Alcott, Dickens, Doyle, Melville, Steinbeck, Hemingway, Austen, and others were all elegantly presented. Karen tended to the coffee bar on one side while Humphrey rang up a customer behind the cash register on the other side. He normally attended to the coffee when he was on duty. He had developed a knack for it, amazingly.

I didn't see Gomez.

After Karen handed a cup of coffee and a receipt to a customer, I was next in line. Karen was short with even shorter blond hair and wore pink eyeglasses. She had been a mainstay at the store since we opened. She and her husband had moved to Myrtle Beach after he'd retired. He fished, but she still enjoyed working. I let her get away with watching Turkish soap operas on her phone during down times, but she never let that get in the way of making sure all her duties were done.

She smiled at me. "Clark, I didn't expect to see you here today. I heard what happened at the marina with the gunfire and all. I was so worried for you."

"You're not the only one," I said. Her mention of a gun firing at me stirred a memory of holding Gomez in my arms while we ducked for cover behind a thick wood piling.

Karen reached across the counter and patted my hand. “So glad you’re safe.”

“Thanks.”

“The usual?” she asked.

I tried to smile. “You know me too well.”

“Coming right up.” She moved to the side to reach under the counter. I kept a stoneware Mickey Mouse mug there I’d gotten from the trip Autumn and I had taken to Disney World in what seemed like a lifetime ago.

When she handed me the mug, she said, “Have you heard what happened with Theresa and Frankie?”

Frankie was the owner of the ice cream parlor. His wife died a decade ago, but he kept running the place despite getting up in years.

"It's like something from one of my soaps," she said. "Theresa and Frankie are getting married and moving to Florida."

On a day of shocking revelations, this news was up there. I had never even seen the two speak to each other. They were both of similar age and single, so it made sense on that level.

"Wow. That's something," I said in an understatement.

"You're telling me."

"What's going on with their businesses?"

Karen always kept her ear to the ground for gossip in and around the Boardwalk. Since this took place literally next door to us, I figured she'd be the first to know what was happening.

"It seems," she said, "that they sold both businesses. Theresa sold it to some guy who's going to open a surf shop, and Frankie sold it to some people who are going to open some sort of exotic restaurant. Like, they're going to make pastries and other dishes from all around the world."

"That's interesting," I said. "It will probably do well since we get so many nationalities who visit here."

"That's what I was thinking," Karen said. "I hope she makes kunefe or baklava."

“I’ve heard of baklava. Is the other one Turkish?”

“Yeah,” she said wistfully. “They eat kunefe in some of my soaps. It always looked so good.”

“Well, I hope you get a chance to try it.”

“Me too.”

A guy came up in line behind me, and I stepped aside to let Karen take care of him instead of my order. He and I nodded at each other. He was of average height and build with curly blonde hair and striking green eyes. He reminded me of someone, but I couldn’t place him out of hand.

“Excuse me,” I said.

“No problem,” he replied. His green eyes weren’t the only thing that was striking.

His voice carried a distinctive ring to it. Like he'd make a good singer. He sounded like a country music artist in town for a gig at the Grand Ole Opry or Alabama Theater.

The bell above the door chimed as Gomez entered. Her eyes were tired, hair uncharacteristically disheveled. She'd had a similar day to mine. I stepped past the guy and met her halfway between the door and coffee counter.

I grabbed her elbow. "What's happened?"

The rims of her eyes were red from tears. She wasn't crying now, but the evidence was there that it was recent. This had been a tough day for all of us.

She brushed her hair off her forehead and out of her eyes. In a voice that was a mix of weariness, strength, and exhaustion, she asked, “Can we talk in your office?”

“Of course. Coffee?”

A scant smile crossed her lips. “Yes, please.”

“I’ll meet you there.”

“Thanks.”

She brushed past me and headed for my office. Her perfume lingered behind.

I grabbed coffee for both of us. I’d served her enough times to know how she liked it. Three creams, two sugars. Oat milk preferably, which I started stocking just for her.

My office was down a short hallway on the left at the back of the store. The right side back held a stockroom full of books. The end of the hall led out to the rarely used delivery alcove. Gomez had left the office door cracked open. I entered holding a cup of coffee in each hand.

A walnut desk took up most of the space. Sunlight streamed through windows set high on the wall. Dust motes danced in the air. Shelves lined the room containing collector editions of novels that I refused to sell and writing manuals. Steven King's On Writing was one that I've read the most. A high-backed leather office chair sat behind the desk. Two comfy, non-leather chairs sat on the other side of the desk.

Gomez had collapsed into the visitor's chair against the wall. The weight of the world was seemingly on her shoulders. Instead of sitting in my usual, comfy seat, I sat beside her and held out a cup.

"Here you go," I said. "You seem like you need this."

She accepted the cup. "Thanks. I wish it were something stronger."

"Sorry. I used to keep a bottle of whiskey in the desk after Autumn died," I down at the drawer where I used to keep the alcohol and then back at Gina. "For days like this."

Gomez looked at me with sad eyes. "I know that had to be so hard on you. What made you stop keeping it there?"

I drank from my mug. "Part of it was not wanting to be drunk at work. Part of it was reaching a point in my mourning where I didn't need it as much." I stopped briefly as a thought struck me. "Part of it was something else."

"What's that?"

In a soft voice, I said, "I met you."

Her lips trembled. She reached out and laid her hand on my arm.

"I remember her from the times I would have to go to the courthouse. Not sure that I ever spoke with her, but she seemed like such a smart and lovely woman."

"More than you know."

Her hand was warm. Comforting on a day of discomfort. We stared at each other. I saw the same conflict in her eyes that was in mine. She had to see it too. It was so strange that, here we were, hours after we learned that her partner and friend had died, trying to make sense of it all, and we were trapped in a moment where we were both trying to figure out what we meant to each other. My epiphany that meeting Gomez a year ago had helped end my depression over losing Autumn, which had driven me to drink during the sad times, told me a lot about how much I cared for Gina. Her vulnerable green eyes didn't bore into mine as much as they tried to penetrate my soul and listen to my thoughts.

As much as I wanted to look into her eyes and tell her that I couldn't stop thinking about her, even when I was with

Andrea, this wasn't the time. There may never be a proper time.

Even if I wished it were, this wasn't the occasion for a deep, personal conversation where we laid all our feelings on the table. I took a deep breath. "What did you learn from Marge?"

She shook her head and drank from her cup. "It's perfect. Thanks."

"Of course."

"She said Moody got home last night, had a cup of tea to unwind, and went to bed."

"And he didn't wake up?"

Gomez bit the corner of her lip. "Just like that. He's gone."

"Did Marge say if he'd talked to anyone or gotten any messages?"

"She said he didn't."

"Did you ask to look at his phone?"

Her jaw dropped. She bit her mouth closed and cursed herself. "No. I should have."

"We need to find out if he talked to anyone after he left my place last night."

"I know." She thought for a moment. "I'll talk to her again."

"I'll go with you."

"Are you sure?"

It would be a difficult time and discussion. If we were able to talk to Marge at all. By now, any family or friends would have arrived to lend her support.

I answered, "Yes, I'm sure. Whatever this is, it involves me."

"Okay. We'll go to his place from here. I'll send her a message."

"Are you going to tell her that you've been put on leave?"

The vulnerability and tenderness in her eyes vanished at the change of topic. A switch from her seldom seen sensitive side to the toughened detective. She'd almost forced me to call her "Gina" instead of "Gomez" when we weren't talking murdery subjects. These past five minutes were a reminder that Gina could be tender and empathetic one moment and Gomez independent and fearless the next.

Gomez was back. "What Marge doesn't know won't hurt her."

"What if Miller finds out?"

"Let her. As far as she's concerned, Moody was a friend of mine too. Not just my partner. I'm just there to lend support."

I liked this defiant, color-outside-the-lines side of Gomez. It reminded me of myself. The new me, that is. The Clark Thomas of two years ago would have stayed in his lane and let the authorities handle it. Now, with Miller in place, I wasn't sure I could.

"Great." I settled into the chair. "What did you and Miller discuss?"

She brought the cup to her lips and sipped slowly, gathering her thoughts. "We talked about Moody's loss and what it meant for the department. She said there was an up-and-coming detective she would pair me with. Jones. He's young, but good. Anyway, she asked me how I was doing, and I told her the truth."

"Not well."

"No," she agreed. "I mentioned what you told me about the last time you and him spoke. When he told you to go to the Register of Deeds and investigate Summit Capital Holdings, even though the case was closed."

"What did she say?"

She removed her hand from my arm and cradled the cup in both hands. "When I said the name "Summit Capital Holdings," Miller's face went blank. It was obvious she knew the name. She said to forget about it. Case closed. When I asked why Moody would have you continue to investigate, that's when she told me to go home for a few days, claiming I was worried about nothing."

I leaned back in my chair. "She knows something."

"Darn straight she does."

A nautical clock on the wall ticked. We stared at each other, letting the implications of Gomez's interaction with Miller sink in.

I broke the silence after drinking the last of my coffee and setting the Mickey Mouse mug on the desk. "When we were at the police station the other night, you and I were talking about Chief Miller in the hallway. Remember that?"

Her head tilted forward.

I said, "We had just apprehended the suspect at the Marina, and you hadn't told Miller we were going to. You told a few of your fellow officers to meet us there instead. You kept her out of the loop. We talked about it in the hallway at the police department, but you said you couldn't discuss it there. You didn't trust Miller, did you?"

Gomez chewed the inside of her lip. "I don't completely."

"Why?"

"It's sort of that same feeling I had about your wife. That she was murdered."

"Intuition?"

"Something like that." Gomez smiled. "My dad was a detective in Hoboken. Right across the Hudson River from Manhattan. He saw about every crime conceivable. Dad was big on trusting his gut and taught me that from an early age. He said I was like him. Told me, listen to yourself. You have great instincts."

"And with Miller, you're listening to your gut?"

Gomez's green eyes bore into mine. "Yes."

"Why?"

She shook her head in defeat. "I don't know yet. Just a feeling I have."

"That feeling had to grow stronger when she had that reaction to hearing Summit Capital Holdings and then told you to adios."

"More now than ever." She blew out a breath that pushed a lock of hair out of her eyes. "But I don't know why."

I placed a hand on her wrist. “I trust you. We need to figure it out.”

She finished my thought. “If we do, it might help us figure out the connection between Zach, Summit Capital Holdings, and Autumn.”

CHAPTER THIRTEEN

GOMEZ FIGURED A SECOND visit to Moody's house to visit his wife wouldn't need advanced notice. Marge liked Gomez. She seemed to think that Marge found her presence comforting. Gomez was a representative from the police department to which Moody had devoted most of his working life.

Gomez offered to drive since she knew where we were going. They say smell is the sense closest linked to memory. Something about where your long-term memory is in your brain in relation to your nose. I didn't think about it until after I had climbed into the passenger seat and caught a whiff of the car freshener and recalled the time she and I had, briefly, made out in this seat. In my mind, I could still feel the door when she had lunged across the center console and pinned me up against the passenger side door.

From the way she was looking at me out of the corner of her eye, she might have been thinking about the same thing.

Breathe in. Breathe out.

I tried to pass that memory out of my thoughts by discussing the matter at hand along the way. We went over what we knew. That is, Moody had tasked me with looking into Summit Capital

Holdings knowing the case where the name was discovered had already been solved. Zach was the one we figured now who sent the threatening text messages to Autumn but was not the apparent murderer, and that both Chief Miller and Judge Whitley seemed to know something they weren't telling. All three were involved somehow, but there wasn't an obvious link between the three.

Except that Tony Bruno had said there was someone running the seedy underbelly of the city.

"After Zach was murdered, Moody and I spoke with Miller in the clubhouse of Swaying Palms. It was about actions needed to proceed with me as part of the investigation. After she walked away,

Moody kept mumbling to himself about something."

"Yeah, he mumbled a lot," Gomez said.

A smile flickered across my face at the memory of one of Moody's personality quirks before it fell. "So, Zach had been murdered, but we didn't learn about Summit Capital Holdings until later. That's when Moody pressed me to dig into it."

"Because he thought it might link to Autumn, right?"

"Yes, but why? What possible connection could he have pulled from such a generically named company?"

Gomez and I were on the same wavelength. She picked up on my train of thought. "He somehow guessed or knew that Zach was a bad customer and played a role in what happened."

We waited at a stoplight on 29th Avenue N. by Broadway at the Beach and Top Golf. Cars crisscrossed in front of us.

"I think he knew but couldn't say," I said. "He wanted me to figure it out."

"Agreed." She shook her head in frustration. "What I can't get over is, if he knew there were crimes being committed, why didn't he say something?"

There was that nagging thought I had since I'd met Moody. I considered myself a good judge of character, and from the moment he shook my hand the first time, I had this thought that I spoke aloud to Gomez. "I wonder if he was on the take."

“Like someone was paying him to keep quiet about their illegal activities? No. I refuse to believe that.”

“Why do you say that?”

“Because I was partners with him for three years. I worked with him every day. If he was doing something on the down low, I would have known.”

The Moody’s lived in The Preserve at Pine Lakes off Robert Grissom Parkway before it crossed over the 17 Bypass and became International Drive. Their home was a new build. After playing half a round of golf with Moody and learning how much he loved to play the game, I was sure he had been satisfied owning a home beside a fairway on the prestigious Pine Lakes Golf and Country Club.

The home builder sign at the front of the neighborhood listed homes in this neighborhood starting at $685K. Having an idea of Moody's salary and knowing that his wife was a unit secretary at police headquarters, it seemed like a stretch that they could afford this place.

I suspected I already knew the answer. In the aftermath of her partner's death, a man she'd worked side-by-side with every day, I didn't want to ask her if she thought Moody was on the take. She had to have a good knowledge of his comings, goings, and interactions. If he was crooked, and I hoped he wasn't, it seemed like she should have known or at least suspected. She hadn't voiced that concern in these past twenty-four hours. The truth was going to come out eventually. Upon seeing where he lived, my hand clinched the door handle.

Gomez navigated through the Pine Lakes neighborhood which was filled with pristine multi-colored homes, yards, cars, and kids playing. The golf course intertwined with the homes. The course was packed today. Golfers and their golf carts were on every hole we passed. After the drenching rains we had on Saturday that had dampened our investigation into Zach's death, I was sure golfers were eager to get back at it.

Moody's home sat in front of a lake on Whitebark Drive beside an empty lot used as a common area between homes where three kids played tag in the verdant green grass. Cars were parked in the street and filled the driveway.

Gomez parked behind a big white Jeep Wagoneer next to the curb.

They lived in a light green one-story home with a two-car garage that had two dormers over top of it, suggesting a bonus room, a front porch with a ceiling fan, and trendy landscaping. It looked like it was finished yesterday. Still had that “new house” smell, so to speak.

We exited the car to find the air filled with the aromas of grilled hot dogs and hamburgers. If I didn’t know any better, I’d swear we’d just pulled up to a Moody family cookout.

“Looks like the family has arrived,” Gomez said as she walked around the car to stand beside me.

“Did Moody have kids?”

She smiled. "A gaggle of them. And grandkids."

The grandkids paid us no attention as they chased each other. A little boy chased two older girls. I didn't know if they were brothers, sisters, or cousins, but all bore a resemblance to Moody. They had the same beakish noses and slumped stature that the late detective possessed.

A tall man with his arms folded across his chest stood on the front porch, keeping watch. He had black hair cut close to the scalp and wore black-rimmed glasses. He had on a white, buttoned up shirt over a pair of light blue seersucker pants. His feet were bare. He was southern relaxed business casual.

Gomez led me up a stone path in the middle of the expansive front yard. The man watched us approach. I took him to be the family protector. The gatekeeper who had final say in who entered. When we got close, he drawled, “Can I help you?”

Gomez answered, “I’m Gina Gomez. Moody’s partner. I was here earlier. You’re Marge’s son, right?”

“I’m Darnell.”

“Right,” Gomez said. “Phil told me how much Marge leaned on you for support after her first husband died. She always spoke about you in glowing terms.”

His serious demeanor cracked with a smile. “I was fourteen when Daddy died. The oldest of three and had to step up and be the man in the family." He tilted his chin at me. "Who's this?"

I stepped forward with an outstretched hand. "Clark. Clark Thomas."

He eyed my hand suspiciously for a beat before shaking it. "Nice to meet you. You work with my stepdad too?"

"Sometimes."

His right eyebrow lowered in confusion.

Gomez explained, "Clark has a knack for solving murders. He worked with Phil this past weekend while I was out of town."

Recognition dawned on his face. "Ah, that's you. Okay. Momma told me about you." He stepped aside. "Go on in. Momma is in the kitchen."

We entered a living room with a high lofted ceiling, big screen TV, and adequate furniture. Nothing too lavish, but tastefully decorated. A baseball game played on the screen. No one was watching. It was just background noise.

Family members milled or sat about in groups, speaking in quiet, somber tones. There would be no squeals of delight in here like we witnessed with the kids out front, which was probably why they were there and not in here. A few people turned our way but didn't speak to us. We were intruders into a private family gathering.

An arched doorway separated the kitchen from the living room. I didn't need Gomez to lead me there, although we walked beside each other. My sniffer detected coffee and cookies. Just what I needed.

Three women worked in the kitchen, preparing desserts and side dishes for a big family dinner. Through the windows, two men sipped beers on the back patio while another tended to the grill. A picturesque lake lay beyond the backyard.

"Back so soon?" Marge asked Gomez as we entered the kitchen. The other two women looked up from where they were mixing ingredients in stainless steel bowls before going back to what they were doing.

"Yeah," she said. "Sorry to bother you again. We have a few important questions that came up that we hoped you could answer." She pointed at me. "This is Clark Thomas, by the way."

Marge took off an oven mitt after she had just pulled out a tray of fresh baked chocolate chip cookies and set it on the counter. Like waffle cones, cookies were also my kryptonite. My stomach grumbled. It had been a long time since lunch. Until now, dinner hadn't crossed my mind, nor where I was going to sleep tonight.

Marge studied me behind thick lenses. "Yes. I think we met at the station. Phil mentioned you once or twice. You were there with a blonde recently, right?"

I wanted to muse over what Moody might have said about me to his wife, but we had more pressing matters. "You have a good memory. I was there to speak with your husband about a guy stealing from a homeowners' association."

She tapped the side of her head. "Got a memory like an elephant." She looked at her family members, and said, "Excuse us for a moment."

Marge grabbed a paper towel, folded it in half, and placed three ooey-gooey cookies on top of it. My pulse surged. "Follow me."

She led us through the living room to an office with glass French doors. It wouldn't be private. The people outside the office would be able to see us conversing inside, but they shouldn't be able to hear us.

Marge popped open a door and led us inside. I followed Gomez and shut the door behind me. The large office contained a wood desk on one side and a bookshelf with some beat-up spy novels, dominated by Robert Ludlum and John le Carré. A sofa flanked by two white side tables fronting a flat screen television was on the other side of the space.

Marge sat heavily on one end of the couch, careful not to let the cookies fall out of the makeshift napkin. I wouldn't have cared. I might have eaten one even if it had landed on the hardwood floor. Five-second rule. Gomez sat on the other end. I wheeled out the chair behind the desk and placed it between where they sat and the TV forming a sort of human triangle.

Marge breathed out a heavy sigh and set the cookies down on the cushion between her and Gomez. "Please, take one. My mom's recipe."

I didn't want to seem too eager, so instead of snapping out my hand like a frog stabbing a fly with its tongue, I did the gentlemanly thing and allowed Gomez to have first choice. She picked up the cookie closest to her and thanked Marge.

Of the two left, I grabbed the one that looked like it had the highest chocolate chip-to-cookie ratio. "Thanks."

"Don't mention it. I needed a break from my sisters anyway. They're overbearing and don't come around too often." In a lower voice, she said, "Not that I mind."

"Glad to help," I said.

"Marge," Gomez said, "I relayed some of what you told me earlier to Clark, but some things have come up that we need to see if you can shed any light on."

I took a bite of my cookie. It was indeed delicious. Not as good as my mom's, but I'd devour an entire tray of these if left to my own devices. That might be my stomach talking.

"Of course," she said. "Not sure what else you would want to know since it looks like a heart attack that got him."

For a woman who lost her longtime husband earlier in the day, and one prior, I had to hand it to Marge. She seemed like a strong woman who dealt with loss in private. Her face didn't display any signs of crying. Her hands were steady. In all, it seemed like a normal day for her.

Maybe the shock of it would take hold later when she was alone.

"We won't take up much of your time," I said, "I promise."

"Sure thing."

"Have you heard of a company called Summit Capital Holdings?"

Marge took a bite of cookie and contemplated. I took the time to have another bite myself.

She said, "Hmm. I'm not sure. Who are they?"

I leaned forward. "That's what we're trying to figure out. Have you heard of them in relation to any of Moody's cases?"

She puckered out her bottom lip. Not the answer we needed. "No. Doesn't ring a bell. What does it have to do with Phil?"

"We don't know," I said. "It came up in the Zachary Lawson murder, and your husband seemed adamant that I check into them."

"Hmm. Have you found anything?"

"Not much," I said. "They're some faceless shell corporation registered in Antigua that had something to do with Zach Lawson. They seem to have purchased several properties in Horry County and other places in South Carolina."

Gomez shifted. "We're thinking that since Zach was a property developer with a real estate license in many states, he might have been Summit Capital's lead agent here."

"Okay," Marge said. "Like I said, haven't heard of them."

"No worries," I said. "We're trying to figure out his urgency in having me check them out for a case that was closed yesterday."

As Marge was Moody's wife and a unit secretary at the police department, she would have some knowledge of what happened over the weekend.

"Did he ask you to do that before or after you caught the murderer?"

"After," I answered.

"Hmm," she hummed again. "Wonder if they have something to do with your wife."

“You know about Autumn?” I asked.

“Of course,” Marge said. “I worked dispatch at the time and was the one who took the call when she died.”

“Oh,” I said. “Well, that’s what we’re trying to learn. Whether Summit Capital had anything to do with Autumn’s death.”

“Hope you do find out,” Marge said.

“Us too,” Gomez said.

It was good to know she was invested in finding Autumn’s killer. This wasn’t the time or place for it, but it struck me that maybe, subliminally, she wanted to help investigate because solving this might release me on some metaphysical level. Like, the truth would set me free.

“Thanks,” I said.

"What else would you like to know?" Marge asked, taking the last bite of her cookie. Mine, sadly, was gone. Gomez still had half of hers, and part of me wished she would offer it to me.

I cleared my throat. "What happened after he came home last night?

"When he came home, he told me to get the bags."

"What bags?"

"We kept two suitcases packed in case we needed to leave the country at a moment's notice. Phil was always the paranoid type. If the country went into disarray, he told me that he'd rather be somewhere, anywhere else. So, I catered to his paranoia."

Gomez asked, “Did he talk to or message anyone?”

Marge shook her head. “Not that I know of. I mean, he could’ve before he got here.”

“Would you mind if we looked at the call logs on his cell phone?” Gomez asked.

Marge pursed her lips. “Can’t. Lucien bagged his work and personal phone as evidence.”

Anger seeped into Gomez’s voice. “What are you talking about? Evidence? They’re not calling his death suspicious.”

“Great question,” I said.

Gomez seemed to accept Marge’s response. There was nothing to be done about it now. “What else did he do?”

Marge sucked in her lips. "He said he was tired and was going to get something to drink and went to sleep."

Her steely exterior cracked, and she began to cry. Gomez glanced at me before sliding across the couch to comfort Marge.

Gomez embraced Moody's grieving wife, causing me to recall the night Autumn died three years ago and the emotions that had poured out of me. I closed my eyes, pictured Autumn's smiling face from that fateful morning when we took a walk on the beach together before going off to our respective jobs. I took a deep breath.

Autumn died of a "heart attack."

Moody's partner, Ed Banner, died of a heart attack a few months later.

And now Moody died in apparently the same manner.

The causes of death, Banner's strange actions inside of Autumn's courthouse office while investigating her death, Tony Bruno's comments about "someone running this city," and Summit Capital Holdings were all linked together. I could feel it deep within my bones.

For all three to die in the same manner, I drew three conclusions. Conspiracy, murder, and poison.

Marge cried into Gomez's shoulder. Here was another person who had to deal with the death of a loved one in whatever was happening in Myrtle Beach.

I lifted myself out of the chair and kneeled on the floor in front of Marge.

Reaching up, I placed a hand on her shoulder. "I'm so sorry for your loss, Marge. Your husband was a good man." Then I paraphrased what Gomez said to me that changed my life. "I think he was murdered the same way I believe my wife was, and I need you to do something for you and me."

I paused as she looked up and met my gaze. Then I had to say it before it was too late, "Authorize an autopsy to prove it."

CHAPTER FOURTEEN

MARGE AND I HAD a real heart-to-heart conversation where I laid out my reasoning and helped her understand the feelings I had when Autumn died. Gomez rubbed Marge's arm in sympathy the entire time and let me handle the talking. If money was an issue, I offered to pay for Moody's autopsy. She said it wasn't.

In the end, Marge acquiesced to the post-mortem procedure. Gomez arranged to have Moody's body taken from the funeral home to MUSC in Charleston for the autopsy to be performed. We'd have our ultimate answer in two days, maybe sooner. Marge said she'd let me know the second she learned the results.

Gomez now had another issue. A work issue. As a detective for the MBPD, if she began conducting a murder inquiry, then she needed to file paperwork to start the process. By not putting it on record, she ran the risk of losing her job if Chief Miller found out.

That was her department. I wasn't going to say anything about it. When I've worked on solving murders in the past, since it wasn't my job, I never had any paperwork to file. Both Gomez and Moody had told me how tedious it was to write up the reports.

When it came to whether she trusted Chief Miller, the answer lay in Gomez's actions. By keeping her boss out of the loop for a second time in as many days, it told me all I needed to know. When Moody had told me last night, before leaving my house, to sleep with a baseball bat under my bed, it wasn't hyperbole. He meant it. There was something criminal happening, and somehow Autumn, Banner, Moody, as well as Gomez and me, were in the middle of it.

We left the Moody residence after the sun had gone down. I hadn't spoken to Andrea today. My stomach was empty, and I didn't know where I would be sleeping tonight. Andrea had offered to let me spend last night on their couch. If I called, that offer might still stand.

After getting the printout from Courthouse Karen about the Capital Summit Holding holdings, I didn't know if I could trust Andrea. If people were watching what I was doing, I needed to confront her somewhere in public rather than in her apartment at Paradise Hideaway. The last thing I would ever want to do is endanger Libby. Nor did I want to speak to her about it over the phone. I wouldn't be able to study her to see her body language.

My feelings with Andrea were conflicted at the moment and wouldn't be resolved until I spoke with her. The thing was, Andrea had never given me a reason to doubt her honesty. A phone call should have been all it took, but with everything that had happened, I couldn't leave anything up to chance. My instinct told me to trust no one, yet I had to let some in only to get answers. Andrea likely could not help with this, being new to the town and all.

The stakes had been raised. I had to rise to the occasion and stay sharp.

When we returned to Gomez's car parked on the street, I took out my cell phone to check my notifications before opening the door. I'm not sure why I chose that moment to do so, but I was frazzled after having the discussion we just had with Marge. That, plus the hunger, meant I wasn't thinking straight. I was light-headed, and my hands were shaking.

Gomez unlocked the car door. I reached for the door handle on the passenger side at the same time I tried to put the phone back in my pocket. With me being all jittery, I missed my pocket and dropped the phone on the pavement. One corner of the phone hit the ground square and the cheap plastic cracked and split open like a thick-skinned Humpty Dumpty falling from the wall. There wasn't a protective case around it. I only used the cheap free phones from my cell phone carrier, so I wouldn't be sad if one broke. Having the latest cell phone was never high on my priority list.

"Aww monkey," I groaned.

Gomez had opened her door but hadn't gotten in yet. With one hand on the door, she asked, "What happened?"

I shook my head in a sad arc. "Dropped my phone. Broke it."

"That's not good. Is it still usable?"

"Let me see."

Sparsely placed streetlamps illuminated the street. The pavement where my phone had fallen was in a shadow created by the Camry. It didn't seem like there were too many pieces to pick up, but I wouldn't get to see them until I was inside the car.

I reached down and groped about until I cradled everything in the crook of my other hand.

"Need me to shine my flashlight on it?" Gomez offered.

I rubbed my hand across the darkened pavement until I was sure there was nothing else there. I hoped Gomez had some hand sanitizer in the car.

"Nah. I got it all, I think."

I opened the car door and climbed inside, careful not to drop anything. Gomez got behind the wheel, turned on the dome light to illuminate the car's interior, and put on her seatbelt. My left hand, the hand I used to feel around on the ground for the phone, was gray with dirt.

"Got any sanitizer?" I asked.

"Yeah." She opened the console between the two seats and fished around.

After getting my belt on, I examined the broken phone in my lap. There were four pieces. The front screen, back cover, battery, and something else. Something metal and round. I had never seen one before but knew instantly what it was. My jitteriness had grown to full-blown shaking upon seeing the extra item in the phone. It wasn't supposed to be there.

Gomez found a bottle of sanitizer and handed it over. She saw the pieces in my lap.

She gasped and held a hand to her mouth. "A bug!"

CHAPTER FIFTEEN

THIS WASN'T ANY OLD bug. Definitely not a Palmetto bug. I would have much rather had one of those things crawling around inside my phone rather than this kind of bug.

This bug was a device to listen to my conversations without my knowledge. Someone had placed it there. What I couldn't figure out in that instant was who?

The bug in question was small, round, and flat. No longer than half an inch in diameter and had a hole in the center. Like a cross between a coin and a small microchip.

Gomez held out her hand. “Let me see that?”

We exchanged the listening device for the sanitizer in her hand. While I pumped a few squirts into my hand and rubbed both together, she held the bug up to the dome light for a better look. A black SUV passed us on the street. Red taillights receded into the distance.

I popped the phone back together, minus the bug, while she examined the device. The phone screen now featured a long, diagonal crack to go along with the other scuffs and scratches it had accumulated in its lifetime. I held in the power button on the side of the phone and blew out a relieved breath when the screen lit.

“Looks like the phone still works,” I said.

Gomez didn’t answer. She held the tiny device side-on, inches from her eyes, like a severely farsighted person trying to read the fine print on a coupon.

“Should we crush it or throw it into the pond or something?” I couldn’t take my eyes off something I’d only seen in spy movies. “Is it listening now?”

Without taking her eyes from it, she said, “It is.”

My throat tightened. We were both aware of what this meant. Whoever was listening knew that their espionage attempt had been compromised. Which meant two things. Either they could go further into hiding, or a scarier thought, come after us.

Gomez flashed a brief smile while continuing to study the device as she rotated it on its side. She muttered a curse.

"What is it?" I asked.

Without responding, Gomez opened her door and stepped out. She looked in both directions before dropping the bug on the pavement and using her shoe to stomp on it. Despite its miniature size, it still made a satisfying crunch on the blacktop.

She bent down to retrieve the remains and climbed back in the car, shutting the door. Holding one hand out flat containing what was left of the bug, Gomez reached into the center console again, pulled out a small evidence bag, and dropped the remnants into it. As she sealed the bag, she said, “It’s worse than I feared.”

My blood ran dry. “How so?”

She furrowed her brow, glanced out the front glass, then back at me. “This entire thing of you needing to watch over your back.”

“What about it?”

“I just.” She paused, composing her thoughts. “I just figured that if someone had it out for you, it would be from some sort of organized crime syndicate.”

“Wasn’t that the subject of the training conference you just got back from yes- terday?”

“Yes. After dealing with Tony Bruno and Stanley Griffin from the Tidal Creek case and having an inkling of what we were up against with Autumn, I signed up specifically for that conference, hoping it could help."

My brain picked out the "we" part of what she just said. It was comforting to know I had someone like Gomez on my side in this. That I wasn't alone. The other thing she said that drew my attention was her going to the conference to possibly help find Autumn's killer.

I looked into her dark green eyes and asked myself, "What kind of person would go through the trouble of doing that for another?"

An answer arose deep within my heart, but I couldn't think about that right now. I tried to shake the thought away. I pointed at the clear bag in her hand. "Beyond the obvious, what's troubling you about that?"

She held it up to her face and studied it again. "What I was getting at was, if anyone would be spying on you, it would be some underground crime organization." She shook the bag. "But this is one of ours."

A jolt of astonishment coursed through me. My gaze fixed on the newfound knowledge.

"How did it get there?" I asked, knowing the answer.

"Someone had to have planted it there," she said. "Has anyone been in possession of your phone? Like, has it gone missing for any length of time before suddenly reappearing?"

"Not that I can think of."

"Has it been out of your eyesight for any length of time?"

Like most people in this new technologically advanced world, my phone has become a part of me. It was always on my person or near me.

A slow, incredulous shake of my head mirrored the disbelief swirling inside of me. Her mention of "time" raised another thought. How long had the bug been inside my phone? It was impossible at this moment to think back on every day and determine when that might have happened. There were times at the bookstore when I would leave the phone at the coffee counter or in my office while busy doing other tasks.

"How long would it take for someone to place the bug in there?" I asked.

"If they're trained at this sort of thing, not long. A few seconds to pop the phone in half, slide this little sucker in there, and put it back together."

I motioned at the bug in the bag. "Do you know if it draws power from the battery, or does it have a finite life span before dying?"

Her eyes went to the bug and back to me. "No, this guy doesn't attach to your battery or anything. It's a mini voice activated recorder. I'd have to ask Lucien, but it seems like they can last for six months or so."

My mouth went dry at the mention of her fiancé. Gomez had great intuition. She'd demonstrated that over the course of us getting to know each other. I considered myself to have the same. I didn't trust Lucien from the moment I'd met him, even after working with him this past weekend. Here was a situation where our instincts conflicted.

I tried to think of a way to avoid doing what she said without alerting her to my hunch about Lucien. There might come a time when that would be unavoidable, but for now, I needed her on my side. A growing sense inside of me, as this day unfolded, was how I was not only close to finding Autumn's killer, but also close to having to confront whatever was happening between Gomez and me.

My eyes shifted to Gomez with a thought that I almost rejected out of hand. I was sure there had been occasions during the past six months where she'd been alone with my phone for more than a few minutes. The suspicion seemed too far-fetched to be real, but Tony Bruno's warning to "Trust no one" echoed through my skull.

"No, no need to do that. A ballpark figure on its lifetime will suffice. The fewer people we loop into this, the better. Besides, he already acted like it was an imposition when we handed over Autumn's cell phone."

Her chin bobbed. "I see what you're saying. So, what now?"

I glanced at my newly repaired and restarted cell phone. "Are there other ways someone can listen to my calls on this?"

“Yeah. There are several programs we and the FBI have access to. It takes a warrant first.”

“Hmm. I can’t think of a reason why there would be a warrant to listen to my calls. I haven’t done anything wrong. The eavesdropping would have to come from somewhere else.”

“Agreed. If they’re using a bug like this, then they’re not sophisticated enough to have access to those programs.”

“Which leaves us where?”

“I don’t know.” Gomez placed a hand across her stomach. “Not sure about you, but I need food. I think better on a full stomach.”

“Great. My stomach is trying to devour the rest of my body.”

“Where should we go?”

It occurred to me that the bug could also have had a GPS signal that allowed them to track my location. Now that Gina had crushed the device, it would have disappeared off their screens, so to speak, then they might get more suspicious and come looking for me. For us.

We had to lay low. I channeled my inner fugitive or spy on the run in one of Moody’s Robert Ludlum novels.

“Do you have cash?” I asked.

“No. I don’t carry cash on me.” She caught on to the reason for my question. “Do you?”

“I keep twenty bucks on me, but I have some stashed at my house in a Crown Royal bag.”

She placed a hand on the steering wheel and looked ahead. “That’ll get us dinner at a drive thru.”

“Okay. Let’s go.”

She put the car in gear and pulled away from the curb. “What are we going to do after that?”

“Head back to the Golden Mile. We need to see if Zach’s wife, Paxton, is home.”

Gomez glanced over at me. “Why her?”

“She might hold the key to all of this and not even know it.”

Paxton had the key alright, just not the key we ever imagined.

CHAPTER SIXTEEN

THE CASH I HAD on hand covered two chicken sandwich combos at the Bojangles off 80th Avenue N near the Publix shopping center. I would have much rather gone across the street and enjoyed a meal at Hook & Barrel, but alas, it was not meant to be. Not this evening. Money and time were not on my side.

Gomez called Paxton Lawson at her beachfront estate on the Golden Mile and told her she needed to swing by and tie up a couple loose ends. Nothing big.

Paxton said that she'd just put her autistic son, Ethan, down for the night, and she had just poured herself a glass of sparkling cider. It was as close to a glass of wine as she could get after suffering a concussion yesterday. Her mom had temporarily moved into a guest room to assist with Ethan. She said to come on by and that she'd open the front gate when we arrived.

Now a widow, Paxton had a full agenda. When Autumn died, I had to take care of the legalities of it myself. It was stressful at the beginning, but some nice people assisted me. Paxton, the aspiring social media influencer, likely had a team of attorneys to handle those matters for her—unless the FBI froze her assets while investigating Zach's web of offshore corporations and possible money laundering.

We scarfed down our sandwiches in the fifteen minutes it took to get from Bojangles to the Lawson estate. The mansion lay hidden behind a tall, brick wall. We pulled to the gate composed of wrought iron bars. Details of the home were difficult to make out in the dark, but landscape lighting gave hints. Still, it was enough to give us a feel for its enormous size.

The gate swung open, allowing Gomez to enter. She curved the car around a stone-paved circular driveway. A grass courtyard lay within the circle, highlighted by a tall water fountain lit from beneath like it belonged on the Las Vegas

Strip. Water cascaded down three tiers to the bottom.

Gomez parked by the front steps. We got out. The sounds of waves crashing came from the other side of the house. Salt air tickled my nostrils.

Just like when Moody and I spoke to her two nights ago, which seemed like an eternity at this point, Paxton met us at her front entrance, consisting of a pair of glass doors with an engraved palmetto tree spanning both. A chandelier hung from the recess above.

Her long, black hair was tied back in a ponytail. She wore a black camisole and a matching pair of pajama pants. Paxton possessed pale skin and an angelic face. It was easy to see why the much older Zach fell for her.

Appearances aren't everything, however. Under the skin, I found Paxton to be self-possessed, aloof, and of what I would consider a questionable lifestyle. Her admission to us during the investigation that she and Zach had an open marriage surprised me at first, until we dug deeper. She was having an affair with Zach's handsome friend from New Zealand, Gideon. Now they could do whatever they wanted to.

By the end of the investigation into Zach's death, I loathed everyone involved, except for Ethan. That little boy stole my heart. Gideon might have been an interesting guy to have a beer with but knowing what he did behind closed doors with his friend's wife made me think twice about that.

Paxton held a goblet filled with sparkling red cider between two fingers as she watched us walk up the stairs to her level. Her cell phone was nowhere in sight. The attention she gave to it while Detective Moody and I asked questions about who might have slayed her husband made me want to chuck it into the ocean. If she pulled it out from her back pocket now, I might be tempted to do so just for the fun of it.

"Hi, Paxton," Gomez said as we approached the top step.

Paxton regarded me without a word and said a cool "Hello" to Gomez.

When we stood on the landing in front of her, she sipped from the glass and savored the dark fluid. The confidence in her eyes that she'd shown on Saturday was gone, replaced by fatigue and anxiety. Okay, I take back what I said about throwing her phone into the waves. I understood what she was going through, and even though she acted like she didn't care, her husband and breadwinner in the family was gone. Her life had instantly gone in a direction she hadn't planned. I didn't know if she was prepared for a life without Zach, but the sun will rise tomorrow. No one is ever ready for that, but we learn that life will go on whether we like it or not. For Paxton, each day would present new problems that called for immediate and potentially life-altering answers.

She finally looked at me and nodded. Now that we were closer, I noticed a thick bandage on the back of her head. A lawyer had come here yesterday afternoon under the guise of discussing Zach's will. Instead, he clubbed her on the back of the head, kidnapped Ethan, and left her for dead.

"How are you?" I asked.

Her stance toward me softened. "Okay. I had a slight concussion and lost some blood. My head hurts, but the doctor prescribed me some pain meds and told me to rest. It throbs, but Mom is here to help with Ethan. Thank you for asking."

"Of course," I said.

Gomez stuck out a hand. "We haven't met, but I'm Gina Gomez, lead detective with the MBPD. I'm so sorry for what happened to you, Zach, and your son, but I'm glad that you and Ethan are safe."

Tears welled in her eyes but didn't cascade down her face. It occurred to me that we were here unofficially. Paxton didn't need to answer any of our questions, but if she didn't know that Gomez had been sent home on leave, then ignorance might be bliss in this case.

Paxton nodded and said to us, "Thank you both for rescuing my son. I don't know what I would have done had I lost him."

"That's what we're here for," Gomez said. "Are you sure you don't mind answering a few questions for us?"

"Sure," she said.

"We found several cheap cell phones in the dresser where Zach was staying in the pool house," Gomez said. "Do you know anything about them?"

Paxton knitted her eyebrows. "No. I never paid attention to what phone he was using. I know he had some he used for business. Why?"

"It's my wife," I said.

Confusion clouded Paxton's eyes as she turned in my direction. "Your wife? What does she have to do with Zach?"

"That's what we're trying to figure out," I said. "Did you hear him talk about a company named Summit Capital Holdings?"

Gomez turned sharply in my direction but didn't speak.

"Yeah. That's one of them," Paxton answered. "He had different companies for different things. Resorts, housing developments, individual homes. That sort of thing. I don't know how he kept track of them all."

When Moody and I picked through the pool house where Zach had taken up residence, we found purchase agreements for properties in Grand Cayman and Guadeloupe with Zach's signature on them. One was to sell. The other was to purchase. The names Zach had used for those contracts were Lawson Luxury International and Salty Sands Holdings. I didn't recall the names of the other parties on either contract. To my knowledge, that paperwork wasn't collected as evidence in the murder case, although the Feds might be interested later.

Gomez asked, "Do you know what specifically Summit Capital was for?"

Paxton took a slow sip from the glass. “I don’t. Why?”

Gomez said, “They are shown as the owners of a house on the golf course near where your husband was killed.”

“And several other places in Horry County,” I added.

“Do you think this group had something to do with Zach?” Paxton asked.

Gomez pursed her lips then said, “We don’t know. That’s what we’re trying to figure out.”

I told Paxton the situation with Autumn in a nutshell, including that the person who sent threatening messages to Autumn the night before she died was likely from a phone Zach owned. “We were able to trace where those messages originated."

"Where was that?"

"Bridgetown, Barbados," I answered.

Paxton placed a finger on her chin. "Zach was part owner of a luxury resort there."

Gomez and I shared a brief, knowing look. This seemed like progress, at last.

I scratched my arm. "Do you know if he was there on March 22nd three years ago?"

"Why that date?" Paxton asked.

I answered, "That was the date before Autumn died and when the messages were sent."

"Okay." Paxton looked into the night sky, trying to recall back that far. Then she did what I hoped she wouldn't do. She pulled a cell phone from her back pocket. "Hold on."

Her fingers danced across the screen in a blur as she held it in one hand and the wineglass in the other. I couldn't see what was on her screen. If it was Instagram again, I'd scream. Whatever she was doing, her thumb moved from left to right, scrolling through something. Had to be her calendar.

"Let's see," Paxton said. "We may not have gotten along in the end, but we always knew where the other was with a shared calendar. I can see every business trip and meeting that he's taken since the early 2010s."

The FBI was going to love that once they started investigating Zach's business affairs.

"Let's see," she said. "Yep. Here it is. He was in Barbados from March 20th through the end of the month on business."

Gomez and I exchanged a quick glance, both thinking the same thing. This confirmed that Zach didn't murder Autumn.

CHAPTER SEVENTEEN

WE ASKED TO TAKE another peek inside the pool house where Zach had been staying before his death. Paxton said that was fine and gave us a key to get in. Since Zach's quarters were still part of a crime scene, I let out a sigh of relief when she didn't ask any questions about why we needed a key to be let in. The crime scene technicians would have one, and I figured that the Feds or police would have taken all her keys to it so she couldn't get in, but perhaps they were more interested in online data or awaited a warrant.

I flicked the light on after unlocking the door. The high-ceilinged interior resembled a dorm room if it were located inside a tropical resort. The counters in the compact kitchen were littered with trash and empty beer cans. Nudie magazines lay on the coffee table in front of a large screen TV and Xbox. A cluttered desk with a computer monitor sitting on top took up one corner. Cables ran out of the back and into a computer tower underneath. Two framed pictures faced whoever would sit in the uncomfortable looking chair at the desk. An unmade bed lay in the back corner with a nightstand and tall chest of drawers. It was there where we'd found the burner phones.

"Gross," Gomez commented.

"You're telling me." I headed straight for the coffee table with real estate agreements. Gomez drifted to the corner with the desk and began carefully going through papers.

This pool house wasn't gone over by forensics technicians like they would in a normal crime scene since the murder had been committed several miles from here. They had come in and bagged the evidence Moody and I had discovered. The rest of the place was untouched from the time I left until now. Maybe the FBI had told the local authorities not to touch anything, that they wanted their people to be the ones who processed the scene. Which still didn't explain how Paxton still had a key. Maybe she was hiding something or didn't trust the authorities to give up all the keys.

I sat down on the edge of a couch next to the coffee table and picked up the agreements. There it was, plain as day on both: **Summit Capital Holdings.**

My mouth went dry. There was the connection. "That's it."

Gomez looked up from the desk on the other side of the room. "What is it?"

I tapped a finger on the documents. "Summit Capital. They're on both contracts. They're buying one cheap and selling the other at what looks like a way overinflated price."

She cocked an eyebrow. "You know what that means, don't you?"

"Money laundering."

"Bingo," she said and looked back down at the desk. She leaned forward and studied one of the two pictures in the frames intently. She placed a hand over her mouth in disbelief. "No, it can't be."

Dread crept through me as I rose from the couch, each step toward her heavy with apprehension. The color had drained from her face. I stepped around the desk and behind her.

She reached up from the chair and grabbed my hand. "Steady yourself."

I gulped. "For what?"

She pointed at the picture frame on the right side of the desk. It was a Coastal Carolina men's soccer team photo. The resolution was somewhat grainy, suggesting the photo was older. Eleven men were depicted in it. Ten wore their soccer uniforms. An older man dressed in a teal polo shirt with a Chanticleer logo on the chest stood in the middle of the back row. He must have been the head coach.

A much thinner and younger Zach stood next to him. We learned during our investigation that he went to CCU on a soccer scholarship. He had put on weight over the years since, but had once been a fit, handsome young man. Kneeling in front of him was his friend, and Paxton's lover from New Zealand, Gideon.

"Yeah," I said. "There's Zach and Gideon alright. What about it?"

"It's not them," Gomez said. "Who's that standing on the other side of the coach?"

I leaned forward over her shoulder to get a better view. The other young guy standing next to the coach was likewise handsome, with a head of nice hair. I squinted. The eyes. There was something about the eyes. They were an intense blue. A set of intelligent eyes destined for greatness.

"It can't be," I said.

"It has to be," Gomez said.

I looked down at her and then back at the photo.

Standing next to the coach with a confident grin was a young man who, in his future, had become the mayor of Myrtle Beach: Sid Rosen.

CHAPTER EIGHTEEN

"WHAT DOES IT MEAN?" Gomez asked after we had time to catch our collective breaths.

I couldn't take my eyes off Rosen staring back at us. "No way. Is it possible he's involved in this? He's the mayor after all."

"Hmm." Gomez pressed her lips together and pointed at the picture. "He wasn't mayor when Autumn died. He was elected the year after."

"Does that matter?"

"Maybe. Maybe not," she said. "To my knowledge, no acting mayor in American history has ever been charged with murder. Since there is no statute of limitations on murder, he'd go down even if he played a small part."

"I think we're seeing that there's more than one person involved in all of this."

We still hadn't stopped staring at the photo. A gust of wind came off the ocean and hit the side of the pool house, causing a creak in the ceiling joists. I searched the faces of the other young men, trying to see if I recognized any of them. I didn't. Using my phone, I snapped a picture of the group photo for future reference. It could come in handy.

I normally don't pay much attention to politics, especially not during the big election season that followed Autumn's death. Since I was a Surfside Beach resident, even though I could practically throw a rock from my house and hit the imaginary line separating my home from Myrtle Beach, what happened here was almost like it was happening somewhere far away. It wasn't on my radar.

"He was an attorney before he ran for office," I said.

"I think so." Gomez twisted in her chair and looked up at me. "As a matter of fact, it seems like he was a real estate attorney."

"There's a good chance he conducted business with Zach Lawson."

"If they were teammates in college and both stayed here after graduation, it would make sense if they were friends."

We were so in sync that not only were we speaking in turns but also finishing each other's thoughts.

I kneeled to the floor next to her seat so she wouldn't have to look up at me. We were shoulder to shoulder. Her perfume invaded my senses. The outside world didn't exist. I fought the urge, despite the topic of conversation, to place my hands on her knees and kiss her. My thoughts and feelings were everywhere right now. The urge to solve Autumn's death and gain closure all while sorting out my feelings had me reeling. I didn't trust myself not to screw everything up.

Our heads were now level with each other. I said, "If they were friends in college, they might be in business now."

"Just because he's mayor, doesn't mean he can't still have open business interests. Yeah, it's a full-time job, but it has a finite lifespan. He could be elected out of office or choose not to run next year."

"Let's think about what this might mean. Hypothetically." Gomez rubbed her hands together as she thought aloud. "Zach has a real estate company and has his good buddy, Sid Rosen, conduct his closings. Zach's way of keeping business coming to his friend."

"What would Rosen be giving back to Zach for all this business?"

She looked down for a beat then back at me with wide eyes.

At the same time, she said, "Rosen helped Zach find holes in the system," I said, “Rosen helped him bury money in the Caribbean.”

We looked at each other for a long moment, letting our comments sink in. Both seemed logical if there was indeed a relationship between the two.

“If he was getting all this money, why would he run for mayor?” I asked.

“Maybe to influence zoning and construction contracts handed out by the city.”

“He attended every meeting I went to when I was a member of the Myrtle Beach Downtown Development Corporation.” They kicked me out last year for something I had done during the Paige Whitaker investigation, but that’s a story for a different day. Gomez was already aware of this. “Rosen had a big say in all the redevelopment plans, but I'm not sure how much he influenced specific building and green space plans. How can we figure out if that's what's happening?"

"Look at who is benefiting from any zoning changes or building contracts within the city limits. See if there's a connection to his old law firm and/or Zach."

A memory from this past weekend at Swaying Palms hit me like a brick. I'd seen Rosen in a golf cart with one of the most famous people in Myrtle Beach, Greg Rowles. Minutes after Zach was found dead in the woods, Moody and I were examining the body. Moody had sent out a text moments before, and I'd assumed it was to Chief Miller, but in retrospect, it had to be to Rosen. How else would Rosen have known what happened or where to go at that point?

When Rosen saw the body, he was visibly shaken. Most people would be when seeing a dead body for the first time. I was. But he seemed more upset than I would have figured. Now, I know that they may have been friends. Not only friends, but possibly business partners. Rowles had been long gone by then, and I hoped he wasn't part of this mess.

When I first met Moody, his demeanor and physical appearance reminded me of someone who would be typecast as a crooked cop in films. Working with him on several cases, and particularly this past weekend on the golf course, allayed any thoughts that he might have actually been a crooked cop. He had shattered any preconceptions I might have had of possible shady side activities. I just didn't sense it in him. Now that I'm realizing his text might have been direct to Rosen, I didn't need to ask myself why. Still, throughout the case, Moody knew very little about all this, only tips based on suspicions of where to find the answers. I had a feeling he was only on a need-to-know basis.

Judge Whitaker primarily presided over traffic and boating violations that had nothing to do with any sort of zoning ordinances or real estate transactions. All this begged the question: "How did this affect Autumn? She would have nothing to do with any of it."

Gomez pressed a finger against her lip. "I'm not sure. We can check with the Register of Deeds and have them cross reference any real estate transactions with Rosen's law firm and Zach's real estate company."

"Throw in Summit Capital Holdings too," I said. "Gideon said that Zach had a web of shell corporations. He could have used any variety of names to acquire property other than Summit Capital and Lawson Luxury International."

"Good thinking. I don't have any contacts at that office, but I'm sure we can figure out how to do it in a way that doesn't arouse suspicion."

I felt the outside of my back pocket, remembering the contact card Karen at the Register of Deeds gave to me earlier today. She seemed eager to help in any investigation, even if it meant bending the rules. I pulled the card from my pocket and held it up.

"I think I have the answer right here."

CHAPTER NINETEEN

CHAPTER NINETEEN

START OF TEXT MESSAGES

We have a problem. The bug in Clark's phone went offline.

I was afraid that would happen. What was he doing when it stopped working?

He and Gomez had just left Moody's home and talked to

Marge. I heard everything through the bug.

Did she know anything?

Didn't seem to, but she agreed to send Moody down to Charleston for an autopsy. They suspect he was poisoned.

Can we stop that from happening?

I don't know.

Figure something out. Clark and Gomez can't get those findings.

What if I stopped them from investigating? They're the only ones who suspect anything.

How would you do that?

Leave it to me.

END OF TEXT MESSAGES

CHAPTER TWENTY

WE DIDN'T FIND ANY further answers in the pool house. I checked over the property transactions on the coffee table but didn't see Rosen's name attached to any.

After returning the key to Paxton, we left through the gate and turned left on Ocean Boulevard. The moon reflected off the waves on a cloudless night. The air was warm and crisp. This would be an ideal night for a romantic moonlit stroll on the beach if it weren't for the fact that we were trying to figure out who might have murdered Autumn, Moody, and Ed Banner. Not to mention I was afraid for my life, had a girlfriend, and Gomez had a fiancé.

I considered her darkened form as she focused on the street ahead as we passed by hotels on both sides.

Her phone buzzed several times. She had looked at the notifications but hadn't done anything about them. Likewise, I'd gotten several messages from Mom, Bo, and Andrea that I hadn't returned.

As we drove past the Dayton House Resort, I scheduled a text message to go to Karen at the Register of Deeds at 8 a.m. tomorrow. I didn't want to disturb her this late. I hoped she'd be able to come through. My laptop was in my travel bag in the Jeep. Once I found somewhere to crash, I'd dig into the Horry County Tax Records website Moody had given me to find out who owned the rental house at Swaying Palms.

"I've gotta get home," she said with a sad resolve.

My heart fell. "Lucien?"

"Yeah, he keeps texting me, wanting to know where I am."

"Do you want to?"

Her chin dipped ever so slightly. "No, but I can't be doing anything suspicious like not coming home."

"I understand." We passed by the Gay Dolphin on our right as we entered the Boardwalk. The glowing Sky Wheel lay ahead on the left. "If there was a listening device in my phone, wouldn't they know you were with me? Whoever "they" are."

She blinked. Her hands tightened on the steering wheel. "I hadn't thought of that."

"If you recognized that the bug we found in my phone was used by your police department, we need to think about who might have access to them."

"They're not my department right now," she reminded me. "I've been put on leave."

That wasn't the answer I expected. "Does all of what's happening have you rethinking your job?"

She took a breath. “I don’t know. Maybe. I was on guard after Chief Miller sent me home. Finding that bug in your phone has me questioning all of it. And yet, I still have the urge to solve crimes. To find justice for those who lost loved ones.” It went unsaid but she meant Autumn and people like me.

I reached over and covered one of her hands on the wheel. “I’m here if you want to talk about it.”

She sniffed. “Thanks. I didn’t wake up this morning thinking that by the end of the day, I’d learn that not only was my partner dead, but there might be a huge conspiracy happening within the city government and police department.”

“You and me both.” We stopped at the light by the Bowery. The light was red.

Tourists crossed on both sides in front of us. It was a busy night on the Boardwalk, but we hadn't noticed.

My bookstore lay a few blocks ahead, and she would have me back to my Jeep within moments. Decisions about what to do next were imminent.

***

When Gomez dropped me off at my vehicle in the lot behind Myrtle Beach Reads, I told her I was going to go grab a wad of cash from the safe in my office. She came with me into the darkened bookstore to make sure it was safe. Nothing stirred inside except for the dust motes floating in the streetlights' glow that streamed through the front windows.

I'd move the money back to the business account when I felt safer, but I hoped it would last me through the next few days. I didn't want to leave a digital trail with my bank card. I was relieved to find plenty of money in the safe. The summer had been good for Myrtle Beach Reads.

From there, we headed toward Surfside Beach. The Quality Inn, next door to the Bar-B-Cue House, had four attractive qualities to me at present. It was cheap, accepted cash which allowed me to stay off the grid, had vacancy, and had parking in the back off the main road. Since I already had my overnight bag, I was able to avoid a potentially dangerous visit to my home. I suspected that, if my phone was bugged, then my house might also be compromised as well. It tugged at my brain as to how any of it had gotten there and who was responsible.

Gomez walked me to the hotel door, I guess to make sure I got there okay. A salty breeze brushed against us.

If it weren't for the death and being on the run, this almost seemed like she was walking me to my door after a date. I used the key to pop open the door. It swung inward. Light from the walkway spilled into the room.

We faced each other in front of the open door, both of us unsure of what to say or what to do next. A slice of light illuminated the front corner of an inviting king size bed. Almost too inviting.

Looking into her emerald eyes as she brushed the hair from the side of her face caused my heart to race. Her neck flushed. She bit her bottom lip and glanced at the interior of the room before coming back to me. I wasn't a mind reader, but it seemed like she was having similar thoughts.

I didn't know what the future held. Neither of us did. Our worlds changed today. How much further would this tension between us go? I didn't know, but deep within my soul, I wanted the woman standing before me to be a part of it. Her actions showed her true feelings toward me. Did my actions toward her convey the same message?

She fingered the engagement ring on her finger, reminding herself of her promise to Lucien.

Then two things happened. One made sense. The other didn't.

She slipped the ring from her finger and placed it in her pocket.

Neither of us had said a word. Traffic flowed past the highway at the front of the motel. Insects danced in the street-lights which crackled with phosphores-cence.

Gomez hadn't taken her eyes off me, nor had I taken mine from hers. Blood rushed through my ears.

She reached out and took my hand and leaned forward, giving me a tender kiss on the cheek. Her head tilted to the in-side of the motel room. "This isn't the time or place."

Deep down, I had the same longing feel-ing. I traced a finger across the impres-sion the removed engagement ring had left on her finger. Begrudgingly, I said, "I agree. What are you going to do about Lucien? We need to accept the possibility that he's involved somehow."

Her shoulders sagged as she uttered the words. The weight in her voice revealed understanding. "I know."

"Does he know where you are? Who you're with?"

"He doesn't. What about Andrea?"

My shoulders lifted then dropped. "Same. I've gotta talk to her."

She gave a hint of a smile, and said, "Lock yourself in here. Get some rest. I'll touch base in the morning."

"I'll do that."

"Answers are coming, Clark."

"They must. Be careful with Lucien."

“I will.” She stared into my eyes, reached down, and grabbed my hand. “You're shaking.”

“I'm scared,” I admitted. “This is not where I expected to be when I woke up yesterday. People are getting killed. Who knows who else died because of whatever conspiracy is going on.”

“Hopefully, no one,” she said in a soothing tone. She'd make a good mother. I already felt better. She reached behind her back and pulled out a sleek handgun. “I know you said you've never fired a gun, but you might need this. I grabbed it out of my glove compartment.”

I stared down at it. I'd touched one other gun in my life. My grandpa's service revolver from the Korean War. Beyond that, I'd never been around them.

She noticed my hesitation. “Take it. Only use it if you absolutely have to. I'd feel better if you had it.”

My body quaked with fear. A thought struck me like a mallet. We were close to figuring out who killed Autumn. It wasn't Zach because he had been in Barbados. There was a connection between him and Mayor Rosen. I didn't see him doing the dirty work, but there had to be others involved. They were out there. Nearby.

I took the gun. It was heavier than I remembered. The steel was cool in my hand. “Thank you.”

Her shoulders sagged in relief. “It makes me feel better knowing you have it. You know, just in case.”

“Yeah. Just in case,” I repeated.

"Keep it on the nightstand. Don't put your finger near the trigger unless you're sure you need it."

"I won't touch it after I carry it inside."

"Good." She squeezed my hand and walked away without another word. I watched her go until she disappeared around the corner of the building.

In life, we hope difficult situations work themselves out without having to face them straight on. What was happening now, between Gomez and Lucien, or Andrea and I, had varying levels of complexity that needed to be unraveled. It would take time.

That time was not the present for me. I had other pressing matters to attend to.

I knew exactly the most important task to tackle first.

CHAPTER TWENTY-ONE

I FIGURED BO WOULD be up late since he'd lived on West Coast time for the last decade. With hesitation, I called him. I hoped his NSA experience would come in handy right now.

He must have been holding his phone. He answered after half a ring.

"Clark, are you okay?"

I laid on the surprisingly comfortable bed, propped up on about fifteen pillows that came in every hotel room, eating a pack of crackers I'd got out of the vending machine in the lobby. The hotel owners had placed security cameras everywhere. In my new, paranoid world, I made it a priority to check. I'd asked for a room at the end of the back corridor of the motel so I could make a quick retreat if it came to it and a camera was perched right next to the door, looking down on anyone who might try to break in. They had two cameras in the lobby and three on utility poles in the parking strip running in front of the rooms.

I made even more moves to protect myself. My Jeep was parked right outside the door. Before settling in, I had removed the license plate and backed into the spot so no one would notice and for a quick, forward-driving escape. I'd checked in under an alias, "Bruce Purdy," and gave them the incorrect car and plate number. Judging by the bored clerk at the check-in desk, I doubted she would bother to check any of it.

It occurred to me since the attractive Gomez had entered the lobby with me when I checked in and I paid cash for the room, that the clerk likely figured we needed the king-sized bed for a few hours. At the time, there was a chance that would be the case, but like many other things on this day, it was not to be. She had followed me here, she said, for my protection. It could have also been for her peace of mind.

I tried not to notice the gun Gomez gave me sitting on the far end of the night-stand on the other side of the table lamp.

"Yeah, I'm fine," I answered. "Holed up at a motel for the night. Been a crazy day and I don't want to get into the details."

"I understand," Bo said at length. "Can I tell Mom and Dad you're okay?"

"Of course. That's one reason I called."

"Cool. What are the other reasons?"

I closed my eyes and reopened them before replying. "It seems that the guy who got killed on the golf course this past weekend and the mayor of Myrtle Beach, Sid Rosen, were in business together."

"Oh. Wow. So, the guy Zach might have contacted Rosen from Barbados after sending those texts to Autumn?"

"Seems like it."

"Which means there's a connection between Rosen and Autumn's death?"

"And several others that we know about."

"Wow," Bo said again. "Can I help?"

"I'm hoping so. Tell me, is there a way you can scour the internet and public records here and in the Caribbean, to try and link Zach and Mayor Rosen together? He wasn't the mayor when Autumn died, but a real estate attorney. I forget which law firm he worked at."

"I can find out where he worked in a snap," Bo confirmed and hummed to himself. Bo always did that when he was doing some heavy thinking. "Each island would likely have their own records. Some of them might not be online depending on how advanced their governments are."

"True. Check local newspapers for property transactions. Some of them might list the closing attorneys."

"I'll do that and see what else I can find." He explained that he would use Open-Source Intelligence or OSINT. A way to leverage open-source intelligence techniques to gather publicly available information on Zach, Rosen, and Summit Capital Holdings and their operations abroad. He'd create a program using Python to scrape the internet for articles and information. "It's more helpful than Google."

"Great. How long do you think that'll take?"

"Hmm. I'll have it to you by morning."

My eyebrows shot toward the ceiling. "That fast?"

"Sure thing," he said, his voice brimming with confidence. "My internal clock is three hours behind yours. Mom and Dad have been in bed for hours, and I'm usually a night owl anyway. I got nothing better to do."

I took in and expelled a relieved breath. Finally, something good that might move in my direction. I needed a win after the day I'd had.

"That would be awesome, Bo," I said. "I'd owe you."

"Nope. You wouldn't. Get some rest. You sound like you need it."

He hung up and got to work.

With a grunt, I removed the back cover of the phone and removed the battery. I'd learned somewhere that if the battery is disconnected, you can't be tracked.

I stared at the ceiling for a long time, trying to rationalize and compartmentalize all that had happened today. First, Moody died. Then going to Conway and running into Judge Whitley and learning that Summit Capital Holdings not only owned multiple properties in the county but that somehow Andrea was also involved. I didn't have time to deal with her today. I hadn't called her with all that had happened. I tried to avoid confrontation, but this was a topic I'd have to meet head-on. Her possible connection baffled me more than anything.

We learned that Zach, the same seemingly random person whose murder I investigated over the weekend, had been the person who sent those text messages to Autumn. I'd tried to rack my brain thinking of how he could have known her and vice versa.

Thankfully, we convinced Marge to send Moody for an autopsy. That would tell us if our suspicions about him being poisoned were correct. The crazy and alarming thing was the listening device placed inside my phone came from the police department. I was aware of Gomez's suspicions of Chief Miller, but the chief wouldn't have bugged my phone herself. It seemed likely that Lucien would have access to such devices, but when would he have done it? The phone rarely left my sight, and I'd had a difficult time thinking about who could have been around it long enough to pop it open, install the bug, and snap it shut without my knowing. My family, Andrea, and the workers at my store were all that came to immediate mind.

The baffling part of it all was learning that Mayor Sid Rosen might have been involved. As a real estate attorney, he wouldn't have had a reason to enter Judge Whitley's courtroom unless he was trying to get himself out of a boating or traffic ticket. Was it possible he was angered over a traffic ticket enough to kill the judge's clerk? It didn't make sense. None of it did.

If the signs were pointing at Rosen and Zach, there were three important things to work out that happens in any murder investigation: means, motive, and opportunity. If Zach was in Barbados, then that left Rosen or some other crony to do the dirty work. It seemed like we were just scratching the surface of the people involved. As we continued to dig, who else might we uncover?

Thinking of Zach, it reminded me of Percy, his lawyer and friend, who had apparently helped in setting up some shell corporations for Zach. Let's say that Autumn, Moody, and Ed Banner were all poisoned. It seemed like the most likely cause of death at this point. How would the poison have been introduced? If Moody's autopsy came back with signs pointing to poisoning being the cause of death, the report should include the toxins found. If so, then it might point to the origin.

As I lay in bed, looking up at the ceiling, I pounded my fist on the bed in frustration. Even if we learned what poisoned Moody, I had no clue how we'd find where the poison came from without search warrants. If I were the person who poisoned the three, then I would destroy any trace of deadly toxins.

The poison would be the means part of the equation. I set that thought aside and tried to think of the opportunity angle which went back to figuring out how the toxin was introduced. I had no way of knowing if Moody encountered anyone else between leaving my house last night and getting home to Marge. If he did, then the possibility existed that the poison was introduced then, either by a needle or inhalant. I'd read plenty of Agatha Christie novels where poison was the weapon used in murders. After the day I'd had, my brain was mush, and I couldn't think of all the methods deadly toxins used.

These thoughts swirled and twirled in my brain. At some point, late in the night, my eyes closed and remained that way until daybreak.

I dreamed of Autumn.

CHAPTER TWENTY-TWO

By the time I awoke, Bo had come through. I put the battery back in the phone, powered it on, and discovered that he'd sent his findings in an email and had texted me to make sure I saw his message.

My habit is to sleep on the left side of the bed. It's something that developed from my childhood when Bo and I used to share a bunk bed. Back then, he was afraid of heights. Now he went skydiving and climbed tall mountains without a care in the world. His fear meant I'd slept on the top bunk. I wasn't afraid of sleeping up there, but I didn't want to roll over in the middle of the night and fall out of bed, despite the guard rail. The left edge of our bunk bed cozied up against the wall. I used to situate myself as far to the left side as possible before falling asleep.

When Autumn and I moved in together after getting married, I explained why I wanted to sleep on that side. I joked to her that I only fell twice in six years when I was a kid, but she didn't think that was as funny as I did.

Even now, after sleeping alone for three years and having this big, king-sized bed to myself, I still went to bed every night with my pillow on the far-left side of the bed.

Sun flowed in through a crack in the heavy curtains that covered the window by the door. An AC unit hummed underneath the window. Muffled footsteps thumped on the ceiling from someone in the room above climbing out of bed.

I rubbed the sleep out of my eyes and took a drink of water from the clear plastic cup on the nightstand. The gun was still there. I tried not to look at it.

I lay back on the pillow and unlocked my phone, lighting up the room a touch, and went to my email app. The message Bo sent was the second one down. The top message was a newsletter from Tidal Creek Brewhouse with their events this week. It didn't seem likely at this point that I would be able to make it to any of them.

True to his word, Bo had delivered. His lengthy email set forth a whole string of shady deals and scandals stemming from his scouring of the internet. He sourced news articles, social media posts, and public statements.

He found a bevy of news articles where he found Zach Lawson named in them. Some mentioned the main real estate business he fronted, Lawson Luxury International, and others we had not come across yet. They included Island Haven Investments, Palm Shores Properties, Blue Horizon Estates, and Salty Sands Holdings.

The hair on the back of my neck stood on end. In the pool house at Zach Lawson's estate was paperwork from a property transaction. The seller was Lawson Luxury International. The purchaser was Salty Sands Holdings. The only sense I made of it was Zach was trying to cover up a purchase with his public corporation's name on it with one he wanted to keep secret.

Bo linked each article or website and gave a brief description for each. His report seemed thorough and orderly. We might have some shared blood after all.

I started clicking through the links. Most were mundane transactional listings from different newspapers scattered around the Caribbean. Others were troubling. Once Bo was armed with the other shell corporation names, he was able to branch out and discover more.

Several times, Zach's organizations were accused by local governments of deceiving officials and engaging in environmentally harmful practices like deforestation, improper waste disposal, and damaging sensitive ecosystems. These places relied on their natural beauty to entice tourists and development, and doing any harm raised significant concerns.

One omission from the list was Summit Capital Holdings. Bo must have found this information using Lawson Luxury International. I scanned the rest of his email, searching for mentions of that specific shell corporation, but didn't see it mentioned. All this did was to prove that Zach was involved in some illegal shenanigans. I still needed a link between him, Rosen, and Summit Capital.

Three articles about Palm Shores Properties accused them of ignoring local laws regarding zoning and environmental concerns in Antigua. Island Haven was guilty as well for shady practices in Jamaica. Blue Horizon Estates abandoned a half-finished resort in St. Thomas after it came to light that they had overdeveloped a parcel of protected land. They had pled ignorance for their mistake, but the damage was already done. They pulled up shop and disappeared off the island in the middle of the night.

Through all of that, Bo saved the best for last in an article dated five years ago from St. Grant's Island. I'd never heard of that island before Antonio Bianchi sold his insurance business in Myrtle Beach and retired there after the tragedy on the Golden Mile with John Allen Howard. Apparently, it was off the coast of Guadeloupe. I'd kept in touch with the former insurance salesman. He loved to talk, and for some reason, despite him being a suspect in a murder case, I kinda liked him. Sometimes I lived vicariously through him after he started sending me gorgeous photos from around his villa by the sea.

I could reach out to him and see if he could shed some light, but Antonio had moved to the island well after this article was dated. That might not be necessary.

All I needed was a single quote.

The reporter had reached out to the owners, or anyone involved in Salty Sands Holdings, about possible bribery charges. Someone with that group had tried to influence the head of the St. Grant zoning commission to allow them to put in a luxury housing development overlooking the sea near the capital city of the island, Russellville.

The reporter stated that he couldn't get in contact with the owners of Salty Sands but had gone to the land records department at the courthouse to search for the law firm who filed the paperwork on Salty Sands Holdings' behalf.

There it was. The connection between Rosen and Zach in doing business together.

A snippet of the newspaper article read:

With accusations of bribery coming out from the zoning committee, The St. Grant's Tribune reached out to Salty Sands Holdings. They refused to comment until the closing attorney on the deal in question, Sid Rosen, responded.

"My client has no comment at this time," Rosen reluctantly said in a terse phone con-

versation from his home in Myrtle Beach, South Carolina.

As kids say nowadays when a plan comes together, "Boom goes the dynamite."

CHAPTER TWENTY-THREE

THE ARTICLE ENDED AFTER that, saying it would be updated when more details became available. I took it from the lack of any further articles, nothing more was learned.

I rubbed my chin and laid the phone down. There it was in black and white. That one of Zach's businesses participated in questionable activities, bribery in this case, wasn't surprising. The man was a loathsome brute with scandalous morals.

Seeing his buddy and pal, Mr. Mayor, involved was the shocking part. Perhaps I shouldn't have been surprised. I didn't know Rosen well and everything we learned recently about him had been suspicious. We'd been at several of the same meetings for the Myrtle Beach Downtown Development Corporation, and I'd shaken his hand at five, soon to be six, commendation ceremonies. Thursday's meetup now carried a whole different weight.

Thinking back on those development meetings brought back a memory that made me close my eyes. At the last meeting I had attended, before getting thrown out, I'd had a brief conversation with Rosen. He told me how much he always admired Autumn's work ethic, or something to that effect.

He was a property attorney, and Autumn clerked for a boating and traffic violations judge. Their paths shouldn't have crossed often, if at all. That goes back to the opportunity issue. She died before he was elected. I didn't know when he would have been around her enough to draw that opinion of her. She’d never mentioned him.

The article Bo sent concerned bribing officials. If Rosen wanted to have something happen, he held a position of influence. It might not be within his power to do whatever he wanted, but he had an agenda. If the bribery allegations from St. Grant’s Island were true, he could have been greasing palms here to get his way or someone else's. From what I could tell, he’d been a good mayor during his time in office with no whispers of scandal. Hints of running for reelection were already in the air.

I don't know if Rosen did it, but after reading the article and Moody telling me to investigate Summit Capital, it seemed like our mayor was somehow involved.

His reaction to seeing his friend's body made more sense now, too.

I still wasn't fully convinced. There was a problem with his involvement. The reason I still had doubt about Rosen having a hand in all this stemmed from him asking me to help solve Zach's murder. If he and Rosen were indeed close and were involved in Zach's schemes, surely he would have thought I might uncover something he didn't want me to find out.

It could have been an instance of keeping your friends close and your enemies closer.

Which meant, I was the enemy.

I sent Gomez a text saying we needed to talk. After setting the phone down on the nightstand, away from the gun, I got out of bed, stretched, and went to the bathroom for a much-needed shower.

Usually, when I go through the mundane motions of showering, my mind tends to wander. I always seem to do my best thinking in the shower or while driving. If I could ever combine the two, I might be able to solve world peace and global warming in the same session.

Now that all we'd learned had a chance to simmer overnight, plus the article about bribery this morning, a possible connection formed in my brain. One that I needed to follow-up on ASAP.

I finished the shower as fast as possible. I hadn't even had coffee yet, and I was jittery with the prospect of my possible epiphany. The list of addresses owned by Summit Capital lay on the motel's credenza. There was something I needed to check.

The message I'd scheduled for Courthouse Karen had already been sent—the one asking her to find a connection between Zach's company and Rosen's law firm. Now, I had more ammo in the names of the other shell corporations. When I got out of the bathroom, I'd send her those names as well. I would work on the second thing while I waited for her to get back to me.

After drying off, brushing my teeth, and running my fingers through my hair to get it in place, I exited the bathroom. When I opened the door, my phone was in mid-ring. I rushed over and grabbed it just before it went to voicemail.

It was Winona. She was supposed to have a heavy day stocking the shelves at Garden City Reads with a huge shipment of books. Margaret was going to help her get everything straight. As a retired librarian, Margaret had done wonders in helping Autumn and I with the layout of Myrtle Beach Reads and had volunteered to help Winona at the new store.

I swiped my finger across the screen to answer. "Good morning, Winona. How are you?"

She breathed into the phone. “Clark! Oh, thank goodness I got you. Have you gotten a call from the police yet?”

A chill swept over me. To my knowledge, Winona had nothing to do with my investigation. I hoped the reason for her call was that someone from the PD had called her to send a message to me. Why would they call her though? Any calls would have gone to her cell phone. HTC hadn’t hooked up telephone service to the new store yet. They were scheduled to come out next week.

It turned out that someone had a message for me, and it wasn’t the police department.

“The police?” I asked. “Why would they call me?”

"Because someone broke in here last night and vandalized the place." My immediate thought was the "place" she referred to was the original bookstore on the Boardwalk. I hadn't gotten used to her running the Garden City location.

A knot formed in my throat. I sat down on the bed. I didn't know what to say.

Winona continued, "I've already called the police. I went to unlock the back door to find it was already unlocked. It was weird since I remembered to lock it when I left yesterday."

We didn't have any security cameras at the new place either. HTC was going to take care of that when they came to install the phones. I hadn't had an alarm set up yet because, until yesterday, there weren't any books in the store.

"Are you okay?" I asked.

"Me? Yeah, I guess. A little shaken maybe, but whoever did this is long gone. I checked the stockroom, office, and bathroom to be sure no one was hiding."

I would have let the police do that, but I wasn't going to council Winona on it now. She was safe and knew nothing about the conspiracy I was embroiled in, and that was what was important. I had to give it to Winona. For a small, young woman, she had guts. That's one of the many reasons I selected her to run the new place.

"Good. What did they do?" I rubbed my free hand over my forehead, expecting the worst.

She grunted. "Not much to tell the truth. The pallet of books we received yesterday is intact. The bookshelves haven't been touched, nor has the register counter."

"Okay. What did they do?"

She breathed into the phone again. "They painted in real big letters on the inside of the front window, **BACK OFF**."

CHAPTER TWENTY-FOUR

I GRABBED THE LIST of Summit Capital addresses, my keys, wallet, and phone. Begrudgingly, I picked up the gun, careful to keep my finger away from the trigger, and tucked it into the waistband of my shorts at the small of my back like I'd seen people do in movies. The gun didn't go off and shoot me in the buttocks like I was Forrest Gump, much to my relief.

I rushed out the door, down to the office, and reserved the room for another two nights before running around to the rear of the motel and into the Jeep. After hurriedly reattaching my license plate, I roared out of the parking lot and sped toward Garden City on Kings Highway, reminiscent of when I chased Brian McConnell in his camper van before it wrecked and exploded in my face. I placed a hand over my ribs at the memory. They still hurt on occasion.

The traffic wasn't bad for this time of morning. I made it to the bookstore in good time. I shot a text to Gomez while sitting at the stoplight near Tupelo Bay. I still waited for Gomez and Karen at the Register of Deeds to get back to me. It was becoming apparent that the conversation I'd put off with Andrea yesterday had to happen today. There was no way around it.

Two Horry County police cruisers with their lights flashing were parked in front of the store on the main strip near the Garden City Pier. We'd gotten a narrow spot in between the Garden City Coffee Shop and the Pavilion Arcade. Two dozen tourists and a few local business owners congregated around at a distance to see what was happening.

After parking the car, I bounded up the two steps to the sidewalk. No one stopped me, but I stopped when I saw BACK OFF spray painted on the reverse side of the front windows. Not only was someone trying to tell me to cease my investigation, but they were also showing me they could get inside my business any time they wanted. I'd have Winona call a locksmith to change the locks and get HTC out here ASAP to install the security system.

The officers were friendly and told me they would try to find footage from any nearby cameras to try and identify the person who broke into the store. I wasn't going to hold my breath. Whoever did this knew what they were doing. They probably had scouted the location and were aware of the lack of an alarm and had the ability to pick locks. Their spray-painting skills needed work. Teen vandals trying to tag something with their graffiti would have had a much more artistic flair than the angry work done here.

With nothing being broken, they asked Winona and I some questions, made some notes, called in the incident, and said they'd follow-up. After bidding us adieu, they left, and the crowd dispersed. Nothing to see here except spray painted glass.

The officers asked what I was being told to back off from and who might have performed the vandalism. Since I didn't know who I could trust, if anyone, I told them that their guess was as good as mine. They eyed me suspiciously but didn't ask any follow-up questions. They said they would increase patrols through here for the next few days to deter any further malfeasance.

Margaret came in, and in her calm, no nonsense manner said that she would clean the glass with acetone and a couple rags. Winona volunteered for the job to let Margaret focus on filling the shelves with books.

While I should have been giddy with the anticipation of opening a new business that was already getting buzz among the denizens of Garden City, the events of yesterday and this morning sought my attention.

The message from the vandal was clear. If whoever was behind this was going to these lengths to keep me from digging further, then one thing was clear.

I was on the right track.

***

I sent Gomez another message about the break-in with the warning message. She still hadn't replied to my first text.

This wasn't like her. It comforted me to know she was a big girl who could take care of herself, but I still worried about the lack of reply. The thought reminded me of the hard metal bulge at the back of my waistband. I'd worn a long shirt to cover the gun and was glad the county cops hadn't frisked me. A search and discovery of the gun would have led to some awkward questions as to why I was carrying without a license, never mind the fact that the gun wasn't mine. The last thing I needed was to wind up in jail at this point, which might be right where they want me. Or worse, in an unmarked grave.

This was a bad idea, but if Gomez urged me to take it for my own protection, then maybe she knew something I didn't know about who or what we were up against.

I told Winona and Margaret that I had some important business to attend to, but to let me know if they saw any suspicious characters around or if there was any more trouble. Winona assured me that they would keep the front and back doors locked while they worked.

The time approached ten, and Garden City already bustled with activity. Golf carts, cyclists, and tourists on foot puttered up and down Atlantic Avenue, connecting Kings Highway to the beach, making the going slow for anyone in a motor vehicle. I hadn't eaten or had my first cup of coffee for the day so stopped by Flapjack's Pancake Cabin near the corner of Atlantic and Kings Highway for a stack of pancakes and a carafe of coffee.

I sat by myself in a corner, mentally planning out my next steps and hoping Gomez would call. Instead, Andrea sent me a text asking how I was doing during the meal. I still hadn't told her what had happened or why I needed to speak to her. I wanted to see her this afternoon. I had another stop to make before that. She sent back that she, Libby, and the remaining Silver Girls at Paradise Hideaway had a pool outing planned after lunch and invited me to join them. I say "remaining" because Dot's mom, and oldest of the group, was in jail for killing two people at the beginning of the summer.

After consuming half a pot of coffee and an Elkmont egg platter with a short stack of pancakes, I asked for a to-go cup for the coffee. I left a generous tip for the waiter and made my way back toward the Swaying Palms golf course.

I needed to speak to the good doctor once again.

CHAPTER TWENTY-FIVE

After skipping over the 17 Bypass and cruising past the Gladiator Games Roman Coliseum, the Hollywood Wax Museum, and Broadway at the Beach while sipping coffee and letting everything roam freely inside my head, I made a left and entered the long, palm-tree lined street leading to the Swaying Palms Clubhouse.

There was little traffic on the street. I owed that to the FBI coming in and shutting down the course after Moody and I had uncovered a loan sharking scheme and the sordid affairs of some of their employees. The thought of what had transpired here made me shiver. The worst of them were now behind bars where they deserved to be.

Before reaching the clubhouse, I made a left on Palm Tree Drive and wound my way through elegant houses and past various holes on the golf course. Despite the beautiful day, it was eerie not to see any golfers out and about here.

The road wound past Gideon's large home. He ran a successful custom surfboard company from his garage, shipping products all over the world. Gideon was one member of the foursome who played with Zach every week and was the person who discovered the body.

Originally from New Zealand, Gideon possessed the confidence of a knight and the sensibility of a nobleman. He had a good sense of humor too.

If it wasn't for the fact that he was sleeping with Zach's wife, I would have thought he was one of the coolest and most interesting people I'd ever met. There are some behaviors that I can't stand, and engaging in infidelity with a close friend's spouse was one of them.

The door was up on his three-car garage, exposing his "home office." He wore a pair of board shorts and goggles while using a planer to carve out another masterpiece of a board. Judging by how close it was to being finished, the wooden surfboard was probably the same one he was working on when Moody and I had stopped by on Sunday. I would love to see the finished product.

The street ended at a three-way stop sign where Water View Lane cut across, leading to more homes in both directions. The Intracoastal Waterway flowed past on the other side of a stone fence. I turned left. The street continued straight for a hundred yards before gradually curving to the left, following the Intracoastal.

Grand homes with glorious water views and landscaping fronted the road, looking out on the water. The curve of the road tapered until it ended just past a colonial style home with a porch running the length of the front. Thick white pillars were spaced out evenly on the porch. An elegant chandelier hung down above the front entrance.

It was the last house on the street and owned by Summit Capital. They'd allowed the grass and weeds to take over the front and back yards and the house to fall into disrepair. I was sure it was a favorite target of the neighborhood HOA, with accumulating fines.

That last thought made me blink. If Genevieve couldn't help me, then I hoped she'd put me in touch with whoever ran the homeowners' association here. They'd be able to contact the owners of the home somehow.

Genevieve's house lay next door to the rental owned by Summit Capital. The tall, thin doctor worked overnight in the ER at Grand Strand Medical Center.

When I met her on Saturday morning after Zach's death, she had just gotten out of bed. I had timed my visit for later in the morning so as not to potentially wake her.

Besides, it's not like I could have gotten here much sooner even if I wanted to. I needed to sit down for breakfast and sleep after everything that had happened yesterday.

I pulled to a stop on the side of the road in front of her house and exited the Jeep. A boat streamed past on the waterway. The gentle breeze blew against my skin. A pair of cormorants fluttered overhead. The sun cascaded down, casting the landscape into a yellow glow. The air carried a slightly fishy odor.

The doctor was in her yard. She wore a pair of green gardening overalls on top of a white shirt, boots, wide-brimmed straw hat, and sunglasses so big they made her look like she had bug eyes.

She gave me a sad wave. She lived alone in this big house after her husband had passed away during a flight to Charlotte several years ago. Tending to the yard was her hobby. The results showed.

"Good morning, Clark," she said.

"Good morning," I returned, "Sorry to bother you again, but I was hoping to ask you a few more questions about the house next door."

She came closer to the white picket fence separating her yard from the street. "I'll try, but I've told you everything I know."

"There's been a development, and I'm following up for Detective Moody."

"Yes, I heard that you caught the killer." She took off her purple and green gardening gloves, stacked them on top of each other, and draped them over a picket in the fence. "That must have been scary with the guy shooting at you like that."

"Scary doesn't begin to cover it. At least no one was hurt, including the little boy he was trying to kidnap."

"Where were they trying to go?"

"I don't know," I answered, "but I'm not sure the murderer knew at that point either. I think he was just trying to escape."

"Why did he try kidnapping the boy?"

That was a long topic that I didn't want to get into at present, so I said simply, "Love."

It was the truth, as twisted as it was.

Genevieve wasn't sure how to respond to that. Slowly, she said, "Okay," and stared at me, hoping I would elaborate. When I didn't, she asked, "Where is your detective friend?"

A pang of sadness struck my chest. I gulped, then said, "He died yesterday."

She raised a hand to cover her mouth. "Oh, my goodness. I'm so sorry. Was he injured while trying to apprehend the criminal?"

Her eyes moistened.

"No," I said. "He died of an apparent heart attack."

Her eyebrows came together. “You said he sent you to ask me questions.”

“In a way he did.”

“I don’t understand.”

I explained how he told me to continue looking into Summit Capital Holdings as the last thing he said to me before he died. I left out most of the details, but ended with, “We think there was a connection between the victim and the rental home, and I’m trying to nail it down.”

“Okay. Why is it important?”

“Because it might have to do with who murdered my wife.”

“Oh.” She shifted her weight from one foot to the other. The subject of Autumn came up when we met three days ago. "Why do you think that?"

"Because of the way Moody reacted when we learned who owned the place and that he told me to keep investigating, even though the murderer had been caught."

"Do you think he knew something about Summit Capital he wasn't telling you?"

"I don't know what he knew, but there's a good chance he did with all that's transpired since then." Over this past weekend, Moody emailed pictures of Zach, Paxton, Gideon, and all the other suspects to me for ease of access in case I needed a witness to identify them. I started with Zach and held up the phone for her to see the screen. "Have you seen this man at the house next door?"

She leaned forward for a better view. “Wait, that was the guy who got killed, right?”

“It was.”

“Now I know why he looked so familiar when I saw his picture on the news.”

“Why is that?”

“He came to that house all the time.”

A tingly sensation ran down my spine. “Do you know if he was the owner?”

“I’m not sure, but I would think his continuous presence should be a signal, don’t you?”

“I do.” There it was. Another solid connection between Zach and Summit Capital. I flipped through the photos, showing her each face. She recognized Archie and his wife, Cricket, despite never seeing them together, and Zoe.

"They would come in together through the backyard from the golf course." Genevieve pointed to the picture of Cricket. "This woman and Zach, as you say, wouldn't be inside together long. Usually no more than an hour. Sometimes as quick as twenty minutes."

"Did they look happy when they came out?"

She tilted her head. "Content. He'd slap her on the behind playfully."

We'd learned of their affair after discovering racy pictures in Zach's pool house. There were three sets of photos. Gideon and Paxton together in bed. Zoe and Archie playing adult Twister, and Zach with Archie's wife. This house was the love nest for everyone but Gideon and Paxton. Their vehicles had been seen at each other's houses while Zach was away for work and their son, Ethan, was at school.

She'd answered what I'd come to learn, and then some. Now that I had the connection between Zach and Summit Capital, my next step was to find an iron clad link to Rosen.

Speaking of which, "One more question and I'll let you get back to your yard."

"What is it?"

"Here's a random question. Have you ever seen Mayor Rosen at the house next door?"

She looked at me like I'd turned into a green alien. "No."

CHAPTER TWENTY-SIX

AFTER LEAVING THE SWAYING Palms area, I hooked a right on the 17 Bypass and headed in the direction of Broadway at the Beach. I needed to think. Normally being the wistful man I am, who enjoyed striking, panoramic views of the ocean and how the crashing of the waves enabled me to clear my mind, I pulled off into the empty Captain George's Seafood parking lot with a "picturesque" view of the 17 Bypass to do it.

I didn't say I was thinking clearly, which was why I needed to clear my head.

The revelation that it was Zach and Zoe that Genevieve had seen entering and leaving the rental home didn't surprise me at this point. I went into the conversation hoping that's what she would say. Now, I have another solid connection between Zach and Summit Capital. Genevieve said she'd seen the "owners" coming in and out of the rental when I first spoke to her after Zach's death. She had to have gotten that sense about them from somewhere.

Bumper-to-bumper traffic flowed by the parking lot on the bypass. Captain George's didn't open for another couple of hours, leaving me as the only person in the front parking lot. With cooler temps hinting at September's approach, it was a gorgeous day in the Grand Strand. It didn't seem like I would get to enjoy any of it.

Bo's research revealed that Rosen had a connection with at least one of Zach's offshore shell corporations. It didn't take a huge leap to think that the two were in league here locally. Karen at the Register of Deeds office had said there wasn't any paperwork involved in Summit Capital's filings. That opened the possibility that the head of that office, an elected official, had done something to hide the paperwork.

I pulled out my phone and did a quick search for who was the Horry County's official Register of Deeds. After a few taps on the screen, I found a man by the name of Michael Evans. I didn't recognize him at first, but as I stared at his eyes, something seemed familiar.

"Hmm," I mumbled, switching apps to my photo gallery. After Gomez discovered the soccer team photo that had Zach, Rosen, and Gideon together in it, I snapped a photo of the photo with my phone. At the time, I figured if those three were still friends, then there might be other members of the team in the loop.

One by one, I searched each player's face, starting at the top row before moving to the bottom. There he was, crouched down in front of Rosen: Michael Evans.

This confirmed my earlier suspicion. Whatever this was grew by the minute.

The complexity of the scandal—if that was the right word for it—took on so many branches that it was becoming difficult to keep track of.

I switched over to my note-taking app and wrote the following: **Zach, Rosen. Summit Capital, Evans. Cell phones. Poisoning. Bug, Lucien? Bookstore vandalism. Suspected bribery by Salty Sands Holdings on St. Grant's Island.**

There was more I was leaving out, but with everything swirling around, I couldn't think of it.

Wait a second.

There was one name not on the list.

I added it: **Andrea**.

After tossing the phone in the passenger seat, I looked out the windshield and took a deep breath.

It was time. I couldn't put off the dreaded conversation any longer. I started the car, pulled out of the lot, and waited a few minutes at the light to be able to pull out onto the bypass. Like Carolina Forest meeting 501, I would not like to live in this busy of an area to wait at this long of a light every day.

When it boiled down to it, I really liked Andrea. She'd come into my life mere months ago, awakening a feeling I hadn't had since I first met Autumn when I was in college. That first time you meet a woman who makes you twist your words and heart go thump.

That's what happened the first time I saw Andrea.

Not so much with Gomez. My attraction to her came over time. With the leggy detective, my fondness for her came while we worked together to solve cases. It was a meeting of minds first. Then it grew. I saw what sort of driven and compassionate woman she is. She was gorgeous in her own way too, evidenced by my frequent recollection of seeing her in the green dress during the fashion gala at the Chapin Art Museum before solving the John Allen Howard murder. That's when my admiration had been upped to a more scandalous level in her car coming back from Charleston.

While my love for Autumn grew from the same type of infatuation I currently had with Andrea, that feeling hadn't come yet in my relationship with her. It had faded to being more companionable. Surely, friendship was the first key. She seemed perfect for me, but why hadn't our relationship progressed? Was it her being too guarded or both of us?

Now, Andrea's daughter Libby? That's a little girl I'd do anything for which complicated matters.

As I headed down the 17 Bypass toward Market Common and Paradise Hideaway where Andrea lived, I pondered the question: has Andrea been lying to me this entire time?

Little did I know, the situation with Andrea would work itself out.

CHAPTER TWENTY-SEVEN

I SENT A MESSAGE to Andrea asking if her invitation to the pool gathering was still on the table. She replied a moment later saying that she and Libby were at the pool with the Silver Girls.

She said I could come and join them, to which I replied:

I need to talk to you in private.

K

It took fifteen minutes to travel to Market Common. I parked in the lot next to Andrea's car. She had two designated spaces, of which she only needed one.

I took a deep breath as I exited the Jeep. This was not a conversation I was looking forward to, but it had to be done. I'd gone through much of my life having the good fortune to never have been betrayed by anyone. I didn't know if Andrea had done that to me, but I had to find out.

If what I suspected was true, I didn't know what it would mean in the grander scheme of things. Hopefully, Andrea would shed some light on the situation. I shuddered to think what would happen if she pled ignorance. How would I react?

She seemed like a genuinely good person who had my best interests at heart. Had it all been a façade?

I passed through the lobby of Paradise Hideaway and through the rear doors out to the grand pool. The complex consisted of mostly retired folks. These old folks loved to party. A big one was going on the last time I was here, and stepping out into the courtyard, it appeared that it hadn't stopped.

A sign with the rules of the pool said in big, bold letters: **NO ALCOHOLIC BEVERAGES PERMITTED.**

The warning was ignored.

Men and women old enough to be my parents were having a good old time. Yes, there were a few younger families sprinkled in. I spotted Libby swimming with a girl around her age at one end of the pool. Andrea sat on the ledge with her feet in the water and her back to me. She wore a blue tankini. Now wasn't the time to lose focus, but the sight of Andrea in a swimsuit would do that to most men. To see her bare shoulders basking in the sun made me warm and fuzzy inside.

Andrea was flanked by two Silver Girls. Dot and Violet. The third Silver Girl, Karen, sipped on a boozy strawberry daiquiri at a nearby table. How did I know it was boozy? I'd had one before and had to pace myself. It's like she doubles the amount of rum in the recipe.

At every moment since leaving my Jeep, walking across the parking lot and through the building to here, I found myself looking over my shoulder, scrutinizing everyone. Looking for anybody out of place or staring in my direction. I gave every person I passed a surreptitious once-over, trying to determine if I had seen any of these people somewhere else. I had the sense that I was being followed.

I tried to shake it off as paranoia, but the events of the past month told me to keep my eyes open for anyone acting suspicious. Of course, if they were a pro at surveillance, I might not notice them. Or, like Tony Bruno had cautioned, they might pretend to be my friend, but had other interests in mind.

Which was why I was here to see Andrea.

My shadow passed over the three women sitting by the pool. Violet looked up at me. “Clark! How nice to see you!”

Dot raised a half-empty plastic cup of daiquiri with a straw sticking out the top. “Go over there and see Karen. She’ll set you up.”

I looked at Karen, then back to Dot, and smiled. It might have been the first time all day I had done that. “Thank you. Maybe another time. I need to chat with Andrea for a second.”

A look of disappointment crossed Dot’s face. “You’re missing out.”

“I know.”

I helped Andrea get to her feet. Her legs were wobbly. She placed a hand on my shoulder to steady herself. My knees became weak when she flashed her thousand-gigawatt smile at me. Focus.

"Claaark," she slurred. "I'm sooo happy you're here."

She placed her arms around my neck and gave me a big kiss on the lips. She tasted of alcohol. How many of Karen's daiquiris had she consumed? If she were even slightly drunk, a state I hadn't seen her in before, then she might be more forthcoming in what I needed to talk to her about.

"Thanks," I said. I wasn't going to lie and say I was happy to be here as well. Anything but. "I need to ask you something."

She caught the way I said it. With a hint of caution, she said, "Sure. What is it?"

I looked down at Dot and Violet and over to Libby playing with her friend in the pool. No one was near the back corner of the pool area. I tilted my head in that direction. “Let’s go over there.”

I walked beside her, holding her arm to keep her steady. She might have been having too much fun this afternoon. I hated to break it to her, but that might be about to end.

This section of the pool lay in the shade of a pear tree.

“What’s up?” she asked.

I had thought about how to frame this question on the ride over. I couldn’t come up with a way to nibble around the edges of the subject. It was best to get straight to the point.

Instead of asking a question, I said, "Summit Capital Holdings."

Her mouth fell open, and the color drained from her face.

"You've heard of it," I said. "I can tell."

She cocked her head to the side with a raised eyebrow. "Yeah, I have. How do you know about them?"

I looked in both directions. No one was nearby. One reason I chose this tucked-away corner was that it was out of sight from the security camera looking on from the back exit of the condo.

When Andrea and I'd first met, we'd had lengthy conversations about losing our spouses. Her husband died in a car accident one night while driving home from a bar. He was intoxicated at the time.

An addiction he'd had; Andrea told me. She was aware of it before they were married, and she had convinced herself that she could get him off the bottle after they wed. That had never happened.

Libby came along shortly before his death. Andrea had said they weren't married long. Only about a year and a half.

"It's a long story," I said, "but it seems like they had something to do with Autumn's death."

She leaned closer. "How?"

"That's what I'm trying to figure out."

My mention of Summit Capital seemed to have sobered her up from whatever amount of alcohol she'd consumed before I'd gotten here. Her blue eyes were more focused. Was it concern, or was it willing herself to remain focused, so she didn't slip up? Was she fishing for information to report to someone about how much I knew?

Because I needed answers, I only relayed the details of my trip to the Register of Deeds to search for information about Summit Capital after coming across their name during the investigation this past weekend. I left out that I did that at Moody's urging. The less she knew at this point, the better—for both of us likely.

"When I left the courthouse," I explained, "the woman working in the Register of Deeds gave me a printout of all the properties owned by Summit Capital."

"And you saw my condo on the list," Andrea said.

At least she wasn't running away from it. That gave me hope that she would be cooperative.

"Yes, I did. How did it end up there?"

She nibbled her bottom lip. "Remember how I said that I took our savings after Libby's father died and bought Coastal Décor?"

"I do."

Her right eye twitched. "That wasn't entirely true."

I took a step away from her, trying to keep my volume under control. "What do you mean, 'not entirely true'?"

She sighed and her shoulders sagged. She leaned in again, but I held her away at arm's length.

For the first time, my movement seemed to upset her. As far as I was concerned, if anyone needed to be upset, it was me.

"When he died, yes, I used our savings to buy my store. That much was true, but it took all the money I had."

"And you needed help to find a place for you and Libby to live." I crossed my arms. "If you were living in Missouri, how did you know Coastal Décor was for sale? I was Sherry's next-door neighbor there, and I didn't know the place was for sale."

Andrea wasn't put off by my defensive posture. If anything, she had softened hers. Was it a ploy? "My uncle told me about it. Said it might be good for me, and he'd help me out with living arrangements."

My blood ran cold. "Your uncle? Who's your uncle?"

Without skipping a beat, Andrea said, "Sid Rosen."

CHAPTER TWENTY-EIGHT

THAT WAS THE LAST thing I had expected Andrea to say. I sometimes have the nasty habit of opening my mouth and speaking before I know what I'm going to say. Instead of immediately responding with something I'd regret as soon as I said it, I held my tongue. I could not let her know I was onto him,

Doing that helped in this instance because Andrea, with a healthy dose of alcohol coursing through her body like a truth serum and seeing my reaction, filled in some blanks.

She placed a hand on my arm. I didn't pull away.

"Look, I never told you he was my uncle because I didn't think it was important. He told me he'd help me move here and start a new life for Libby and me if I didn't tell anyone where the money came from." She started rubbing her hand up and down my arm.

It didn't comfort me.

Andrea continued, telling me how "Uncle Sid" always helped her mama out when daddy couldn't pay the bills. Her mom was Rosen's older sister.

As she spoke, everything she said became white noise. The words coming out of her mouth sounded like Charlie Brown's teacher. Several of the separate threads I'd been chasing twisted together to form an entwined string. There was so much more that there would be a threaded rope by the time I was finished. I just hoped that rope didn't hang me.

I'd come to notice something about Andrea. What I first thought of as a nervous tic might not have been the case. Like a tell in poker, every time her eye twitched, it came before she said something that might be a lie. A moment ago, her eye twitched before she revealed that Rosen had helped her buy Coastal Décor and move from Missouri to Myrtle Beach. When I first met her, she didn't say anything about needing help. Only that she had used savings to come here.

She'd done that before. Like when I came into her store and found her in the office composing an email on her computer—which she abruptly minimized when I entered—and told me she was doing some paperwork. Who had that email gone to? Rosen?

First, she moved into the business next door to mine—after "Uncle Sid" helped her buy it. Then there was the bug in my phone. After wracking my brain as to who had the opportunity to place it there, the only logical conclusion was that it had to be Andrea. She was the only person I'd left alone with my phone for any length of time. There had been times when we'd had dinner, and I'd gotten up to use the restroom and left my phone on the table.

It didn't seem like it would take long to plant the listening device in a phone. In the spy novels I've read, it seems like you just pop the back cover off the phone, activate the tiny spy, place it near the receiver, and snap the cover back on. It could take less than a minute to install the bug if she knew what she was doing.

Sometimes, Andrea acted like the elevator didn't go all the way to the top. Her pronounced deep South accent tended to make her sound like a back holler yokel. The type that causes people to assume they weren't the brightest. She may not be, but I now thought she had pretended to be dumber than she was. When not engaged with Libby or others, she always had a magazine or book in front of her. She'd shown me enough in our conversations that she was smarter than she let on, which led to some terrific thought-provoking chats.

If she was the person responsible for placing the device in my phone, then the only conclusion was that Rosen instructed her to do it. If that was the case, then she wouldn't be dumb enough to agree to do it without asking why she was doing it. That meant she was placed in my life to spy on me and was part of this conspiracy.

I had to admit, Andrea shared several of Autumn's physical attributes. Andrea's hair wasn't auburn like Autumn's, but it had a similar wave to it. Autumn didn't wear glasses while Andrea did. They had similar face shapes and bodies. Even their first names started with the same letter. If what I was thinking was true, having an available niece like Andrea would be awfully convenient to distract me with my “type.” Too bad my type was not fully physical but more mental.

Andrea had been inside my home several times. Had she planted devices to spy on me there? At this point, I didn’t want to go home and find out. I had the paranoid feeling that someone would be parked down the street, waiting to see if I came home.

It occurred to me that I didn’t know when I would be able to go home again.

Andrea was still talking, defending herself for not telling me about her uncle sooner. I hadn’t heard a word she said, so lost I was in my thoughts.

I blinked, seeing her in a new light. My heart ached.

I took her hand off my arm.

That annoyed her. "What? Are we okay?"

"I don't know."

"What are we going to do?"

I looked into her eyes and decided. This was too important to beat around the bush. If what I was about to ask was not correct and out of line, I would be in danger of her never speaking to me again. If I was correct, then I might not ever want to speak to her again.

"Did Rosen tell you to spy on me?"

She opened her mouth. Closed it without answering.

Before she finally answered, her eye twitched.

CHAPTER TWENTY-NINE

SHE TOLD ME SHE didn't know what I was talking about and denied my allegation. I wanted to believe her, but that eye twitch when I'd asked plus the other circumstantial evidence suggested otherwise.

Instead of calling her out on it and causing a public scene (which I should have), I pretended to accept her answer with a nod.

She asked me if I was ready to grab a beverage and hang out with them, but I had more to say. What I wanted to say, I had to do so with an element of caution. If she was passing on information about me to Uncle Sid, then I had to consider every word carefully. A slipup could prove costly, maybe my life.

It still bugged me as to why Gomez hadn't replied to my texts or called. That troubling thought remained at the back of my mind while Andrea stood in front of me.

After the moment of silence, she spoke. "Where have you been? Besides last night, I didn't hear from you at all. I want to hear about you solving that murder and getting shot at." She rubbed my arm tenderly. "That's so heroic."

I brushed the accolade aside. It seemed like she said it to make me feel like she was on my side. Which, I must admit, she could be despite my growing concerns over her loyalty. But where was the concern over my welfare most girlfriends would mention if their boyfriends were shot at?

“Thanks,” I said. “I was the right person in the wrong place at the right time, I guess.”

“Don’t be so modest. I can’t think of any normal person doing what you did outside of movies.”

I changed the subject. “I dropped my phone last night.”

She looked down where I had the phone in my pocket. “It still works, though, right? You texted me somehow.”

"It does. Got a few scratches and a hair-line crack."

"That's better than completely broken."

"Yeah, it is." I reached into my pocket, withdrew the phone, and held it up. "It was interesting when it broke open after hitting the pavement."

She eyed the phone before asking, "What was so interesting about it?"

"I found a listening device inside."

"Unh-uh," she said with a slow nod of the head. "Someone's listening to your conversations?"

"Apparently so."

"Why?"

If Andrea was indeed part of this, then it wouldn't hurt for me to cast a line and see if she bit.

"I think it has something to do with Autumn." I'd told her all about how Autumn's death three years ago went from unsuspicious to suspicious. Every detail. Now that I suspected her of trying to wiggle her way into my life by way of Sid Rosen, if Andrea was spying on me, that meant he knew everything I had told her. More, if you count the phone bug. There were conversations I'd had with Gomez and Moody that Andrea wouldn't have been around to hear.

"Why would someone want to do that?" she asked.

"I guess to make sure I'm not getting too close to the truth."

"What would happen if you did?"

"Probably nothing good would come of it, at least for me."

"Are you saying that you think what might have happened to Autumn could happen to you?"

At this point, I threw the "might have" in her statement out the window. I still didn't know how or why, but with all the signs pointing to Rosen, I think I knew who.

And Andrea was now linked to whatever scheme and to him.

No matter how much she denied it, right now, I couldn't trust her.

To answer her question, I said, "Possibly."

If she was afraid for my life, she didn't show it. At least she seemed to take me seriously.

"Should you stay here?" she asked. "Maybe you need to get away and let the dust settle on whatever is happening."

"No," I said, setting the bait. "Things are coming to a head, and I think your uncle has something to do with it."

She removed her hand from my forearm and crossed her arms. "Are you accusing my uncle of murdering your wife?"

"I'm not." At least not yet, but I didn't want to say that to her. "I'm just saying that something smells fishy, and the source of the smell seems to be coming from city hall."

She took a step away. “You can’t mean that.”

“I don’t know what else to say, but I do mean it.”

Andrea tapped her bare foot on the concrete. “What are you going to do now? Go after him?”

“No. It’s just that what I’ve learned about him, and his friend Zach may be linked with the people who sent Autumn the threatening text messages.”

I didn’t want to tell her all the details.

This was all information I didn’t want Rosen to know I was onto. Yet.

There was something that had happened that I was fairly sure Rosen and Co. wouldn’t know about yet. If I mentioned it to Andrea and it got back to me through nefarious means, then I would know Andrea was passing along information to her uncle.

"Did you hear that Detective Moody died yesterday?"

Her eyebrows shot up and her pupils dilated at the unexpected statement. "No, I didn't"

I shook my head. "He dropped me off at my house after we left the police station the other night, went home, and died in his sleep."

"Goodness. That's so sad. What do they think he passed away from?"

"He had a history of heart problems. Survived a major heart attack a while back. The coroner said that was the cause, but his wife is sending the body in to have an autopsy performed."

"Why?"

"To see if there were any signs of foul play."

"Why would she think that?"

I shrugged. "He'd been around Myrtle Beach for a long time and apparently poked his nose into a few places maybe he shouldn't have. She thinks that maybe someone had had enough and wanted Moody removed."

She arched an eyebrow. "If he died of a heart attack, how could he have been murdered?"

"Poison."

"You're kidding."

"I'm not." Time to cast the lure and see if I caught something on the other end. "I'm thinking maybe Moody had figured out who was behind Autumn's death and his former partner's as well. All three died of supposed heart attacks."

Andrea didn't know how to respond at first. She wasn't a person who was familiar enough with how murder investigations worked to be able to connect the invisible dots. But she could tell someone else about it and let them do the figuring. Which is what I hoped would happen.

"That's quite a coincidence," she said at length.

"Exactly. That's why I think it's all connected."

Her chest swelled with a deep breath as we locked eyes. She stepped forward, placed a hand on one side of my face and kissed my cheek on the other side. Her breath was warm just before her lips made contact. I didn't move to wipe the moisture from her mouth away. "You need to take care of yourself," she said, drawing back. "It sounds like you've gotten yourself into something dangerous."

"I agree." I touched her elbow, drawing her close. At this point, while I was aware that this conversation would make her suspicious, I didn't want her to think that I saw her as an enemy. Which I did.

"I'm not going to tell you where I'm going," I said. "Just know that I need to see this thing through."

“I understand. Please, be careful and let me know you’re okay when you can.”

I grabbed her hand and kissed her on the lips. “I’ll do that.”

I was beginning to understand what undercover spies went through with the cloak and dagger and half-truths. It was an icky feeling, but it had to be done in this case. On the other hand, it could all be part of the game of her uncle placing her in my life.

The only thing for sure, at this point, was that I couldn’t trust her. At least not for now. I hoped that the mistrust of her on my part was misdirected, but I had to play it safe for the time being.

We parted hands and ways. She told me to be careful again as I walked away.

***

I walked back into the lobby at Paradise Hideaway and trotted through to the front exit. There was something I wanted to see before I left. Something that might confirm my reservations with Andrea.

The doors whooshed shut behind me as I stepped onto the sidewalk at the front of the condo. At a brisk pace, but not brisk enough to arouse suspicion, I walked the length of the building down the left side and circled around to the back.

Large, green dumpsters sat at either end of the back lot. A Carolina Cool service van was parked near a rear exit. The rear doors were left open. No one was inside the vehicle. At least I didn't spot CIA listening equipment inside the van.

A six-foot tall fence lined the back of the pool patio to keep out random onlookers. A strip of green grass about twenty yards wide separated the back alley from the tall chain-link fence surrounding the Myrtle Beach International Airport. After a while, the residents tuned out the constant arrivals and departures of the passenger planes.

Near the side of the dumpster on this end of the alley rested an empty five-gallon paint bucket. I grabbed it and took it with me to the fence by the pool. I wasn't tall enough to peek over it even standing on my tippy toes, but the bucket should do the trick.

I turned the bucket upside-down and stepped onto the flat surface of the underside. Careful not to place my fingers over the edge of the fence so less of me could be seen, I looked over the top to the spot Andrea and the Silver Girls had taken.

Andrea wasn't with them. They weren't looking for her.

But I was, and I spotted her over in the same quiet corner where she and I had our conversation. Her back was to me, but it was obvious what she was doing.

She had her cell phone up to one ear. Her hand covered her mouth as she spoke into it using a hushed voice.

No doubt about it now.

She had to be on the phone to Uncle Rosen or some other crony.

Either way, the trap had been set. Now to see if I caught my prey.

CHAPTER THIRTY

I CLIMBED INTO MY car, tossing my phone in the passenger seat, and left the parking lot immediately.

I still didn't know who was responsible for the whole scheme, but the mayor of Myrtle Beach sat squarely in the middle. After reflecting on it, Autumn and Andrea shared physical similarities. Rosen himself had told me that he admired Autumn's work ethic. For him to think that, he must have been around her at the courthouse. He would have known what she looked like and some of her personality traits.

He must have one sick mind to think to himself, "Hey, my poor niece Andrea out in Missouri recently suffered the sudden loss of her husband. She resembles this other woman I murdered (maybe). I should buy my sweet niece and my precious little grandniece a home and business next door to the chump who used to be married to the woman I murdered (probably). Then I wonder if I could get her to spy on him and tell me if he's getting too close to learning the truth behind his wife's seemingly innocent death (whatever that is)?"

Right now, all signs pointed to him, but I had no way of proving it. Means, motive, opportunity. That's what mom drilled into me during my first murder investigation. If you had all three, then you would have a good idea who committed a murder.

The only conceivable means I imagined that could have killed Autumn, and possibly Moody and Banner, was poison. I wasn't an expert on the subject like Agatha Christie. The results of Moody's autopsy should come tomorrow. When it did, it would tell me if he was murdered and what traces of poison were left in his blood. If he was murdered, that is. It's just as likely that he genuinely had a heart attack, and I was jumping at shadows.

It seemed now that those shadows were cast by something real and ominous, and I was only just now scratching the surface.

I passed by Tidal Creek Brewhouse heading out of Market Common, trying to think of how to dig deeper. As I sat at a stop sign waiting to turn onto Farrow Parkway, a possible solution struck me like a brick. Cars passed in both directions.

I reached over, grabbed my phone, and went to the email app.

An impatient tourist honked their horn behind me. I looked in the rearview mirror and gave a thumbs up to the driver behind me as a way of apologizing. I turned right and pulled into the first parking space available along the street fronting the colorful row homes of the area.

The guy who had been behind me zoomed past after I pulled into the spot.

He held up a different finger to me from the thumb I had given him. Whatever. It didn't surprise me that he had a license plate from a state up North known for having aggressive and impatient drivers.

I pulled up Bo's email and found the article from St. Grant's Island where Rosen commented. It was dated five years ago, and I hoped the reporter still worked for the paper.

His name was still in the directory on the company website along with his phone number and email address. Some of these small-town reporters made their private numbers public in hopes of getting news tips. The constant news cycle churn had to be stressful for someone looking to fill space in a column.

I called the number trying to remember if I had international calls added to my cell phone plan. This was the first one I'd made outside of the country, and I didn't care if my cell provider charged me out the yin-yang to make it.

He answered after three rings. "Steve Koch. How can I help ya?"

I waited for a loud motorcycle to roar past before speaking. "Hi, I'm calling from Myrtle Beach in South Carolina, and I was hoping you could answer a few questions for me."

An audible groan came from the phone speaker. "I get this all the time. Ya need to call the St. Grant's tourism cowncil."

I pulled the phone from my ear and checked the screen to make sure I'd di-aled the correct number. He'd already identified himself as the person I sought, but you never know. "Excuse me?"

"This happens all the time," Koch said. "My phone numbah is one digit off the tourism cowncil's. I get these wrong numbahs all the time. Hang up and dial a six at the end instead of a five. Have a wicked good day."

Before he hung up, I said, "No, no, no. Mr. Koch? I called to speak to you."

"Okay. Got a news tip? What's this about?"

He didn't have an island accent if such a thing existed on St. Grant's Island. It was more Boston. Heavy Boston.

"I'm not sure if it's a tip, but I have some questions about an article you wrote."

"How old is the article?"

"Five years."

He whistled. "Five years? I write about ten articles per week for the papah."

"Busy guy."

"That's the truth. I retired from the post office a decade ago in Quincy, Mass. and moved with my wife here to St. Grant's. Wanted to get away from the wintahs."

"I grew up in Southern Ohio," I said. "I can relate. One of the many reasons why I moved to Myrtle Beach."

"I've been there," he said. "Nice place."

"It is." I'd struck some common ground with Koch. Now, I hoped he'd be able to help me.

"What is someone from Myrtle Beach callin' me fwor?"

"Do you remember a company called Salty Sands Holdings who got caught for trying to bribe their way into some property?"

"Hmm," he mumbled. "Let's see. I think so. They tried to purchase a wicked big tract of land up on the north side of the island for development. The deal went through at first. We're not a large island, and that was some of the lone remainin' untouched land on it. I've been up there. It's really a beautiful piece of land. I was surprised no one had tried to do anything with it before."

"What went wrong?"

"Some of the local officials wanted government researchers to comb the site for anything historically significant that might get erased if Salty Sands went through with their plans of addin' a luxury resort."

"I take it they found something."

"Oh baby. Boy did they evah."

Koch explained that the soil on that part of the island is acidic, which makes it difficult to find salvageable remains. Salty Sands had no problem with the Institute for Preventative Archaeology Research going through the property as they didn't think they'd find anything. What they discovered was ninety-seven pre-Columbian graves dating back to between the 11th and 13th centuries. St. Grant's sits near Guadeloupe which itself is a string of six Caribbean islands all brought to life by volcanic activity. The bodies were buried in such a way through layering of limbs that the bodies remained undisturbed in the soil. Hundreds of post holes from long gone structures along with shards of pottery, tools, and animal remains were also found.

"When the discovery was made, Salty Sands tried to keep it out of the press," Koch said, "and then tried to bribe officials to basically sweep the entire thing undah the rug and forget aboudit so they could proceed with their project."

"How nice of them."

"Yeah, just anothah crooked developah in this part of the world," Koch said. "They think they can come to these small islands down here and do whatevah they want. Sometimes they find out the hahd way that it's not that easy. Is that what you wanted to know?"

"Yeah, that helps," I said. Trying to bribe their way through a historic finding the way they did sent a shock through my system that I'd explore more. For now, I needed to learn something else. "Your article said that you couldn't get in touch with anyone from Salty Sands for comment, and you ended up contacting their attorney, Sid Rosen."

"Correct," Koch said. "I stumbled onto the story aftah Salty Sands pulled up stakes and left the island. The government didn't want the people to know that bribery was even a possibility heah."

"How did you learn about it?"

He laughed. "The same way I get a lot of my stories heah. Sitting at a café. There's one on the cornah near our apartment that always has some good gossip. It's a place where locals hang out. Not very many tourists, thank goodness. A couple guys were talkin' about findin' the graves, before that discovery became public, and how this American company was trying to covah it up so they could build."

"That's one of the things I love about coffee shops."

"Exactly. So, I asked these guys who the company was, and they told me Salty Sands. I went ovah to the government centah heah in town and started going through property transactions until I found 'em. There were two names on the contract besides the sellahs. Salty Sands was owned by some guy, I think his name was Zachary, Zacharius, or something and their lawyah's name, Sid

Rosen. I couldn't get in touch with the first guy but caught Rosen at his law office. It was obvious that he didn't want to talk to me and regretted takin' my cahll. I pressured him into makin' a statement and that was that."

Goosebumps prickled on the back of my neck. I had Rosen and Lawson linked in a property transaction and bribery scandal outside the States.

"That's interesting," I said. "Did you know Rosen got elected as mayor here in Myrtle Beach about a year after that happened?"

"Shut the front door. You're kiddin' me."

"I kid ya not. He seemed to be doing a pretty good job of it, too. Myrtle Beach has done well under him."

"I take it since you're callin' me to ask about 'im, that he's done something fishy. What is it you said you do?"

A chuckle escaped my mouth. This was always a fun answer to that question when I'm investigating murders. "I own a bookstore on the Myrtle Beach Boardwalk."

"Ah. Did he do somethin' to ruffle yaw feathers?"

"You could say that. I think he was involved with murdering my wife, if he didn't do it himself."

He let out a long whistle. "That's definitely fishy, my friend."

I gave him the nutshell version of events leading up to my phone call with him as traffic passed me by, including how

I hadn't been able to find a way to link Rosen to Summit Capital. The afternoon progressed and the shadows began lengthening across Farrow Parkway from the buildings and trees.

"I've seen that name," Koch said when I finished. "Summit Capital."

My mouth went dry. "Where?"

"Hmm. I forget exactly, but I can look through my notes."

"You keep notes about articles from that long ago?"

"Yes, sir. This is proof that ya never know when you'll need 'em. It might have even had to do with this failed development project, I forget. Give me a few hours and I'll get back to ya."

"Hey man, I'd appreciate that so much. I'd owe you a drink if I ever made it to St. Grant's."

"Bah. Fuhgeddaboudit. This is fun for an old scribe. Who knows? It might even make for a story here."

"Hopefully, for you, it does."

"That's right." He paused. "I just checked the time. I'm about to take my wife out for some dinnah and dancin' at this place in town. Might be tomorrow before I get back to you."

If I live that long. "Any help is appreciated."

"Sure thing, my friend."

Before I ended the call, I had a stray thought that had nothing to do with the previous subject. "You wouldn't happen to know another expat by the name of Antonio Bianchi, would you?"

"Oh man. Antonio? That guy's the life of the pahty."

Somehow, I wasn't surprised.

The call ended. I took a deep breath. Finally, a possible link between Rosen, Zach, and possible illegal activity with bribery at its heart.

For the first time, the dots in what happened to Autumn started to connect, along with a possible motive.

At present, the most concerning part of all was, where is Gomez?

CHAPTER THIRTY-ONE

CHAPTER THIRTY-ONE

START OF TEXT MESSAGES

Andrea's cover is blown. He knows. What do you want me to do?

Take care of him and Gomez.

Him, I don't mind. I'm not comfortable harming her.

Do it or I'll reveal your secret. Then she'll hate you anyway. Make it look like an accident.

If you insist.

I do.

END OF TEXT MESSAGES

CHAPTER THIRTY-TWO

WHILE I WAITED FOR Koch and Courthouse Karen to get back to me, I had nowhere to go. I could hide out in the motel but didn't want to stay in one place for too long. Although I was outright ignoring the warning spray-painted on the windows of Garden City Reads by continuing to investigate, I wanted to lay as low as possible in case I was being watched.

During the murder investigation at Tidal Creek Brewhouse at the beginning of

June, I was aware of the security cameras used at Paradise Hideaway. I kicked myself for not thinking about them while I was there, or I would have done a better job of avoiding them in case someone was watching. Slinking around the rear of the condo and peeking over the fence while standing on an upside-down bucket didn't look suspicious at all. Yes, there was a camera at either end of the building. I'm such an amateur at times.

The thing about me was I learned quickly and rarely made the same mistake three times. Maybe four. Sometimes only twice if I was lucky.

At any other time, Gomez not returning my call or text wouldn't have been so bothersome. Usually, it meant she was working. This time, she had been placed on leave, and we were in the middle of trying to figure out if her partner had been murdered.

As I cruised up to where Farrow Parkway turned over to Socastee Boulevard after going under the 17 Bypass overpass, it occurred to me that there was one person I could contact about Gomez. He was also the person who might have placed a bug in my phone meaning that he might also be involved in whatever scheme was taking place in Myrtle Beach.

Lucien.

The light turned red at the three-way intersection leading out to a McDonald's and WBTW television station. I bit the inside of my bottom lip. I didn't want to do this, but I saw no alternative.

I didn't have Lucien's number saved in my phone. I had no reason to, but I had a thought on how to get it. I checked through the emails I'd received this past weekend. Because I was officially part of the Zach Lawson murder investigation, I'd been included on emails to and from Moody and the forensics department. Kevin had been the person who sent most of them, but one time, Lucien responded with a "Thanks."

His emails had a saved signature that included his contact information under his name. I pulled up that email, held my finger on his number, copied it, and pasted it into the screen to make a call.

There are times in this crazy universe where something happens that you can't explain. Maybe you're cruising down the highway, listening to your favorite radio station, and as one song starts to end, a random song you haven't heard in years pops into your head. Then, right as that happens, it comes on the radio. It is so weird at that moment. Such a coincidence.

When coincidences occur during a murder investigation, they are almost always not as random as they seem. I've learned to distrust coincidences.

Right when I had my finger poised over the button to call Lucien, the phone first vibrated in my hand before his number disappeared and a box popped up on the screen with an incoming call from the same phone number I was about to try.

Lucien was calling me. The light turned green. Traffic resumed.

I answered the call. “Hello?”

Without preamble, Lucien said, “Have you seen or heard from Gina?”

My throat went dry. “No. Not since yesterday.”

“She didn’t come home last night,” he said. “I’ve tried calling her. Texting her. Everything. I know it could mean something bad if she is, but I was hoping she might have been with you.”

I didn’t know where things would stand with Andrea after all of this would shake out. Part of me hoped she was an innocent dupe because I want to believe the best in people, and it was too late to tell Uncle Sid “no” when he asked her to keep an eye on me. Allegedly. No matter the outcome of all this, I'd made up my mind to stop seeing Andrea. There was no way I could after what happened earlier.

After Gomez removed her ring last night when she began to suspect Lucien of having something to do with what was happening, the other part of me longed for her. When I lay in the motel bed during the wee hours of this morning, I found myself conflicted. After the scene at the pool with Andrea, that conflict evaporated.

The prospect that Gomez might break off her engagement with Lucien cast a possible bright future with her that I hadn't foreseen going into last weekend.

That is, if Gomez wanted to pursue anything with me. One mustn't assume.

If Lucien had been listening to my calls or every conversation through the bug in my phone, then he would know his fiancée and I would have been to Moody's house and spoken with Marge. He would be aware that we saw his death as suspicious and that an autopsy was currently being performed. It's also possible, if she was the informant, that he was already aware of the conversation Andrea and I had by the pool. I didn't know, but she could have been talking to Lucien and not Rosen.

He wouldn't like what I was about to say, especially knowing he was the jealous type.

"Gina and I visited Moody's wife yesterday to see how she was doing."

"I'm aware."

He'd be aware if he was tracking my phone. If he was doing that, then I wouldn't put it past him to keep tabs on Gomez in a similar fashion.

Speaking of which. "Have you tried tracing her phone?"

Working for the police department and running a forensics lab had its perks, and I assumed that included having access to cell phone tracking software. Bo might be able to use his skills to find Gomez.

He groaned. "I have. No luck. It must be off."

"Or gotten destroyed."

"Why would you think that?"

"Maybe she was involved in a car accident on the way home."

"She wasn't. I've checked." He hesitated. "Let's let bygones be bygones and cast our differences aside. She's missing, and I hoped you knew where she was. She's been acting strange since she got back from that conference in D.C., and I thought it might have something to do with you. After talking to you, I'm not so sure. Right now, I'm just concerned for her safety."

"Why? Do you think she's in danger?"

"Her job always puts her in danger. You never know when some dude she put away five years ago gets out of the pen and comes at her with a vendetta."

He didn't give any hint about the current unfolding drama with Zach, Rosen, or Summit Capital. Our first thought when we found the bug in my phone was that it must be Lucien behind it. He had the means, motive, and possible opportunity to plant the bug.

Like with Andrea, I had to ask myself if I was jumping at shadows and open myself up to the possibility that Lucien had nothing to do with this. He may just come off seeming like a scuzzball and may not actually be one. Who knows? He might be a nice guy after all, and I was the one who had jealousy toward him. I mean, Gomez had to see something endearing enough in him to agree to marry Lucien.

I swallowed. "What are we going to do?"

Yes, I used the word “we” in that question. It was a difficult thing to say, but if Lucien’s concern was genuine, and he wasn’t involved, then it seemed like the two of us working together might be a good thing for Gomez’s sake.

On the other hand, if Lucien was involved, I was playing right into their hands.

CHAPTER THIRTY-THREE

IN THE END, WE decided to stay in touch and to let each other know if we heard anything. I think we both realized that we'd "stay in touch," meaning when I eventually heard from Gomez, and if Lucien was innocent, I would contact him. If she came back on the radar and contacted me first, and we continued to assume Lucien was involved somehow, then he could take a hike.

I figured him suggesting staying in touch was more of a way for him to keep track of me. That is, if he had been tracking me from the beginning and now couldn't.

I pulled off into the narrow True BBQ gravel lot. It occurred to me that I'd now been to more than one barbecue joint in the last two days. Barbecue restaurants were almost as plentiful as pizza places in the Grand Strand. I'd walked up to the window at True BBQ several times in the past and loved grabbing something to go.

As depressing as a thought it was, right now wasn't the time for brisket or pulled pork.

Well, maybe. We'll see.

I'd been kicking around the idea of bugs and tracking devices in my head since last night. It made sense that whoever was behind the installation of the listening device that fell out of my phone would have also used it to track my location. If I was a person with bad motives keeping track of little old me, I'd have a backup. They may not be able to listen to my phone calls, but there were other ways to track my travels.

It was time to see if my raised level of paranoia was justified.

I took off my seatbelt and climbed out of the Jeep. I was parked between a large silver Chevy Tahoe and a black Nissan Altima. True BBQ didn't have a dining room, but they had placed a few picnic tables out front where a large Hispanic family was currently enjoying a feast.

Going around the vehicle, I ran my hand under each wheel well, searching for a tracker someone might have planted there. I'd parked where the SUV shielded me from the road so the crazy guy feeling around his undercarriage—me—wouldn't be seen. The underside of the car frame where I ran my hands had bumps on it. Occasionally, I'd knock off a clump of dirt stuck there. This was one way to detail a car I'd never considered.

On the third wheel I came to, the front passenger side, my hand brushed across something hard and small. Something that hadn't been in the first two wheel wells. It was stuck there by some sort of adhesive. I squeezed my hand around it and pulled. It came out with some effort.

It was black and rectangular, about the size of a pack of gum. The surface of it glinted in the sunlight.

I glanced at the families eating at the picnic tables. They weren't paying any attention to me. The Tahoe further obscured their view of me.

A genius idea struck. Whoever these people were had gone out of their way to plant a bug on my phone and a tracking device on my Jeep. This was an opportunity to turn the tables. It was high time to gain some of my own power and take away some of theirs.

I ducked down and eased over to the rear driver's side wheel well of the Altima, reached under, and stuck the device to the underside.

After confirming that the device wasn't going to fall out, I stood up and wiped the dirt off my hands by rubbing them together. For a moment, I considered that my gambit might put someone else in danger, but surely whoever was trying to keep tabs on me would figure out fast that the owner of the Altima wasn't me and put two and two together.

I checked the last wheel and under the back bumper but came up with nothing else.

Satisfied that I'd now thrown my antagonist off the scent, I climbed back in the Jeep and motored out of the lot.

Little did I know my fingers had come within inches of discovering something I wouldn't learn about until much later.

A backup tracker placed on the underside of my gas tank.

CHAPTER THIRTY-FOUR

MY PHONE BUZZED WITH a message tone on the seat next to me. I ignored it because I was caught in traffic on the 17 Bypass. I was no longer wandering around aimlessly. Time to get to the center of this. Time to go to City Hall and confront Rosen.

Our scheduled meeting for the commendation wasn't until tomorrow, but I'd walk in like I had the wrong date and time. He was known for keeping regular office hours and being available if not tied up in meetings or having other commitments. Running Myrtle Beach was a full-time job, and I respected his work ethic, although not the man himself.

I exited onto 501 and headed downtown. Traffic was miserable with all the tourists using 501 as the main route to get to the beach.

As I sat at a stoplight, I quickly checked my notifications to see who had sent me a text. It was from a number my phone didn't recognize. Knowing my time was brief, I didn't read the message, and instead sent a message to Bo, asking him to try and locate Gomez using her phone number, which I included in the message. After about two miles, I swung a left onto Oak Street before veering off onto Broadway Street.

The revamped and remodeled Myrtle Beach City Hall lay at the end of a sort of triangle. It had the classic look of any small-town city hall built in the mid-1900s. A new green space with neatly manicured lawn and oaks fronted city hall. The bus depot had been moved during redevelopment allowing the city to create a new traffic pattern and build a new common hub for city services. A new residential center rose above the trees beyond the hub. It had been built through private investors after approval from the city. The goal there was to create an area of more affordable workforce housing.

Live oaks provided shade to visitor parking on the street in front of the city hall. Palmettos lined the street facing Broadway Street. The old city hall had been remodeled and expanded with two new wings during the redevelopment of downtown. The goal was to integrate several government offices and the municipal court into one building. Autumn would have wound up working here if she were still alive.

The main entrance fronted Broadway Street. If I went through there, I would have to navigate through various channels and guards to get to Rosen's office upstairs. Technically, I wasn't supposed to go up there without an appointment or clearance from the city manager. As I'd been there several times over the past year, I hoped the security guard at the rear employee entrance would allow me access. The proposition was a fifty-fifty chance at this point, but I didn't have anything to lose.

As this was a government facility, security cameras were everywhere if you knew where to look. Some obvious. Some not so much. I spotted the openly visible cameras at each corner of the building. There were also six on the roof. Two facing the exterior front and back and one on each side facing the sides.

My phone buzzed. Bo had done quick work trying to find Gomez through her cell phone. It wasn't good news. He said it was offline, like someone had removed the battery from her phone or thrown it in a lake so it couldn't be tracked. The other new message from the unknown number still sat on my notification bar unread. It was probably just my pest control guy telling me when he was coming to spray for bugs. I wish he could kill mechanical ones as well.

My house probably had more of them than Palmetto bugs at this point. The bug man, or whoever it was, could wait. Might be my weed control guy, come to think of it. He could wait, too.

I locked the door to the Jeep and headed to the back steps. I passed a smiling woman with medium length brown hair and glasses, clutching a stack of manila folders.

"Hello," she said with a smile as we passed each other. The ID on the lanyard around her neck identified her as "Shelly."

"Good afternoon." I returned.

Salt air blew in off the ocean a couple hundred yards away. It always seemed windier in this part of downtown since they tore down the old Pavilion. I missed going there with Autumn when we were dating. The leaves of the oaks and palms fluttered in the steady breeze.

Just before I hit the buzzer to alert the security guard inside that someone wanted in through the employee entrance, I remembered my phone had buzzed with a message tone on the way here that I ignored twice

I pulled it out of my pocket and checked it. The message came from an 843-phone number that wasn't saved to my phone. Most of the time, random messages were spam, but ones from the local area code were usually legit.

I checked it. It was Mike Dame. The police officer who clothes lined me on the Boardwalk while chasing Shelly down in the death on the causeway caper. He and his partner Battles were big dudes who Gomez seemed to trust. On Sunday, when we went to apprehend Zach's murderer at the marina, after the death on the back nine investigation, she had contacted those two for backup instead of calling for backup through traditional means. Gomez had already begun to distrust some of the people operating within her police department, including the new chief, Sue Miller.

Gomez had called the ones she trusted to help us in arresting Zach's killer.

His message read:

Found Gomez's car in a lake off McDowell Shortcut Road in Murrells Inlet. Get here ASAP!

He attached a GPS pin of the coordinates where he found her Camry.

A shudder of fear crept down my spine. The message didn't communicate if she was safe or injured or worse.

The door to enter city hall stood in front of me. I was right here, right now, and needed to confront Rosen. His car was in the lot. He was here. My heart hammered in my chest. I wanted to confront him with all that I had learned, how his name kept popping up, and see his face when I did it. See if he cracked.

I stuck the phone back in my pocket and clenched my fists, trying to decide what to do.

There was only one thing to do.

With one last look through the window inset in the door, I turned on my heel and bounded down the stairs back to my Jeep.

Gomez was in trouble, and I had to try and help her.

CHAPTER THIRTY-FIVE

On my way to Burgess, technically Murrells Inlet, and McDowell Shortcut Road from downtown, my phone buzzed again. I didn't keep my phone linked to the infotainment screen like normal people, so text messages didn't pop up on the display.

With an adrenaline rush and my foot heavy on the gas, I screeched to a halt at a light near restaurant row in Surfside. Sign boards for Cookout, Bojangles, Taco Bell, and others beckoned my nearly empty stomach. Why did it seem like I was always hungry when working a case? Maybe murder and food go together in my book.

Even though I don't normally look at my phone while driving, considering the urgent text message from Mike that I didn't see for fifteen minutes after he'd sent it, I reached over and grabbed my phone.

The message was another one from an 843 number I didn't recognize. I had hoped it was Mike letting me know Gomez was okay, but it wasn't. It was from Karen Polhemus at the Register of Deeds with an update on her findings.

Didn't find other shell corps, but something VERY interesting

about Summit Capital. The prop they own on Oak St. I can't say why, but you need to ask Whitley about it. Saw you talking to her in the hall. Hope this helps. Sorry I can't tell you more. You'll understand. STAY SAFE!

Traffic began moving before I responded. In fact, for one of the rare times in any Grand Strand motorist's life, I didn't get stopped at another light before navigating my way to the coordinates Mike had sent me.

McDowell Shortcut started and ended at two separate parts of 707 in Burgess. The road contained an almost endless stream of cookie cutter subdivisions, a recycling center, and skirted the Indigo Creek Golf Club.

I rounded a sharp curve near the golf course at a snail's pace as I approached the pin on the map. When I reached it, I didn't see Gomez's car, the police, a tow truck, anything. I pulled onto the rocky shoulder and stopped. Several cars swept past me who had been behind me. I hadn't paid them any attention, but they had apparently noticed my lack of speed.

One of them blew the horn and flashed a similar gesture to the Northerner from Market Common earlier today.

Trees and a fence lined the road on this side. A wide field spread across the other. Cars moseyed past. Clouds covered the sun.

Then I saw it. A chain-link fence ran along the perimeter of Indigo Creek, keeping freeloaders from sneaking onto the golf course and playing for free. A hundred or so yards ahead of me, there was a break in the fence.

I slipped the gun into the glove compartment, got out of the Jeep, slammed the door, and ran along the shoulder to the break. It was hidden from where I had pulled to the side, but now that I was seeing it from the other direction, several cars were clustered around a pond through an opening in the trees fifty feet in.

Although I didn't know exactly where Gomez and Lucien lived, it seemed like she had described it as being near Nelly's Pizza on 707. If that was the case, it left a large question in the air: If her car was in the water beyond the vehicles in the gap in the trees, why would she have been going in that direction? She would have been going away from her home.

I stilled my shaking hands and legs and summoned the courage to climb over the broken fence. Three separate tire marks went from the main road into the woods. Two of them had turned into the cut from the same direction I had come from. A set of tread marks on the black-top veered across one lane, through the shoulder, and cut a deep gouge in the earth heading off to where the vehicles sat.

One of them was a Horry County police cruiser. The other was from the Myrtle Beach PD. This was outside their jurisdiction. Their lights weren't flashing.

I trampled through mud and tall grass. Tall loblollies lined the cut just wide enough for a car to pass through, although one was never meant to. Gomez had blazed her own path.

My stomach was queasy. I'd seen several dead bodies in the last year or so. Only one, the first one, had been a friend of mine. She was more of a casual acquaintance.

I didn't know what I would do if I came up and saw Gomez's lifeless body. Just the thought of it made my stomach want me to expel its contents. I pushed the urge down and pressed forward.

Officers Dame and Battles had their backs to me as I approached. They wore their traditional black uniforms. Two Horry County officers, a man and woman, stood next to them wearing gray shirts and dark slacks.

Battles was the first to notice me. "He's here," he said to the other officers.

They turned to face me, exposing the rear end of Gomez's blue Camry buried halfway in the mud and water of a pond. She was nowhere in sight.

They must have seen the color drain from my face. The queasiness in my stomach almost won.

Dame was the first to speak: "We were on patrol when we got a call from my buddy here at Horry County. They responded to a report of a single vehicle incident, ran the plates, and called me."

The woman, who had a sturdy frame and her blonde hair tied back in a ponytail, said, “Mr. Thomas. I’m Officer Susan Duncan. This is my partner, Beauregard Hall.”

Beauregard was my middle name, but this wasn’t the time to bring up the common ground.

“Hello,” I said. “Is there any sign of Detective Gomez?”

Beauregard shook his head. He was wet up to his waist and his boots were covered in mud. “There’s not. I waded in and checked to see if anyone was inside. It appears as if she swerved and ran off the road and into this pond.”

“There’s a lot of deer around here,” Duncan said. “She’s fortunate she didn’t hit a tree. By examining the skid marks, it looked as though she was traveling at a high speed. Well over the limit.”

My chest heaved with each breath as I tried to think it through. "Okay. Why did you call Dame and not whoever it was you needed to report this?"

Duncan shifted her eyes to Dame and back to me. "We'd heard about Gomez being sent home yesterday after her partner's death. That isn't unusual. When you work together every day, it's common for a partner to have some time to grieve in the event of the other's death. We haven't called for a tow truck or anything yet because," he gestured at the submerged Camry, "It's not going anywhere, and we wanted to bring you all in first."

"What we heard," Beauregard drawled in a thick Southern accent, "was that she didn't want to go home. That she wanted to open an investigation into Detective Moody's death. Miller told her no. He died from natural causes. Gomez protested and Miller put her on leave anyway."

Battles said, "They'd heard rumors that you and Gomez had gone to Moody's house to try and get his wife to do have an autopsy done, checking for poison."

I took it all in and digested it. At least my stomach agreed with that. "Yeah. That was after Chief Miller sent her home."

"Look man," Dame said, coming over and putting a meaty paw on my shoulder. "We've heard some things. Gomez explained to us after arresting Zach Lawson's killer why she called Battles and I and didn't follow protocol by not calling for backup over the radio."

"What did she say?" I asked.

"That she'd had a long car ride back and forth to D.C. for that police training conference and had a lot of time to think," Battles said. "She'd thought about some of Miller's actions since taking over for Kluttz, and how Miller might have an agenda."

"That led to her not trusting the new Chief," Dame said, and gave us a conspiratorial eye, "Maybe Gomez has an agenda of her own. She's been around long enough that she could practically run the place if called upon."

Battles grunted in agreement. I didn't think that was the case, but I wasn't going to disagree.

Duncan and Beauregard listened to the juicy gossip without saying a word. Their faces remained impassive.

"Did Gomez say what kind of agenda?" I asked.

"She didn't know," Battles said, "she was going on a hunch."

"We know from our end and being around Detective Gomez," Duncan said, "that she's good at her job. If she had a strong instinct about this, then there might be something to it."

"Tell us what's happening," Dame said. "We're here to help. You can trust us."

I eyed each of them. They had no clue as to what we'd uncovered connecting Zach Lawson and Mayor Rosen and several shell corporations operating illegally in the Caribbean. I'd hold that close to my chest for the time being. I didn't want to go around spreading accusations against Rosen unless I had solid evidence to connect him with illegal activities here in Horry County. Plus, if Gomez trusted them, she would have told them.

For the time being, I wanted to keep all that off the police's radar. If I laid everything out to these four police officers, I couldn't be sure the information fell on the wrong ears. I'd been around Dame and Battles enough to know their trustworthiness. I hadn't met Duncan and Beauregard until now. Whatever was happening seemed to be confined to Myrtle Beach.

Still, telling them everything scared me. I feared for my life and Gomez's. If my enemies had gotten inside my bookstore, then it wasn't a leap to believe they could break into my parent's house. It likely wouldn't be difficult for them to get to Andrea since she was Rosen's niece. He probably had a key to her place. Whether she was innocent in this or not, which I didn't believe after seeing her speaking in hushed tones after our conversation earlier, there was still Libby to think about. I'd do anything to protect that little girl.

That idle thought caused me to long to be a dad and have a family, even standing here in the muck next to a pond with a wrecked car and four police officers. Perhaps Libby reminded me of the unborn child Autumn was carrying when she'd died–was murdered. A future that was taken from me. The brain had the ability to play all sorts of tricks on a person at any time. Stupid brain.

I shook the thought away and focused on the present.

"Here's what I know," I said, and then proceeded to tell them about the vandalism at Garden City Reads, finding the listening device in my phone, and GPS tracker on my Jeep. I left out the Rosen/Zach Lawson/Summit Capital Holdings parts—the actual conspiracy of why I was likely under threat.

They listened closely and shared concerned looks with each other. When I was done, Battles said, "Why do you think this is being done?"

"It has something to do with Autumn, but I don't know what yet," I said.

"Who's Autumn?" Officer Duncan asked.

CHAPTER THIRTY-SIX

I TOLD THEM THE story about Autumn and how Gomez had informed me of her suspicions surrounding the night of her death. How, over the last year, we'd uncovered more that led us to believe she'd gotten mixed up in something sinister. Since we learned about Moody's death, she and I had been trying to get to the bottom of it, only to discover that someone had it out for us.

Eventually, Beauregard called the submerged car in to dispatch.

Before another Horry County cruiser and tow truck arrived to fish the car out to the pond, we walked back to the road. Duncan found evidence of footprints coming from where the car splashed into the pond and heading back to the road.

We followed the trail back to the road where the prints ended in the tall grass beside the gravel shoulder.

“Look,” I said, pointing at the ground. “The person used their foot to brush away their prints.”

“Appears so,” Battles agreed.

Beauregard followed the imaginary path from the edge of the grass to the pavement, went to a spot, and crouched to get a better view. “Looks like someone picked Gomez up.”

"I wonder if she'd hit her head and has amnesia or something," Duncan suggested. "Someone took her to a hospital. Maybe she didn't have an ID on her, and they registered her under Jane Doe."

"That doesn't compute," Dame said. "You still would have gotten a call from whoever picked her up or from the hospital of the incident."

"True," Duncan conceded.

"Wait a minute," I said. They looked at me. "Why was she driving in this direction? She left me in Surfside late last night. Wouldn't she have been traveling the other way toward her home?"

"That's right," Dame said. "She and Lucien live over by St. James Middle School."

“Hmm.” Battles placed a hand on his chin.

“You’re right,” Beauregard said. “That doesn’t make sense.”

“Hold on,” I said and trotted back to Gomez’s car.

“Where are you going?” Dame asked over my shoulder.

“To check something,” I called.

When I reached the edge of the pond, I pulled my shirt, shoes, and socks off. I had clothes in the Jeep if needed. I didn’t care if the four saw me in my skivvies at this point. I’d gone swimming in ponds as a kid. Sure, there might be muckety-muck to clean off later, but that didn’t stop me from wading in. Based on what we'd seen, I had a strong feeling about this.

The water came up to the rear passenger seat. They were right. She was not inside, but there was one thing I wanted to check.

The officers followed me but stopped at the edge of the pond.

The water was warm and had a fetid odor of earthiness and decay. Something brushed past my leg, startling me for a beat. I waded to the driver's side door, clutched the handle, and tried to open it. The water inside the car was cloudy. Her seat wasn't visible. The position of it was important here. All the water pressing against the door made it extremely heavy.

I'd rode with Gomez enough to know she has the habit, despite having long legs, of keeping her seat most of the way forward. I didn't know how she did it, but when she drove, the steering wheel was always on top of her. Maybe she was a little bit farsighted and tried to get as close to the road as possible to see.

Finally, I was able to open the door enough to feel down on the seat cushion. It squished beneath my fingers. It was hidden from view, so I ran my hand to the front to see where it ended.

"Aha," I said when my fingers reached the edge.

An edge much farther back than when Gomez drove.

"What is it?" Dame called from the bank.

I turned with relief etched on my face. I announced, "Gomez wasn't the driver."

Which led to two enormous questions: who was driving and where was Gomez?

CHAPTER THIRTY-SEVEN

Beauregard and Duncan told us to adios. Dame and Battles were out of their jurisdiction, and I shouldn't have been here to begin with. The county pair were going to start a search for Gomez and have her Camry taken in for processing. Battles said he'd make a call and get everyone involved in the search. Duncan told Dame she'd keep him in the loop. He told her he'd do the same. I told them to talk to Gomez's fiancé, Lucien. They said they would.

I ducked behind the Jeep while they were talking and making calls to change out of my wet, stinky shorts and underwear. Didn't want anyone to see a full moon in the middle of the day.

I agreed to follow them to Nelly's Pizza on 707. A pizza was waiting for us when we got there. I figured Dame had every pizzeria in the Grand Strand on speed dial. He took the box and laid it on the hood of their patrol car as vehicles sped by on the four-lane road. I had washed as much of the pond stench off my legs in the bathroom while Dame grabbed Cokes from the cooler by the door on the way out.

With my stomach growling, I accepted a proffered slice from Battles.

"Thanks, man," I said and took a bite. I hadn't eaten here before, but it was love at first bite. "Mmm."

"I know, right?" Battles said before devouring half a slice in one bite.

While we chewed, Dame didn't mind talking with his mouth full. "Tell me what's really going on. You can trust us. Gomez did, remember?"

"I do," I said after swallowing my second bite, which was as good as the first. "That's why I figured I wasn't walking into a trap when you sent the message."

"Paranoia getting the best of you, is it?" he asked, not in a sarcastic manner, but in a form of sympathy. Dame might act like a big kid, but he seemed to have a huge heart.

The pizza the size of a wagon wheel slowly disappeared, slice by slice, as I laid out the entire story, including Rosen's ties. The sun lowered in the sky behind the tall pines. Dame and Battles listened mostly, only jumping in to ask for clarification on various details.

At the end, Battles wiped the grease off his lips with a napkin. He was the quiet one of the two officers but seemed like the deeper thinker. "What you're saying is, this all started three years ago with your wife dying and that the guy who died at Swaying Palms, whose murder you investigated, is tied to all of it?"

"Correct," I said. "Not only tied to all of it, but he may be the ringleader in it all. If not Lawson, then possibly Rosen is the head honcho. The evening after we wrapped up the case at Tidal Creek, Tony Bruno told me to stay on my guard. He'd heard through the grapevine that there was someone underhandedly controlling this city and that he knew who the second in command was, but not the guy on top."

"Or gal," Dame added.

"Right, or gal," I said. "Thanks. That's another point. Let's say that Rosen and/or Zach are behind all of this. What I don't understand is why they would be up to something so nasty that they'd kill over it. Not only once, but multiple times. Not to mention sending someone out to vandalize my bookstore."

Dame grinned at me like I was a small child about to be taught an important life lesson. "Money makes the world go round."

"Exactly," Battles said. "Let's use Zach, for example, with his real estate development. You say they'd tried bribery on some island to try and get their way. Maybe that's what they do or do worse when they can't get their way."

My head bobbed. "Which would make sense if their reasoning for resorting to crimes was to get something built which would make them a lot of money."

"And Bingo was his name-o," Dame said.

The content of Karen Polhemus's text message came back to me. "Hold on."

I walked around to the passenger side door of my Jeep, opened it, and reached under the front seat for the printout of addresses she'd given me yesterday at the Register of Deeds. I returned to where Battles and Dame stood. "These are the addresses in Horry County that Summit Capital Holdings owns."

"How did you get that?" Dame asked.

I shrugged. "I have my ways."

He and Battles glanced at each other and then down at the list I'd laid on top of the car's hood.

Tracing my finger down the list, I said, "My source sent me a text message on the way here, telling me to pay special attention to the property they own on Oak Street."

"They have a place in downtown Myrtle?" Battles asked.

"Apparently," I answered. "Let's see here. Here it is. 905 N. Oak Street."

"Hmm," Battles hummed.

"What is it?" Dame asked.

"My mom just moved in there," Battles explained. "The Castello delle Onde. She was fortunate to get one of the few residential units. It's a hybrid luxury hotel that offers some rooms for sale. The bottom level has retail, a restaurant, and a spa. Mom likes it because there are shuttles always leaving for the beach."

"I know the one you're talking about," I said. "Has the white Italian stone type of exterior. Looks like something from the Amalfi Coast."

"That's the one," Battles said.

"Sticks out like a sore thumb down there," Dame said.

While they talked about that, I reflected on the meetings I'd attend as a member of the Myrtle Beach Downtown Development Group, over a year ago being my last. I'd had the opportunity to give a voice to the direction that the city wanted to take in bringing an aging downtown to a new century and give tourists and locals alike a new place to enjoy while also bringing many of the city agencies to one place.

Rosen had been a member before and after he was elected mayor. He didn't seem to have an agenda, but I recalled when the plans were being made, that there were two small sections of Oak Street off 9th Avenue North that were still undeveloped. The plan was to have lower priced housing for people who work near downtown located along the fringes of the overall project, but that left one additional space closer to the middle of downtown. Rosen suggested taking bids on that lot for a building that would cater to those with higher budgets.

"Oh no," I said in the middle of Dame and Battle's back-and-forth.

They stopped. Dame asked, "What is it?"

"That's it," I stared at the empty pizza box in concentration.

"What's 'it'?" Battles asked.

I looked up at them. "Summit Capital Holdings. I'd heard of them before. They won the bid for there, but there was a holdup in the starting phase of the build."

"Know what it was?" Battles asked.

"Not off the top of my head," I answered. "But it seems like the holdup happened once they broke ground. Like they started and had to stop for some reason before they could continue."

"I wonder why they had to pause?" Dame asked.

At that moment, I recalled the second half of Courthouse Karen's message. "I'm not sure, but I think Judge Whitley would know."

The script was starting to come full circle.

I finally believed I knew the link between Autumn and Rosen.

Moody's last words to me had been that if what he'd discovered were true, then this city might burn to the ground.

If I were correct, Moody's parting statement might come true. These findings certainly seemed like flammable material.

Little did I know that Myrtle Beach wouldn't be the only thing that got burned because of this.

CHAPTER THIRTY-EIGHT

DAME AND BATTLES HAD to leave to aid in the search for Gomez. As I sat in the Jeep, I pondered my next move as their patrol car exited the Nellie's Pizza parking lot. Going after Rosen before I had all the pieces had been a rash thought. I was glad the police inadvertently deterred me. I wanted him to be trapped like the rat I believed him to be and have no way out.

Perhaps my next move wasn't a destination as much as it was an internet search. The next thing I needed to do would be better done by using a computer rather than a cell phone. I used my phone to create a mobile hotspot and set it on the dashboard. I retrieved my duffle bag from the cargo area and pulled out my laptop. Like a true mobile warrior, I opened the computer and connected to my phone via Bluetooth. Viola. Instant research center. A couple of families came and went from Nellie's while I pecked at the keyboard. Never mind the oddball sitting here doing a routine search for zoning permits in front of a friendly neighborhood pizza shop.

I used the web browser to get on the City of Myrtle Beach official website and found the page for the Planning and Zoning Department. For good measure, I opened an incognito browser tab that could not be tracked or recorded in my browsing history. The last thing I needed was for some programmer somewhere to know it was me doing these searches on their website.

Scrolling down past the Director and Staff contact information, I found an Overview & Quick Links section where there was a link to the GIS Zoning Map.

The browser opened a new tab after I clicked and a map of Myrtle Beach loaded, centered in the middle of the city. It was divided into colorful shapes depicting various business developments and districts. Most of the odd shapes were shades of green. Each had red letters layered on top with designations like "RMH, WM, MUM, MUMBTW, PUD, RDZ, etc."

I wasn't sure what they meant, but the area I was looking for was easy to spot in DOWNTOWN: ART, which stood for the Arts & Innovation District. I zoomed in closer to 905 N Oak St. When I did, there was a small, square, white block in the middle of the brownish green of the Arts District.

When I clicked on it, a box appeared with lines of text inside.

2019-47 FID 85

OBJECTID_1 5097

OBJECTID 0

GDO_GID 0.000000

ORD_NO_1 2019-47

ORD_NO_2

ORD_NO_3

ORD_NO_4

ORD_NO_5

ORD_NO_6

ORD_NO_7

ORD_NO_8

ORD_NO_9

ORD_NO_10

ORD_NO_11

ORD_NO_12

ORD_NO_13

ORD_NO_14

ORD_NO_15

ORD_NO_16

ORD_NO_17

ORD_NO_18

ORD_NO_19

ORD_NO_20

ZONING_DIS MUMV Mixed Use Medium Vertical Density Updated 3/27/20xx, 10:00 PM

Shape__Area 312117.306641

Shape__Length 3273.399441

The Castello delle Onde had gotten its zoning approval four days after Autumn's death. Recorded well after closing hours.

There was a white arrow at the top of the box indicating there were other entries for this property. I clicked on it and an identical box appeared with much of the same information with a big exception dated the day before Autumn's death.

ZONING_DIS MUMV Mixed Use Medium Vertical Density Application Delayed Pending Possible Historic Designation

Updated 3/22/20xx, 8:00 PM

"Gotcha," I said to myself.

There it was, on the screen. A bona fide link between Summit Capital, Rosen, and Judge Whitley.

There were now two arrows at the top of the box. One to return to the previous record and another to an older entry. I clicked to see what had come before.

ZONING_DIS MUMV Mixed Use Medium Vertical Density

Updated 1/23/20xx, 8:00 PM

I clicked around to various properties to make sure my instincts were correct. All of them were time stamped for 8:00 PM. The only one that wasn't was the entry dated after Autumn's death which was recorded two hours later—possibly when no one was looking.

So, Summit Capital had gotten initial zoning approval in January of that year. I remembered that address being nothing but an overgrown, grassy lot. At some point soon after that, they would have broken ground on the Castello delle Onde.

In the days before Autumn's death, they might have discovered something in the lot that caused them to stop. I wasn't sure what the process was for having a site designated as historic, but I imagined that it took longer than the four days between the delayed designation and reapproval.

The same period when Autumn died.

After learning that Zach and Rosen may have tried to bribe officials on St. Grant's due to a zoning conflict, it seemed logical to me that they might try that here.

And who was head of the historic commission in Myrtle Beach? Autumn's old boss, Judge Whitley.

There was the motive I'd been in search of for over a year. Now that I'd made the connection, I didn't think it would be difficult to prove motive and opportunity. What I needed was the last piece of the puzzle: means.

If I found it, the problem became how to get this out into the world and get Rosen and any helpers locked up without getting myself killed.

Of course, if Moody's toxicology report came back the way I believed it might, then there would be another way to get Rosen if I could prove he was behind it.

I'd have to work that part out.

I put the Jeep in gear and left Nellie's.

Time to get to the heart of it all.

For once, the universe made my next two moves convenient. The new layout for Downtown and the Arts & Innovation District had consolidated Judge Whitley's courtroom into City Hall. I'd make it there before the court let out if I hurried.

It took ten minutes for me to return to the 17 Bypass from McDowell Shortcut. That's how long it took for Dame to make a few calls and get back to me with some news.

"Lucien called in sick to work," he told me over the phone. "It's something he apparently never does."

"Great." How convenient.

"That's not all. Battles and I swung over to his place and knocked on his door to tell him about finding Gomez's car. He wasn't home."

"Or he didn't answer the door," I suggested.

"Negative," Dame said. "He wasn't there. He drives a big, red Chevy crew cab truck that sticks out like a sore thumb. It wasn't there. If it wasn't, he wasn't."

"Great," I repeated, but this time drew the word out. "Try calling him?"

"I did, but he didn't answer. Dispatch is trying to contact him now. Meanwhile, we have officers on the lookout for his truck. If he's around, we'll find him."

"What about Rosen? Is there anything you can do about him?"

"Not currently. We'd need something more substantial than what you have now."

"Like what?"

"Someone to come forward or a smoking gun would be nice."

There wouldn't be a smoking gun in this instance, and hopefully it wouldn't come to that. The thought of a gun reminded me of the bulge in the small of my back. I'd found the link between Rosen, Zach Lawson, Summit Capital, and an illegal angle having to do with their Oak Street property. If Moody's autopsy results came back the way I feared they would by being poisoned instead of dying by natural causes, then perhaps there was a way to link the mayor or Zach to him.

"I'll work on it," I said.

"No, you need to lay low," Dame said.

I pressed my lips together. "Can't do that."

My thumb pressed a button on the steering wheel ending the call. I wasn't going to follow Dame's instructions. He likely knew me well enough by now to realize he was wasting his breath.

Lucien was the one lying low. I tried to replay how Gomez's car ended up in that pond. The car came in the direction of her home, not from 17, which was the way I made it to the scene. She'd left me at the hotel late last night. It didn't make sense for her to go home to Lucien and then come back out. It would have been well after midnight.

Unless they got into an argument, and she was on her way back to my room.

The thought stopped me cold and almost caused me to rearend the car in front of me as I stopped at the light by the Coastal Grand Mall. Gomez had taken off her engagement ring while we stood outside my room. Maybe she told Lucien that she wouldn't marry him, or he'd noticed the ring missing from her finger, and they'd had a fight, causing her to leave.

Even so, where was she? She'd apparently walked away from her crashed car, and someone might have picked her up. Surely, she would have reported the crash or gone to the hospital to get checked out if she were injured. The seat was in the wrong position too, which opened the possibility that she wasn't driving the car. The conspiracy theorist in me realized that Lucien would have driven with the seat all the way back like I'd found it. An uneasy sensation settled in the pit of my stomach.

Along the way to downtown Myrtle Beach, a method of exposing Rosen and Summit Capital formed in my mind.

CHAPTER THIRTY-NINE

FOR THE SECOND TIME this afternoon, I exited 17 at 501 and maneuvered toward the ocean as the sun slowly descended toward the horizon. Check-in time for most hotels starts at four o'clock. If I had thought traffic was clogged earlier, it was now in need of Drain-O with motorists getting into town in the nick of time.

Before I'd left, Battles had placed a hand on my shoulder. "Let us handle finding her. You stay safe."

“I’ll do my best,” I’d said. Battles' earlier words of comfort didn’t alleviate my concern and growing dread as I sped back to Downtown Myrtle, to this traffic jam.

I tapped my thumb nervously on the steering wheel as traffic inched along. Time and daylight were wasting away. I kept glancing at the side and rear-view mirrors, scanning to see if a big red truck was following me. If one was, I didn’t think Lucien would be ignorant enough to follow me to the center of government for Myrtle Beach and the myriads of security cameras present.

People were starting to flow from the front entrance on the side of the expanded city hall where the municipal court took place when I arrived. When Autumn used to work for Judge Whitley, they would be in their offices taking care of paperwork sometimes well after court adjourned. Since I'd seen Her Honor yesterday in Conway, I hoped that her caseload this week was light, and I wouldn't have to wait long for her to exit through the employee portal in the rear of the building.

After parking in the public lot out front, I circled around city hall to the back where various employees and court officials were heading out for the day. I clenched my fists, hoping that I hadn't already missed Whitley, and I was in luck. She exited alongside a young woman of Asian descent with dark hair, pleated navy skirt, and modest white blouse. Whitley wore a bright pair of flowing slacks with a light blue and pink floral pattern and a pink top. In the courtroom, you can never tell what judges wear under their robes.

They were deep in conversation when I walked up and stopped them on the sidewalk. The other woman stopped speaking mid-sentence.

“Excuse me, Judge Whitley,” I said.

The Judge’s eyes grew big. “Oh, Clark. What are you doing here?”

“Who is this?” the other woman said.

“Phoebe,” Whitley answered, “this is Clark Thomas. The husband of your predecessor.”

“Oh. Okay,” Phoebe said. “I’m sorry about what happened.”

“Thank you,” I said. “Can you excuse the judge and I for a moment? I need to ask her a few questions about Autumn.”

Phoebe opened her mouth and turned to Whitley.

The judge held up a hand to her assistant. "It's okay, Phoebe. I ran into Clark yesterday and he's putting together something for Autumn that I said I would help him with. Go home. Tell that little boy of yours hi for me."

"I'll do that," Phoebe said. "See you tomorrow."

"Yes," Whitley said. "See you then. Don't forget we have to get an earlier start tomorrow with that Harper case on the docket."

"I'm on it," Phoebe assured.

The assistant said goodbye to me and hopped off the sidewalk, heading for her car in the lot.

Whitley's eyes were droopy, and her shoulders sagged after a long day of court. It might seem like an easy job to sit up on the bench and pass judgment, but I recalled from Autumn's days of working for her, it took a lot out of them. This might either be the best time to talk to her or the worst.

"What's going on, Clark?" Whitley asked. She tried and failed to hide the annoyance in her voice. "I gave you my number so you wouldn't have to track me down."

"I know." I guided her to the side under a tall oak and out of earshot from the flow of foot traffic leaving city hall. When we were far enough away that no one should hear us, I got straight to the point. "Summit Capital Holdings."

Her eyes fluttered, and she took half a step back. “I-I’m not sure what you mean.”

Whitley’s reaction told me the opposite. From where we stood, the top floor of the white stone exterior of the three-story Castello delle Onde stood above the surrounding buildings.

I pointed at it. “I think you do. They own that building.”

Her Adam’s apple bobbed. “Okay. Good for them. I’ve heard it’s grandiose inside. What about it?”

“That place came up in relation to what I’m trying to figure out about Autumn’s death. It used to be an unused grass lot before it was bought by Summit Capital. The filing I found at the courthouse showed their purchase as three months before her death."

Her posture changed from cautious to defensive. She crossed her arms. "What does this have to do with me?"

"The day before Autumn's death, their zoning approval got delayed."

She tapped her foot impatiently on the sidewalk. "Come on, Clark. You're wasting my time. My spouse is at home waiting for dinner."

Judge Whitley had gone from a helpful, open book to wanting to escape in a matter of seconds. I held out a hand. "Bear with me here for a minute. Here's where you come in. Their zoning request was delayed because of a possible historic designation. You're the head of that commission, yes?"

She gulped. "I am."

"You would have heard about this, yes?"

"Yes, I would have, but there are requests like that coming across my desk all the time." She slipped up and tried to cover her tracks, but it was too late. "What I mean is, there's no way I can remember one random request from three years ago."

"What if it involved the recently deceased Zach Lawson and Mayor Rosen?"

Whitley took a step back and started looking around for help. For an excuse to escape. "What are you implying? Be careful of your next words or you'll face a lawsuit for libel or slander."

Her words signaled that the string I was pulling was the right one. I was far enough into this that I was confident she couldn't sue me for telling a false truth in legalese because I was right.

"Ah, it's almost like you know what I'm going to say. Defensive all of a sudden, are we?"

"No," she protested. Then she said the part she'd cautioned me against saying. "I don't like for people to implicate me in someone's death." She placed a hand on my arm. "Look, I adored Autumn. She was great at her job. It's a tragedy what happened."

I closed the step she'd taken away. "Yes. A tragedy. A tragedy that she was killed because she was in the wrong place at the wrong time and wouldn't keep quiet."

"What are you saying?"

Here it was. Time to lay out my theory.

"I think Summit Capital purchased that lot to build Castello delle Onde. It was a legit purchase. Then, they found something after they broke ground that caused someone working there on the construction crew to report it. They did it because it was the right thing to do. Let's say they found evidence of habitation from a long time ago and caused a stoppage. Then that person, let's say the job foreman, filed an initial report to the historic commission—you—and their initial zoning request got temporarily put on hold pending further review. With me so far?"

"I am," Whitley admitted, "but it's gibberish."

"Sure," I smiled. She hadn't offered a defense so far. Maybe she didn't have one. Maybe I was exactly right. I continued, "I found a report from an island in the Caribbean where one of Lawson's construction groups was accused of bribing officials after 500-year-old graves were uncovered during development. Rosen was the attorney that the local newspaper had gotten a statement from." I gauged her reaction. "I can tell you're not surprised."

"I still don't know what you're talking about. Still gibberish."

"You might say it's gibberish, but you haven't walked away, have you?" It was a rhetorical question. I didn't want or need a response. I was rolling now. Thankfully, there weren't any security guards on patrol. It would be the teensiest bit suspicious to see some dude giving a vertically challenged judge an ear full.

After my initial onslaught, she regained her composure. She stepped forward and said in a low, harsh tone, "I'm sorry your wife died in my chambers, but I had nothing to do with it. I'd gone home early that night. Even brewed her a cup of tea before I left as a way of saying thank you. I left her with a huge pile of paperwork that wouldn't wait until morning, but it had to be done. I don't know how you think she was murdered, if she was murdered, but I assure you I had nothing to do with it."

"So, neither Rosen, Zach Lawson, nor anyone associated with Summit Capital

Holdings tried to bribe you into dropping the Historic filing on that property?"

Her mouth twitched. "No."

I held her gaze, waiting for her to flinch. She didn't.

Whitley hoisted the strap of a bag on her shoulder. "Now, if you'll excuse me, I have dinner waiting for me at home."

She walked through the lot and opened the door on a sporty black Infiniti sedan. Whitley faced me as she tossed her leather bag into the passenger side seat. Before climbing in, she shook her head and gave me a sad smile.

The car exited the lot. Whitley served as a defense attorney before becoming a judge. Like this past weekend when interviewing a different attorney, as a suspect, it became apparent that Whitley was also excellent at verbally dancing around any subject that might make her look suspicious. She had to know more than she let on, and I couldn't think of a way to dig deeper about her role in the on again/off again Castello delle Onde historic designation. It might come to me, but I had bigger fish to fry.

I turned and looked up at City Hall. I'd been inside on the second floor where the city officials and supporting staff ran Myrtle Beach. I'd been in the mayor's office twice to receive commendations. From where I stood, Rosen's office was on the far left in the middle section of the remodeled courthouse. A conference room lay between the outer wall and his inner sanctum.

The horizontal slats of the blinds inside one of the two conference room windows moved. A shadow passed behind them and faded.

Rosen had watched my conversation with Whitley.

I clenched my fists and jaw and started toward the rear employee entrance.

Time to fry the proverbial fish.

CHAPTER FORTY

I WALKED UP THE concrete back steps to a door with inlaid glass. A sign to the side indicated office hours. I had twenty minutes before today's time ended. An ocean breeze rustled the leaves of live oaks.

A round, black camera encased in a heavy-duty plastic dome watched like a sentinel over the landing on which I stood. I gave it a wave, hoping whoever was on security would recognize me and buzz me in. If that was Rosen watching me from upstairs, it wouldn't have surprised me if he sent out an armed response to meet me. If he did, the move would raise questions why he'd do that. The people who worked here were familiar with me.

As I reached to press the buzzer, the door opened, and a woman exited. She had dark hair that hung past her shoulders, wore a red blazer over a black blouse, dangling earrings, a necklace made of black-and-white jewels that matched a same-colored hounds tooth patterned skirt. The black strap of a business satchel hung over her shoulder.

She saw me and put a hand over her chest. "Oh, Clark. Goodness. What are you doing here? I didn't think you were going to see Rosen until tomorrow."

"Hey, Michelle." Michelle Shumpert was the Chief Financial Officer of Myrtle

Beach. She had an office two doors down from Rosen. We'd met at several functions and made easy conversation. "I was in the area and needed to ask the mayor something about what happened this past weekend."

Michelle gave me the briefest of suspicious glances. She still held the door open. "He's up in his office."

"Mind if I try to go up and see him?"

She turned and looked at the interior. A short hallway split off in three directions. The guard station was situated in the middle of the nexus. A man with slicked back dark hair and an above average seriousness to his demeanor, sat in a tall stool behind the stand.

"If Rob will let you go up there, sure."

"Thanks, Michelle," I said. "Appreciate it."

"No problem, Clark. We appreciate all you've done for us."

"Thank you."

She placed a consoling hand on my arm. "Hopefully, you won't have to deal with murders anymore."

"I wish that were the case."

Michelle gave a puzzled expression. "Y-yeah, me too." She stood aside with one hand holding open the door. "Anyway, I gotta run. Go on in."

"Thanks, Michelle." I veered through the door, passing a secretary on her way out. We nodded at each other as we passed by. A set of stairs with brass railings led the way up to the second floor.

Rob and the guard station were beside the bottom stair.

If a person wanted to get to the upper level, you had to go through Rob. I'd spoken to him before. He was serious, but compassionate. He was also not one who I would consider a bender of the rules.

The problem was, I needed him to bend one for me.

He was studying a printout when I tried to sneak by.

"Mr. Thomas," Rob said. "How can I help you?"

There was no sense beating around the bush. "Hey, Rob. Do you mind if I go up and ask the mayor a question?"

He cocked an eyebrow. “Is it important? He’s getting ready to leave for the day.”

“It’s of utmost importance.”

He sat up on his stool and folded his arms. “I’m not supposed to allow anyone up there unless they have an appointment or permission from the city manager.”

I’d heard that before. I pleaded, “Come on. Just be a moment.”

Rob had been present every other time I’d been here. He’d seen me shake hands with the mayor and his staff and pose for pictures after getting commendations for helping the police department solve murder investigations. I’d become aware over the past year that my standing in the community had grown. People had started recognizing me in public, which was weird, but I was always met with a smile.

I didn't like taking advantage of my new-found meritorious respect, but I was making an exception in this case. It had to be done.

A blonde woman bounded down the stairs with a leather tote slung over her shoulder. She told us to have a good evening and walked out the door.

Rob looked up the stairs and made a clicking sound with his tongue. "She was the last one up there besides Rosen. It's just him now. He's usually the last to leave besides me. Are you armed?"

The question almost stopped me cold, but I remembered to stash the gun Gomez had given me in the glovebox before coming in. The last thing I needed to do was set off the metal detectors before confronting Autumn's possible killer.

I managed to laugh and tried to hide my nervousness. "No, sir. I'm not. Never fired a gun in my life, as a matter of fact."

Rob cast a suspicious eye over me. He reached inside the guard station and pulled out a black wand. "Hold your hands out at your shoulders."

I complied.

He ran the wand up and down both sides of my body and then the back and front. The wand moved without a peep.

"Okay. You're clear," he said. "Go up. Make it snappy."

I let out a breath. "I'll do that. Thanks, Rob. Coffee is on me next time your wife swings by the bookstore."

He smirked. "I'd enjoy that." He fluttered his hand. "Go on. Scoot."

I turned and began my ascent up the stairs. My footfalls echoed in the stairwell. The place had an old house feel, despite new flooring and fresh paint on the walls. That was all that had changed in this part of city hall in the last twenty plus years.

A desk with an L-shaped gray granite top greeted me at the top of the landing. It was vacant, as were the rest of the offices. The lights were off. Slanting rays from the setting sun streamed through the windows, providing the only source of light. Dust motes danced in the light. Paintings from Myrtle Beach's history decorated the walls. A high ceiling gave the impression of more space than there was.

Straight ahead of me lay the City Manager's office. I made a sharp right and came to a hallway that stretched in either direction. To the right was the City Attorney and her assistant's offices. Michelle, who had let me in downstairs, had her office directly in front of me.

To my left, past the Director of Public Information's office was Rosen's chambers. His door was half open, but I didn't see him inside. It was a large office, so he could have been in a different part of the room. His office had oak paneled walls, an oak desk, two comfy chairs, a cabinet, and a leather settee opposite the desk.

After rapping on the door frame and peering in, I found him sitting on the settee.

“Come in,” he said.

I took a deep breath and crossed over the threshold to face Autumn’s possible killer.

CHAPTER FORTY-ONE

Light from a Tiffany lamp on a side table next to the settee illuminated Rosen. Whiskey, neat, sloshed around a glass in his right hand. His left hand was draped casually over his left knee, his legs crossed. He wore gray slacks, a white buttoned-up shirt, and a pair of brown loafers. The top two buttons of the shirt were undone, a vision of casualness at the end of a long day of heavy decisions in running one of the fastest growing cities in the United States.

Rosen had steely gray hair and piercing blue eyes. He was fit, trim, and oozed confidence while being a man of the people. He wasn't tall, nor short, but somewhere in between. His face was unlined, no doubt the effects of regular Botox injections.

"Clark," he said in a friendly tone when I entered. "What brings you here?"

If Rosen was indeed at the top of the totem pole of whatever conspiracy grasping Myrtle Beach, then he would know exactly why I was here. Someone had gone to great lengths to listen to my conversations, and he may be responsible for uprooting Andrea and Libby from their home in Missouri to bring them here to insert them into my life.

The list of atrocities this man looked to be responsible for imparted the same sense of loathing I'd had while questioning suspects involved in Zach Lawson's murder this past weekend.

Before I could answer, he held up a finger. "Hold on. I have something for you."

He set the whiskey glass on the side table next to the lamp base and reached around to the small of his back. My heart was already thumping in my chest. His movement made it want to break out from my ribcage. Was he reaching for a gun?

"W-what is it?" I asked.

To my relief, he reached into his back pocket and pulled out a brown leather wallet. He unfolded it and pulled out a crisp one-dollar bill and reached it up to me. "Here, this is what I owe you from working the murder investigation of my friend, Zach."

Rosen had just made his first mistake, and I tried not to show any reaction.

On Saturday morning, while I played in a group at Swaying Palms—with my brother, Detective Moody, and his friend, Tom—Zach Lawson had been playing with the group ahead of us. Lawson was drunk the entire time. Someone murdered him on the eleventh hole.

Moody and I rushed to his body. A few minutes later, Rosen appeared. He had been playing with Greg Rowles, and I had seen them on a golf cart earlier. Gomez had been away at a conference, which left Detective Moody working solo. Since I had a history of aiding

Moody and Gomez in investigations, and I had been near Zach all morning, Rosen asked me to help on the case as a consultant and told me that they'd pay me to do it. I told him my fee was one dollar.

At the time I shook Rosen's hand, I figured his request was out of respect for the help I'd given during the past year to the police. He didn't mention that he had a personal stake in the matter, that he and Zach were friends.

Rosen inadvertently admitted to being connected to Lawson. Which I had already learned, but he didn't know that.

Over seventy hours later, we'd caught the killer, Moody had died, Gomez had disappeared, and we'd uncovered a litany of corruption and death that seemed to be centered around the man in front of me. The question was: why? Why would a man of his stature involve himself in such a mess?

I stared at the dollar bill he proffered between two fingers. “Keep it.”

He cocked his head to the side. The corners of his mouth curved downward. “It’s what we agreed to. I just want to make sure that I cover my side of the deal.”

“I don’t want it.”

The mayor drew in a large breath and tucked the bill back in the wallet. “Suit yourself.” After he tucked the billfold in his back pocket, he picked up the glass on the side table and held it up to me. “Tea? I just brewed some. Or would you like something stronger? Whiskey?”

A drink cart sat under a window facing the front lawn and Broadway Street. Glass decanters, a gleaming silver ice bucket, and bottles of alcohol of varying sizes sat on top. As tempted as I was, I needed to keep a clear head. Perhaps that's one reason why he offered me a drink.

"No thanks."

"Your loss. I've heard you like whiskey. I have some fantastic 12-year Glenfiddich single malt you're passing up."

My hackles rose. "Where did you hear that?"

His head wobbled. "I'm not sure. From someone."

He opened the proverbial door for me to rush through it. "You mean, Andrea?"

If my question surprised him, he didn't show it. He played it cool. "Andrea who?"

"Andrea Crispin." I tipped my chin and said in my most sarcastic and angry voice, "Your niece."

Rosen smiled, showing zero reaction to my tone. "Oh, yes, of course. That Andrea. Might have been from her."

"Were you two talking about me behind my back?" I stood with my hands by my side, clenching and unclenching my hands. He pretended not to notice. Without him inviting me, I sat in one of the seats facing the settee to get on level ground.

"You may have come up."

My hands rested at the ends of both arms of the chair. The cushion was quite comfy. If Rosen had been sitting behind his desk, I would have thought I'd entered a scene from the Godfather.

I pointed my index finger at him. "That's funny."

He sipped from the glass and smacked his lips. "What's funny?"

"That I've known Andrea all this time, and she never mentioned Uncle Sid until today."

"Oh?"

"Oh, yeah. I would think that if I was getting to know someone new in town, it might come up in passing. Like, 'Hey, want to come over for dinner with my adorable daughter and me? Oh yeah, by the way, the mayor of Myrtle Beach is also my uncle who paid for me to come here. Did you want soup or salad with our meal?'" I glared at him. "Sound accurate?"

"It would seem logical to me," he conceded. "But that poor girl's been through a lot. Maybe it just slipped her mind."

"Seems like a pretty big factoid to forget to mention."

"Yeah, well, Andrea never ranked near the top of her class, if you know what I mean."

It was true. Andrea did have some dingy moments, but she wasn't loopy enough to forget to mention Rosen. At least, I hoped she wasn't. If Rosen had placed her here to spy on me, then he must believe she was mentally capable of handling the task. Heat flared at the base of my neck at his slight against Andrea.

Even if there was some truth to it, you don't go around putting down other people's intelligence. I did still care about her, but maybe he said that to try to draw the Freudian protective response out of me to cloud my thinking. He was playing checkers. I was playing chess. We had the same board, but we were playing different games. I hoped that my perception of the metaphorical game wasn't the other way around.

I didn't comment on his putdown of Andrea. "Be that as it may, she didn't tell me."

"Why would it concern you anyway?"

"Because I think you or someone associated with you has been watching me."

"Why would you think that?"

He didn't outright deny my accusation which gave me a pleasing sensation. "Because Andrea and Autumn share similar features. It's an almost unbelievable coincidence that you have a family member who resembles my wife. If Autumn would have had blonde hair, they could have passed for close sisters. Almost twins, if Autumn's eyes hadn't been green."

"I admit, they do bear a resemblance now that I'm thinking about it."

"Also," I said, "I found a listening device in my phone. One that detective Gomez identified as likely coming from the police."

"I'm not the police."

"Yeah. They just work for you. Some more than others." I let the comment dangle. Rosen didn't take the bait. I continued, "There was also a GPS tracker hidden on my Jeep."

"Clark, I'm not sure what you're getting at, coming up into my office and leveling vague accusations like this at me." He sipped from the glass and savored it.

He swirled the contents of his glass and studied it. Shifting the subject, he looked up at me. "Your wife was a fine woman and a diligent worker."

"That's true. I was thinking about just that."

"Just what?"

I pointed a finger. "That. You've told me that before. How much you admired Autumn. It got me thinking. You were a real estate attorney before taking office, correct?"

"Yes. I'm still a member of the bar. My partners agreed to let me take a hiatus from the firm while I served as mayor. Once my time is done here, I'll rejoin them like nothing happened."

That is, if you're not in jail, I almost said. "What I'm getting at is Autumn clerked for Judge Whitley who oversees mainly vehicle and boating violations. Your paths shouldn't have crossed often if at all. Certainly not enough for you to form that opinion of her."

Rosen tilted his head. "You know Judge Whitley is head of the Historic Commission in Myrtle Beach?"

I acknowledged it by tilting my chin.

Rosen explained, “Sometimes, I had to handle property transactions where the issue of preservation came into play, and I’d have to confer with Whitley in her chambers. That’s when I was around your wife. I remember Whitley telling me how hard of a worker she was, and I’d spoken to her on several occasions. That’s how I formed that opinion of her.”

I had to hand it to him. His reasoning made sense. He might not have been a court attorney but like every skilled lawyer, he knew how to argue effectively. However, I homed in on something else he had said.

“Ah, like for the Castello delle Onde?”

For the first time, the confident veneer cracked, and he squirmed in his seat.

He sat forward. “I’m not sure what you mean.”

I leaned in. Our faces were close together. “You know exactly what I mean. That beautiful, white three-story hotel down the street. You signed as the closing attorney on the purchase agreements on that deal.”

I didn’t know that for sure, and I was taking a gamble to throw that out there like it was one hundred percent the truth. Just because Summit Capital owned Castello delle Onde, it didn’t mean that Rosen was necessarily the person who signed the papers.

He feigned forgetfulness. “Oh, that one. Yes. Quite a lucrative project for my client.”

"By client, you mean Zach Lawson, right?"

"I assume you know the answer to that question."

"You and Zach were old buddies, is that right? You played soccer together at Coastal?"

He didn't ask me how I possessed that bit of knowledge. "We were. His loss is a tragic one for the community. He did so much with his charity work."

"His wife tells me that his autism charity was as much as a way for him to look like an upstanding, giving citizen as it was for him to fleece donors."

His eyebrows lifted. "Paxton said that? Figures. She was only after his money."

I batted the comment aside with a hand. We weren't here to talk about Paxton. I had let him win his first move in this game. It was a mistake to mention a source, particularly one he could discredit. "Be that as it may, our findings this past weekend has the FBI looking into Zach's charity and his offshore accounts."

Rosen didn't flinch. He had to know that his name would come up eventually in the investigation. If it did, he likely had an excuse ready to go to cover his tracks, which was how he didn't seem flustered at the prospect of the Feds digging around. "If Zach was involved in any wrongdoing, they'll find it. We tried stopping him, but he always skirted the law."

"Why didn't you do anything about it?"

"You met him. Would you want to tell him he couldn't do something?"

"Yeah, but you're the mayor. If he was taking part in illegal activities, then isn't it your job to see that he's held responsible?"

"Not if his wrongdoing took place outside the borders of the US. It's none of my business."

"Did you do any work for him outside the country?"

He leveled his gaze at me, trying to gauge how much I knew. "No. He had other attorneys he worked with in those deals."

"That's a lie."

Rosen sat back in his chair. His hard gaze turned soft. He chuckled. “Ha. Whatever. I didn’t do anything with him outside the country.”

I had one thing to say to that. “St. Grant’s Island.”

CHAPTER FORTY-TWO

ROSEN WASN'T DUMB ENOUGH to deny never hearing of the obscure island. He had to know that if I had mentioned it specifically, that I'd made the connection already.

He rubbed his chin. "Yes. That was the one that I'd help Zach navigate through the local laws and customs. A shame it fell through. How did you learn about that one?"

My lip curled. Even though I was a combatant in an arena I'd never stepped foot in before, I was keeping my cool and holding my ground. "Like you, I have my sources. Did you try to bribe the officials or did Zach?"

He jumped to his feet. "Get out of my office before I have you arrested. You're treading in dangerous waters here."

I looked up at him and raised a finger with every name. "Summit Capital Holdings, Salty Sands Holdings, Island Haven Investments, Palm Shores Properties, Blue Horizon Estates. Any of them ring a bell?"

Rosen didn't answer me. He leaned into the doorway and called down the stairs. "Rob! Get up here!"

I got to my feet and looked Rosen in the eye. "No need to throw me out. I'm leaving anyway."

His face turned beet red. “I should have you arrested for coming here and accusing me of being involved in whatever scheme you’ve cooked up in your mind.”

“Go ahead. Arrest me. That’ll look good, won’t it? We both know how the people of Myrtle Beach feel about me. Wouldn’t that raise some questions about why you had me arrested? Assumptions that I know information you don’t want to come to light?”

We stood toe-to-toe. “Like I said, you’re playing a perilous game here, Clark. You should forget about it if you know what’s good for you.”

“That sounds like a threat.”

“Take it however you want. It’s my word against yours. You mentioned how the people of Myrtle Beach feel about you?

Did you know that I have the highest approval rating as mayor in Myrtle Beach's history?"

I didn't follow politics close enough to be aware of how exactly the public viewed Rosen. I had the sense that he was doing well because I didn't hear as much grumbling from fellow business owners as I did under the other regimes.

"Good for you."

As I started to walk out the door, he said, "Look, I'm sorry about your wife. I really am. I know you're doing this in some attempt to reconcile her death, but you must let her go and move on."

I stopped and turned to him. "Did you lose sleep when she was murdered?"

His forehead wrinkled. “Murdered? Wait, why would I lose sleep?”

I was maybe two inches taller than Rosen and I stood to my full height, looking him in the eye. “Because I think you had something to do with it.”

His face remained impassive. “Clark, even if that were true, you couldn’t prove it.”

CHAPTER FORTY-THREE

IT TOOK EVERY OUNCE of my being to not slug Rosen in the face. The arrogance in which he challenged me said that A) he did have something to do with Autumn's death, and B) he believed it couldn't be traced back to him.

Rob escorted me from the building. He pretended like he didn't hear our conversation while our voices were raised.

I stood in the parking lot at the base of the stairs leading to the employee entrance after Rob closed the door at my back. The world spun around me so much that I had to grasp the railing to maintain my balance. All the signs Gomez and I had uncovered in the last two days pointing to Rosen being the possible murderer proved correct. Even if he didn't personally poison Autumn, Banner, and Moody, he had their blood on his hands.

As much as I hated to say it, he was right. I didn't have the evidence to prove it. At least, not yet.

The sun had almost completed its disappearing act below the horizon. The sky was cast in hues of pink and yellow. The air had a slight chill to it.

The call of police sirens rang out into the air, heading in my direction. I jumped into the Jeep and hightailed it out of the parking lot in case Rosen had called them to arrest me.

With my paranoia reaching its peak after my “chat” with Rosen, I kept my head down as I waited at the stoplight to turn right onto Kings Highway at 9th Avenue N.

Two squad cars with their lights flashing zoomed around me and veered left onto the main artery running through the business side of Myrtle Beach, away from the direction I was about to turn.

A sigh of relief escaped my lips.

After all the subterfuge, Rosen was too smart to sic the police on me. We both knew how it would look to have me arrested. Like he’d said, it was his word against mine. That could run negatively in either direction. If I came forward, then his ability to preside as mayor might get called into question or worse. On the flipside, if I was wrong—and I didn't think I was—then I would be liable for slandering a public official and face punishment. I wasn't sure of the legal code in South Carolina, but I imagined that being found guilty would carry a hefty fine and possible jail time.

I had too pretty of a face to go to jail.

Traffic along Kings Highway was bumper-to-bumper. At present, I had three thoughts running through my head. One of them I'd have to hold off until later. That was trying to connect Rosen to Autumn, Moody, and Banner. The two other thoughts were getting something to eat—I was famished—and finding Gomez.

Then a phone call from Moody's wife eliminated all of that.

***

I wasn't a fan of fast food, but it had its uses. Detective Moody and I had gone through a CookOut drive-thru two nights ago. This time, I grabbed a chicken sandwich from Chick-fil-A on Mr. Joe White Ave on my way out to the 17 Bypass. Throw on some Polynesian sauce—no pickles—and I was good to go. With waffle fries and an Arnold Palmer, of course.

While I waited in the drive-thru line, I sent Dame and even Lucien text messages seeing if they'd heard from Gomez. Lucien hadn't responded, but Dame got right back and said they were searching. A tow truck had pulled her Camry from the pond. They'd found her phone, badge, police ID, and wallet inside.

I'd tried to reason out where she would have gone after seeing the tracks near her car in the pond off McDowell Shortcut. It seemed like someone had picked her up. If I had gone off the road like she had and careened fifty yards through the woods before splashing into a pond, it was possible I would have bumped my head, woke up, and walked away. If that's what happened and we hadn't heard from her, it was possible she had amnesia, or someone had rescued her from the car and taken her to an emergency room. Without any way to identify her, unless her roadside savior knew who she was, then she would be checked in as a Jane Doe.

I was sure Dame and Battles were calling all the ERs in the area. What about the other emergency care clinics? I asked Dame via text, and he said they were focusing on the bigger hospitals. Many urgent care centers were around and used as a way for patients to seek treatment at lower prices. I'd gone to the Brava MedSpa in Murrells Inlet plenty of times for that reason.

Using Google Maps, I drove around to all the medical facilities and clinics trying to find an amnesiac Gomez. It was futile, but I needed to do something. Yes, it would have saved me so much time and been much easier had I called them all. I wasn't thinking straight. Everything

I'd gone through in the past forty-eight hours, scratch that, the last three years, were starting to overwhelm me. I didn't feel like it was safe to contact my family. I couldn't trust Andrea. I didn't want to endanger my surrogate moms in Karen and Margaret at the store. I tried calling Chris, but it went straight to voicemail.

There was one other person. Marilyn. She owned the We Got Issues comic book shop near the Gay Dolphin one block south of the SkyWheel. I'd known Marilyn to be one of the more analytical people I'd met. We got along well when I was a member of the Downtown Development group. She had a funky style but was one of the more fun people to speak with in the group.

If I didn't hear back from Chris, I'd contact Marilyn in the morning.

My blood practically vibrated through my travels with a mix of endorphins from facing Rosen, trying to find Gomez, and general exhaustion. I was running on fumes at this point.

After I exhausted all the different clinics, I still hadn't located Gomez, and heard nothing from Chris, Lucien, or anyone associated with the police. Even Dame had gone silent.

Speaking of exhaustion, that was me. These last three days had sucked all that I have out of me. I felt like Keiffer Sutherland in that show, 24, minus the threats of terrorism, shootouts, and explosions. At the rate this was going, I wouldn't be surprised if any or all those things occurred before this was over.

Along the way, Moody's wife called. The initial results came back from Moody's autopsy, and they confirmed my suspicions.

Poison.

Since the late detective had a history of heart trouble, it had seemed plausible that he died of a heart attack.

Except he didn't.

The color drained from my face. Marge told me that Moody displayed cardiac arrhythmia, and gastrointestinal symptoms pointing at a poison called digoxin. The coroner suggested that this toxin was found in plants, specifically fox gloves and oleander. A one-hundred percent overdose of digoxin from an oleander/foxglove combination causes specific cardiac arrhythmias which were found in Moody. I recalled fox gloves being used as a poison in an Agatha Christie novel, Appointment with Death. I'd also seen them referred to as "dead men's bells." If Rosen was indeed behind this and ended up getting the death penalty, then in a way, he'd rung his own bell.

I told her to call it in. Since Marge worked as a unit secretary for the police, she would know who to contact. At this point, I didn't know who would be called upon to open an investigation with Gomez missing and Moody dead. She said she'd do that and forward me the report.

Now that I'd learned about the toxins that killed Moody, I racked my brain trying to discern how it would have entered his system. There was a thread my exhausted brain wasn't grasping.

With no other options for finding Gomez and most of Myrtle Beach being in bed, I needed to find somewhere to sleep as well. Although I'd paid for more than one night at the motel in Surfside, it was too risky to go back. The GPS tracker on my car would have told whoever was watching that I had stayed there. They might have gone and talked to the clerk and figured out what room I was staying in.

There was one place where I felt safe, but I would have to employ some cloak and dagger tactics to go there.

CHAPTER FORTY-FOUR

I HEADED BACK TO downtown Myrtle Beach and the Boardwalk. Some of the tallest buildings in South Carolina were right here. In between those tall hotels are smaller venues. Some of them were places where you wouldn't want your worst enemy to stay for fear of something incomprehensibly terrible happening to them. It was only a matter of time before they were torn down to be replaced by another tower.

Brave tourists on foot were walking from the attractions on the Boardwalk back to their hotels. The bright lights of the Sky Wheel dominated the landscape. Neon lights cast a purplish glow to the ocean along the water's edge.

After parking in the lot for the Flood Tide Inn, I reached into the glove compartment and retrieved the gun. Several people were milling about. They say to never judge a book by its cover, but the people who say that had never seen these people. Two men wearing tattered clothing, but expensive Air Jordans idly watched me from beneath the overhang over the lobby entrance, beside a rack holding various brochures and coupon books for Myrtle Beach. One had an afro. The other sported a Mohawk. Both had tattoos escaping their shirt collars and creeping up their necks. Both smoked those cheap, thin cigars you get beside the register at a gas station. On the other side of the lot were two scantily clad women watching traffic go by. I didn't want to get close enough to them to make out any details. All I know is that they had a lot of skin exposed.

This was why I didn't like to go out at night.

I tucked the gun into the small of my back and draped my shirt over it before climbing from the Jeep and locking the door. In my mind, I had pictured the two men planning on how they were going to rob me and leave my body in a dumpster around back. However, they were discussing the Carolina Panthers prospects for the upcoming season. Training camp was due to begin later this week.

One of the floosies—I refused to assume more—whistled at me, but I ignored the catcall. Avoiding eye contact with the two men outside the door, I stepped through the double doors after they whooshed open.

The only thing I liked about motels like this was that they accepted cash with no questions asked. I paid for a room, signed my name as "Frank Kaufman," took the key, and left the lobby. The real Frank owns a bookstore in Cherry Grove called Beach Bookshop & Video. He was always entertaining to speak with, and I was sure he'd get a laugh knowing that I used him as an alias.

On the way out, the two men were still talking about football.

"Look," I said, getting their attention. "The Panthers are only going to go as far as their offensive line will take them. Gotta keep that QB upright."

The guy with the big afro nodded slowly and held out a fist. "You got that right."

I gave the man a fist bump. He had tattoos on each finger.

His friend smiled. He had a gold tooth. "Don't do no good to pay that quarterback all that money if you're not going to protect him. It's ludicrous."

"No doubt," I said and started to walk toward the sidewalk on Ocean Boulevard. "Have a great evening fellas."

"You too, man," they said in unison.

The guy on the right yelled, “Go Panthers!” His voice echoed between the towers to the left and right of the Flood Tide Inn.

Maybe you can’t judge a book by its cover after all.

After grabbing my overnight bag from the backseat and locking the doors, I left the Jeep in the lot, whispering a silent prayer for it as I walked away. I parked it near the lobby in the hopes that it would be close enough to the road and the security cameras that no one would touch it. Doubt those intimidating Panther fans would let anyone touch my car while they were out there. It was unclear when they’d go inside.

One thing was clear, I might have paid for a room, but I wasn’t going to sleep in it. I preferred to sleep alone. Not with a thousand Palmetto bugs, in poorly washed, stained sheets, paper-thin walls, and a half-working A/C. I picked the Flood Tide Inn for a reason. It was on the opposite end of the Boardwalk from Myrtle Beach Reads.

I strolled the Boardwalk, staying in the brightest lit areas, heading for my bookstore. The Gay Dolphin was shutting down for the night. Grub N' Go Eats was still serving burritos. A few night owls were in line.

I made my way past the beach volleyball courts, past the 8th Avenue Tiki Bar, Daddio's Ice Cream, Sharkey's, and Holiday Sands before arriving at the Shops on the Boardwalk and the bookstore.

The ice cream shop and I Heart MB Tees stores on one end were closed. Permanently now. There were signs of progress from the new tenants. I looked forward to meeting them, whoever they were. The lights were out at Andrea's Coastal Décor as they were in my book-store next door.

Nobody jumped out at me from around the corner. Barring a single taxicab streaming past, Ocean Boulevard was empty on this stretch of the Boardwalk.

With a sigh of relief, I unlocked the front door to the bookstore and went inside. After disarming the alarm and rearming it, I locked the door and moved through the store and the dark racks. This had been my second home for the last three years following Autumn's death. Sometimes, I even slept here. I kept an extra change of clothes in my office. The armchair in there folded out into a bed.

Despite finding the tracking device on the Jeep and the bug in my phone, I still needed to play it safe with where I holed up for the night. The possibility existed that they had other means of keeping tabs on me. I'd beefed up security with new cameras. The back door was heavy and made of steel. After the vandalism at the Garden City location, I had new unpickable locks installed in both stores. No one was getting through it without a battering ram.

The weak spot was the front with the glass entrance and windows facing the street. The alarm would sound if someone tried to come through the front door or shatter the windows to get to me.

After my confrontation with Rosen, I needed to be extra cautious. I was sure if he had minions, they would be searching for me. Now that I'd played my hand, he knew I was on to him. He didn't outright deny my allegations of his involvement, but only challenged me to prove it.

During all of this, something was tugging at the back of my mind. What was Moody hoping to learn that he was going to tell Gomez and me at the Bar-B-Cue House? There was a chance I'd already uncovered what he wanted to say but hadn't gone far enough down the rabbit hole to connect Rosen and Zach to Autumn, Banner, and now Moody's deaths.

It was after midnight so technically it was now Wednesday morning. We held a Veteran's Coffee Hour every Tuesday morning where we'd provide coffee and pastries from Benjamin's Bakery to Vets. They would come in, grab what they liked, and sit around the café talking about old times. Tonight, I was in luck. A big chocolate chip muffin and apple turnover were left over from this morning. Karen had placed them in a cabinet at the coffee bar where we usually held extra food and supplies.

I grabbed both and a bottle of water from the fridge, but not coffee for once in my life, and wound my way through the stacks back to the office, thinking about Andrea, which made my stomach gurgle uncomfortably. She had taken my breath away the moment I'd met her over there at the coffee bar. Then, as I'd got to know her, it seemed like we synced. We got along well, and I was attracted to her. It broke my heart that she might have been too good to be true. She might've been planted here to keep an eye on me. I'd spent sporadic moments of the afternoon sorting out my feelings for her. There was more sorting to do. Adding up those moments, I made up my mind.

The office was less cluttered than usual. I normally did much of my paperwork on Mondays and Tuesdays. It hadn't gotten done this week. I wasn't procrastinating. I was busy.

Two panes of glass were inlaid high on the outside wall. I didn't flip on the overhead lights because I didn't want anybody outside to see a glow coming from the windows to signal my presence. My thinking with parking and paying for a room at the Flood Tide Inn and coming back here to sleep was that if someone tracked my Jeep there, they wouldn't find me in my assigned room.

Speaking of which, I removed the motel key from my pocket and tossed it on the desk where it landed with a clink. A streetlight stood near the windows so enough light streamed through them to illuminate my office enough that I wouldn't go bumping into the furniture. I set the water and pastries on the desk and dropped my overnight bag into one seat facing the desk. Feeling some of the tension ebb, I went across the hall to the small public restroom. Inside there, I splashed soapy water over my face and armpits and dried with paper towels to alleviate the dirt and odor. After putting on deodorant, I headed back to the office and transformed the easy chair into an ad hoc bed.

I'd done this enough that I kept a throw blanket and a travel pillow inside a file cabinet. Once I retrieved those, I laid down on the bed with the muffin in one hand and my phone in the other.

After what I'd learned and with the day's revelations, I had a guess as to where I might be able to find evidence of poison, and, if my hunch proved correct, it had been in my house the entire time. It was something that if I had the time or energy, I might be able to track down myself. I didn't mind doing grunt work. There was nothing like the satisfaction of getting your hands dirty, figuratively and literally, and seeing the fruits of your hard work. However, I'd learned to admit when I needed help. And right now, I needed it.

Bo, per usual, was still on West Coast time. He might be game for another search mission.

I called his number. He answered on the second ring.

"Clark, please tell me you're okay."

"I'm in one piece, but tired as all get-out," I admitted. "I'm not going to tell you where I am, but I called so you can let Mom and Dad know I'm safe."

The tapping of a keyboard came through the phone speaker. "Let's see. You're at your bookstore, right?"

After seeing his wizardry in tracking down Zach's burner phone to Barbados, I shouldn't have been surprised he'd been able to trace this call so quickly. "I'm telling you Bo. You need to offer your services to private eyes or something."

"I'm thinking about it," he said. "I gotta find a new gig. This is fun and all—I mean, it would be if my brother's life wasn't in danger."

He admitted on Sunday that he was broke despite netting millions of dollars after selling his stake in Uber. He decided to stay with my parents while he figured out what to do next. He'd put his multi-million-dollar mansion in La Jolla up for sale. Once that went through, he would have a nice piece of change to fall back on. I hoped he would learn to budget his finances better.

"I'll help you if I can."

He laughed. "Tell your friends."

In all seriousness, I said, "I might just do that."

If Lucien was as dirty as it seemed, then there might be an opening on the forensics team at the MBPD soon. Not that Bo would do that sort of work. There were other uses for his computer skills.

"Cool," he said. "Is there anything I can do for you in the meantime?"

"There is. Can you put together another program to search for something specific for me? I have an idea that, if it's correct, could tie all this together."

If my assumption proved true, then one of the last things Detective Moody said to me might come true. Myrtle Beach may in fact burn to the ground. Figuratively this time.

"Sure thing," he said.

I relayed to him what I wanted him to do, and he said he'd get right on it. We ended the call, and I finished the muffin. I took a sip from the water bottle and set it on the floor where I could easily reach it if I woke up parched in the middle of the night.

The answer came to me as I lay there, racking my brain trying to decipher what connected Autumn, Ed Banner, and Moody. It was like trying to do a mental Venn Diagram. They each represented three circles. What I hadn't been able to figure out was what would make the three of them overlap.

Banner had investigated Autumn's death at the courthouse. Moody was Banner's sidekick who couldn't go with Banner the night of her death. That was how Gomez became involved. She got the call to join Banner at the courthouse.

There was the overlap between Banner and Moody. They were both members of the police, but Moody didn't accompany Banner to see about Autumn. While I'd been so focused on trying to find a thread connecting the three involving investigations and corruption, there was one link between the three that seemed miniscule in comparison.

Until now.

Autumn died after drinking tea at her desk.

Banner died on his back porch one morning after drinking tea.

Moody had a cup of tea to wind down before he died.

Myself, I enjoyed drinking locally roasted coffee. I wasn't going into Food Lion and buying a bag of ground coffee. Autumn had similar tastes regarding her tea. Sure, Twining's or the Charleston Tea Garden teas would do in a pinch, but she indulged in sourcing her tea blends locally from the farmers market and Beach Dreams Market in North Myrtle.

While I didn't think it was possible that all three would have picked up poisoned tea via retail (others would have been poisoned too), it caused me to wonder if there was a source connecting the three victims.

Early in our marriage, on our third anniversary if memory served correctly, I'd bought Autumn a cast iron tea pot. It was green and had dragonflies on it. She used it every day and kept it on top of the fridge when not in use. I hadn't touched it since her death.

On the morning of Autumn's death, she and I had sat out on our back deck, sipping our drinks of choice, looking out over the lake. Then we'd gone for a walk on the beach before parting ways for the last time. Whatever tea blend she had used that morning would still be in the mesh basket. I'd risk it and go first thing in the morning to retrieve it.

I would also get in touch with Marge Moody and Brenda Banner to see if they had any leftovers from their husband's last cups of tea. That task might be much easier for Moody's wife since his death had just happened. Banner died a few months after Autumn.

As for Moody, if he'd been poisoned, why now? Was it over what he was trying to find out to tell Gomez and me?

I'd played it passively long enough, allowing others to make their moves on me. Gomez still hadn't appeared. This gnawing sense in the pit of my stomach screamed that something terrible had happened to her. There were three, and now possibly four people dead. Enough was enough. I wasn't going to stand for it any longer.

Time to go on the offensive and fight fire with fire.

CHAPTER FORTY-FIVE

WHILE I WASN'T THINKING about fighting fire with literal fire, someone else was, leading to a rude awakening thirteen minutes after two A.M.

Amid troubled dreams, I'd sensed a continual buzzing nearby that persisted long enough to wake me. When I rolled over and opened my eyes, the phone screen was glowing while vibrating before going black. I rubbed my face and the sleep out of my eyes. I'd laid the phone on the desk near the bed with a white noise app running to help me sleep on the stiff pullout bed. My legs dangled off the end if I left them stretched out, so I slept in a near fetal position.

I put both feet on the floor and reached over to grab the phone. The lock screen showed two missed calls and several missed text messages. I checked the time and groaned. I'd put the notifications on silent but left the vibration on, hence the nightmare of bees attacking me.

One call was from an unknown number, but it had a local 843 area code. The other was from Battles. He'd also sent me a text saying it was urgent that I call him.

I did. He picked up halfway through the first ring.

"Clark! Thank goodness you're okay." There was a tangible sense of relief in his voice. "We've been trying to get a hold of you."

My mouth went dry as I expected to hear news of them finding Gomez's body somewhere. His news wasn't as bad as that, but it was still life changing.

Battles called about a fire.

***

I threw on my clothes and shoes before literally running out of the bookstore, arming the alarm before leaving. The night was still. Waves crashed onto the beach across the street. The tang of salt clung to the air. Lights on poles kept this part of Ocean Boulevard illuminated. No cars or people were about.

Summoning the fit body I had during my baseball playing days at Coastal Carolina, I ran all the way through the Boardwalk to the Flood Tide Inn. None of the vagrants or night owls stopped me. Thankfully, my Jeep wasn't up on cinder blocks with the wheels gone when I arrived. It was untouched. Lights from the lobby glowed through the windows, casting a yellowish light on the pavement.

I climbed in the Jeep, peeled out of the lot, and turned on my emergency flashers. It normally takes about fifteen minutes to go from the Boardwalk to my home in Surfside Beach. I cut that time in half, flying as fast as the engine would allow. There weren't many vehicles along the way. Tires droned on the pavement.

As I passed by the Neighborhood Wal-Mart on Kings Highway at the border of Myrtle Beach and Surfside, a glow coming above the trees somewhere near but behind a tall water tower tied my stomach in a knot. I started to cry.

I veered right onto 544 for a hundred yards and turned left onto Village Drive before getting to Lake View Circle.

Fire and smoke licked the sky as embers pirouetted in an updraft. My house was engulfed in a ravenous inferno, and I was helpless to do anything about it.

Four fire trucks and support vehicles were parked on the street as firefighters fought to control the blaze. I parked down the street and dashed toward the house as the roof on the left side of the house caved in, crashing down in a maelstrom of embers and wood. Smoke billowed from the windows. Golden ripples danced across the lake behind the house, mirroring the orange and yellow flames under the stars.

My neighbors had come out and were standing on the street at a distance watching the drama unfold. Dame and Battles were there. Bo had borrowed Mom and Dad's golf cart to get here and stood with them. He had been awake, looked out the window from the desk in my parents' upstairs bonus room, and had seen my house ablaze in the distance.

Blood thundered in my ears as the house burned. We watched it burn all the way to the ground. They comforted me and kept me from having a panic attack. Bo's hand gripped my shoulder the entire time. Battles said reassuring words I didn't hear through the roar of noise in my head, but his tone was soothing. They were relieved I wasn't inside. I would have been dead, for sure.

Two news vans appeared in the pre-dawn glow. I instructed Dame and Battles to keep them away from me. My time for speaking on camera was coming, but it wouldn't be right now. They'd gone too far.

The fire was finally extinguished as the sun climbed above the horizon.

CHAPTER FORTY-SIX

MY HOUSE WAS BUILT over forty years ago. Autumn and I had bought it after some house flippers purchased it and completely renovated the interior. The shell was several decades old, but the inside had been brand new. We spent the first year living there adding our own touches. We'd put in a fence in the backyard to keep our future children inside and safe. All the kitchen appliances were replaced over time with better equipment.

Autumn picked out the interior paint colors and decorated the place herself. I was merely the chief furniture mover and picture hanger. Everything was placed according to her exact instructions. She had an eye for interior design and had talked about quitting the courthouse to start her own service before her uncle had died and a small inheritance came along allowing her to live her dream of opening Myrtle Beach Reads.

I hadn't changed anything in the house since her passing. She was also responsible for decorating Myrtle Beach Reads with a similar nautical motif. I left it untouched as well.

Now our house was gone. Burnt to cinders. Her teapot and any evidence it contained was destroyed.

The fire marshal came and did an initial inspection to try and locate the source of the blaze. It didn't take him long to find it. Arson was the cause, which didn't surprise me. His initial suspicion was that someone had thrown a Molotov cocktail through both windows on the front of the house. The arsonist had firebombed my house with glass bottles filled with either gasoline or a napalm-like mixture (the ensuing investigation would determine which) lit by a burning cloth wick.

I never thought I'd be targeted with paramilitary weapons, but here we are.

Throughout the morning, I had to deal with officials from the fire department, homeowners' insurance, and the Horry County police. The house was in an unincorporated zone, so the county had jurisdiction here. Dealing with them had to be done. Thankfully, Bo and now Dad were there to assist.

Officers Duncan and Hall arrived at some point and congregated with Dame and Battles. After I gave them the entire story about yesterday's events that culminated in Rosen's office, they called in the Horry County Chief of Police, Nelson Pendleton. He personally came to the scene.

He was tall and dark. His facial hair was bushy but under control with flecks of gray. Most of his face held a serious demeanor, but his eyes conveyed kindness and sharp intelligence. He wore a tan cowboy hat like you'd expect the Police Chief of the largest county in South Carolina to wear. He looked and played the part well. One thing was apparent. He held the respect of his officers and Dame and Battles. He had a career in law enforcement spanning four decades, spending half of that time in his current position.

And he knew all about me.

He shook my hand and, finally breaking the grim set of his mouth, said, "I've heard about what you've done during this past year for Myrtle Beach. Officers Duncan and Hall filled me in on your discussion yesterday." He placed a hand on my shoulder. "Rest assured, son, we're going to get to the bottom of this."

I looked him in the eye and tilted my chin. After what Gomez and Moody told me about MBPD Police Chief Miller, I didn't know if I could trust her. They didn't seem to because she was an appointee of Rosen's. One look at Pendelton was enough to tell me that he was a trustworthy man.

He meant business. Serious business. I wished I'd met him a year ago.

I stepped closer and lowered my voice. "I know this is going to sound crazy, but I think Mayor Rosen was the one behind this."

Instead of being shocked or laughing at me, Pendleton didn't bat an eyelash. "Tell me what makes you think that."

***

Two other county cruisers arrived. All uniformed officers huddled with Pendleton. He gave them a situation report before they dispersed to start their investigation. Pendleton took me, Dad, Dame, Battles, and Bo aside and told me that they were calling SLED. The State Law Enforcement Division. The "big guns," in other words. Their primary mission was to provide additional manpower and technical assistance. They were the best the state had.

I recalled from the Connor West investigation that the attorney general and state governor had to sign off on them coming. SLED had several agents in Horry County who worked remotely, instead of being stationed at headquarters in Columbia. Each had various responsibilities, including agents covering

Drugs, Firearms, Tobacco, and Alcohol. The SLED agent in Horry County for Major Crimes was on her way. She was coming to assess the situation and determine if backup was needed. If so, it would take several hours for them to arrive from their headquarters in Columbia. The situation had escalated, and I was in the middle of it.

Through all the noise and kind gestures, I kept thinking. Thinking. Thinking. **THINKING**.

This wasn't an accidental fire. Not after what occurred yesterday. I didn't believe that Rosen would sink to the level of coming out here and personally setting fire to my house. Someone must have committed arson at his command. The name that kept popping up in my head over and over was Lucien. I'd told Pendleton my suspicions of Lucien's involvement and that there may be more on Rosen's payroll, including Chief Miller. It was difficult to say, but I included Detective Moody among the people who may have had some knowledge of Rosen and Zach Lawson's scheme.

He put on a sad face at the mention of Moody's death. The two of them had worked together for the MBPD during the 80s. Pendleton considered Moody a friend.

Pendleton took a call and walked away, leaving the five of us huddled in a group.

Dad's eyes were red from tears. Bo was white in the face, which was a magnificent accomplishment with his fading spray tan hiding the brunt of it. Battles had spoken with Chief Miller against my better judgment, due to police protocols. Because of my Surfside Beach address, I was out of their jurisdiction. There was little they could do now since the Horry County police and SLED were investigating the fire. They would assist if needed but work like this was usually left to the big dogs.

***

Smoke from the house continued to stream to the clouds. The neighbors had gone home. A chance of rain was in the forecast for this afternoon. That should stop the smoke.

The insurance company opened a claim ticket and were going to send someone out as soon as possible. The representative assured me that my policy covered the rebuild costs, but it might take up to three months to process the claim and provide a payout. It all depended on the arson investigation as well.

Dad offered me one of the other upstairs bedrooms at his house. Bo had already claimed one for himself. There were two others. I may take dad up on it after this matter with Autumn was resolved. If it was resolved, I'd need somewhere to stay.

As the fire department officials poured over the house remains and Pendleton directed personnel traffic, I said to Bo, "Did you find anything?"

His eyes lit as he ran a hand through his immaculate hair to make himself look pretty. "Oh, yeah. I emailed the results to you. You were dead on."

A tingle of elation wound through me. The evidence, tangible evidence, against Rosen was starting to come together.

"Think you could help me again?"

"Of course," he said. "Anything."

I told him what I wanted him to do. He hopped in the golf cart and drove back to Mom and Dad's house. Dad remained behind to offer emotional support. At some point, Chris MacInally arrived on his Harley with his slicked back hair, burly chest, and sleeves of tattoos. He swallowed me up in a big hug. We'd become good friends since I accused him of murder. That was the kind of guy he was.

Chris told me that he and Erin were about to depart for Los Angeles to take care of some matters concerning her father's music. John Allen Howard was a world-famous Hollywood composer who had left behind an enormous legacy. He'd been the composer for several blockbuster films and movie series. Now the movie studios were making sequels to movies he had scored for, and Erin was flying out to meet with the directors and producers in hiring someone to rework and continue her father's musical legacy.

He said he only had a few minutes before they were supposed to leave for the airport but wanted to come by and offer his support and something else.

"Here, take these." He raised his hand and held out a set of keys.

I eyeballed them but didn't reach out. "What are these for? You know I don't know how to ride a motorcycle."

Chris grinned as the others listened in on our conversation. "No, dummy. These are for my apartment in Market Common. We want you to stay there for as long as you need. Erin and I are going to be gone for months. No one will be there."

"She agreed to this?"

He placed a paw on my shoulder. "After what you did for her family, she'd buy you a new house if you needed one."

I accepted the keys. A tear sprang to my right eye. “I don’t know what to say. Thanks man.”

We hugged again before he climbed back on the Harley and roared away. I placed the keys in my pocket.

“That was nice of him,” Dad said, “but you can stay with us too if you’d like.”

In the days following the resolution of all this, I might need to stay with them for emotional and possible physical support. I’d already resigned myself to the fact that I might not make it out of this in one piece. My house with Autumn was gone.

My phone buzzed in my pocket. I pulled it out and looked at the screen where it displayed a text notification. A text came from an unlisted number. It read:

You were warned. Stop. Or you're next.

The vultures are circling. It's you who's going down.

CHAPTER FORTY-SEVEN

I SHOWED THE TEXT message to Pendleton. Whoever sent the text did it to scare me. Now, it only emboldened me. He said they'd try to trace it, but not to hold out hope. I sent the phone number to Bo. After the computer wizardry he'd pulled these last two days, I had as much hope in him as anyone.

They say the coverup is worse than the crime. There were at least three dead, starting with Autumn. Rosen had already shown to what lengths he would go to stop me. He could have me killed, but he had to know that if I died, that would be a signal stronger than throwing a vocal political opposition leader out a high-rise office window since I had already informed the authorities of my suspicions and what Gomez and I had uncovered.

Speaking of which, Battles said they still hadn't heard a peep from her, but they had officers out looking. Lucien had gone off the grid too. They were going to send someone to speak to Andrea and find out what she knew. I suspected she would be able to tell them little. She was a minor cog in the bigger inner workings of Rosen’s ticking clock.

Even though they'd begun an official investigation, the weight hadn't been taken off my shoulders. I wasn't the type of person who sat back and allowed others to do the heavy lifting. At least not now. A year ago, I may have. But now, this was bigger than Autumn.

Major Sidney Paulson with SLED came by and met with me in private—as private as possible while standing near a smoldering home. Her blonde hair was tied back in a ponytail. She was thin and of average height. Her most defining characteristic was a pair of beaver teeth up front and center. They made an appearance every time she spoke. For someone with such a serious job, she smiled a lot. The prominent front teeth made her endearing and someone I trusted instantly.

She seemed competent, capable, and serious. Major Paulson was ready to roll after Pendleton and I filled her in, making sure to mention how I believed Autumn, Banner, and Moody had been poisoned. She made some calls to Columbia to request the assistance she thought she needed.

“Can you do anything about Rosen?” I asked her.

She tightened her thin lips. “Not at present, but one thing I can immediately do is use our ALPR network to see if this Lucien guy is out on the road.”

“What's ALPR?”

“Our Automated License Plate Reader. We use it in surveillance to track vehicle movements. If he's out there, we'll find him.”

“What if he switched his license plate?”

“That presents a different problem, but we have facial recognition set up in a few spots around Myrtle Beach.”

“Anything near the lower end of the Boardwalk?” I gave her the address of my bookstore.

“Not down that low,” she answered. “More so in the heavier trafficked areas.”

That wasn't the answer I wanted, but if Lucien walked past the arcade or Ripley's on his way to Myrtle Beach Reads, it would pick him up. Of course, by the time someone saw him, it would be too late.

She excused herself to take a call from the Attorney General and to coordinate with Pendleton and Columbia. After a while, I was forgotten about by the police types. They rallied around their units and had discussions about next steps. I was left out of their loop.

I had my own loop to deal with.

***

I stayed until the fire trucks and support personnel began to leave. I was eventually allowed to walk through the wreckage. Not everything had burned, but most of my worldly possessions were ruined or in cinders. I tramped through the remains in a haze. All of it was familiar, but because nothing was whole, or would ever be again, it was like my mind was only allowing me to see parts of my home. Our home, I reminded myself.

The fire marshal accompanied me, making sure I didn't get hurt. A murder of cawing crows congregated atop a nearby tree, adding to the eeriness.

It was a numbing experience. It was like I'd stepped into a fresh nightmare but still retained the familiarity of living here for the last decade or so.

Not only had the arsonist taken away my home and everything I owned, but they had also taken away my last physical connection to Autumn. I hadn't washed her pillowcase since her death. Every now and then, I'd roll over and be able to smell her essence. Over time, the fragrance from the perfume she wore every day faded from the pillow. That didn't mean that I wouldn't give it a good squeeze to try and push out any remaining scent.

I made my way back to where our bedroom used to be. The ceiling had collapsed, leaving bits of blackened wood and drywall everywhere. Her pillow was gone, reduced to ashes. The metal from our bed frame was warped and gray with burn marks. The wood of the headboard had likewise been reduced to ash. The rest of the furniture was much the same way.

In the corner were the remains of our dresser. It too had burned with vigor. Drywall from the ceiling had fallen on it. As I stared into the wreckage, something glimmered in the sunlight. I stepped over and brushed the debris aside to reveal a warped picture frame.

The tarnished silver frame contained my favorite photo of Autumn. The photo had been taken during a vacation in Destin. The sky was a mélange of orange and yellow with the setting sun. Autumn was sitting on a log that had washed up on the white sandy beach, wearing a black sundress and flip flops. Her windswept auburn hair responded effortlessly to the soft breeze. Her foot dangled in the sand. The right one was perched on the log. The look on her face was one of contentment, happiness, and desire all rolled into one.

I brushed the splinters of wood, ash, and bits of sheetrock aside to expose the frame. The glass had broken, and the metal was warped, but the 4x6 photo remained largely intact. I pulled off the back and withdrew the picture. This picture was saved digitally somewhere in my Google Photo archive, but finding the physical copy brought a sense of relief in this tragedy. Something had survived.

Holding it in both hands, I gazed at Autumn's beautiful face and said, "I'll find who did this and make sure they get what's coming to them."

I stood there amidst the wreckage, clutching the photo to my chest for a long time.

The fire marshal walked away and let me grieve in peace.

CHAPTER FORTY-EIGHT

Word spread rapidly through social media and the local news about my house burning down. I'll never forget the outpouring of support the Myrtle Beach community displayed to me in the days that followed. Friends I'd forgotten about and those who I hadn't called or texted, nor had they attempted to do likewise, were now offering help and words expressing consolation.

Karen at the bookstore called and said her husband saw the story on the news. I hadn't thought about calling the store to tell them I wouldn't be coming in today to work—although I might be sleeping there again. She said she and Miss Margaret would handle the store for as long as I needed. With Garden City Reads now having two employees besides Winona, I said this might be a good time to have them come and get some sales floor training.

On top of employees, neighbors I had spoken to occasionally or never at all came out to express their sympathies. Each of them spoke with investigators. No one had seen anything. It's a sleepy neighborhood with many retirees. Most had been in bed for hours when the blaze was thought to have started.

While I was at the burn site, Mom went shopping at her favorite store, Hamrick's. Not specifically for herself—although she picked up a cute new blouse—but for me. I've worn the same size clothes since high school, so it was easy for her to pick me out several new outfits and underwear. The clothes I had on were blackened with soot and reeked of smoke. The other set in my overnight bag that I wore two days ago was starting to decompose. At least that's what they smelled like they were doing.

At some point during the afternoon, after being urged to get some rest for the third or fourth time by members of the fire department, I took Dad to his house. He told me along the way that Bo saw my house ablaze from an upstairs window during the night while he was on the computer. That's how close we lived to each other.

I crashed in one of the guest bedrooms.

When I awoke after a fitful nap, it was nearly one o'clock. I'd turned my phone off to keep people from waking me up. I hit the power button and opened the bedroom door. No one was upstairs, but fresh, clean, new clothes sat on the floor outside the bedroom door.

Mom had picked out a Greg Norman golf polo, matching shorts, and Hanes boxers from Hamrick's. A note on top of the pile read that she'd left some shampoo and a bar of soap in the bathroom. A not-so-subtle hint to wash the stink off. Mom will always be Mom.

Inside the bathroom was a smorgasbord of toiletries. New toothpaste, toothbrush, hairbrush, deodorant, soap, and shampoo. The works.

By the time I shut the shower off, the hot water had begun to grow cold. I needed every bit of it.

My family had heard me stirring about. Bo sat at a computer desk in the upstairs den, typing away at the keyboard on his laptop. Even with the cane, Dad had made it upstairs. He sat beside Mom on a green loveseat. They cradled mugs of coffee in their hands. A full, steaming mug lay on a side table next to a plush easy chair they'd saved for me.

"How are you doing?" Mom asked as I entered the den.

I ran my hands through my still partially damp hair. "Better now. Thanks."

"Of course," Mom said.

Dad motioned to the recliner. "Take a load off. Talk to us."

"We've been so worried about you," Mom said.

"Me too." I plopped down in the chair and reclined, putting my feet up. The coffee was from their Keurig. Still not what I was used to, but it would do. "Thanks for everything."

"Of course," Mom repeated. "We're just glad you're here and you're okay."

"Me too," I agreed.

"Can you tell us anything that's going on?" Mom asked.

Bo turned to see my response. We made eye contact. I'd told him to tell them very little about my situation and whereabouts.

"It's obviously something big," Dad said. "That house didn't catch fire by itself."

"Nope," I concurred. "The fire marshal thinks a couple Molotov cocktails were to blame."

Mom held a hand to the side of her face. "Who would want to do that?"

I looked at Bo. He shook his head a little.

"I'd rather not say at this point," I answered. "I'll just say that this is bigger than I ever imagined. There are some big players involved who are trying to scare me off."

"I'd let them," Mom said. "Whatever this is, it isn't worth your life."

I disagreed. “It is if it means that the person responsible for killing Autumn is brought to justice.”

Bo took this moment to interject, asking, “Have you read that email I sent you?”

His words were weighted with seriousness.

“I haven’t had a chance,” I answered.

He glanced at Mom and Dad before saying, “Let me sum it up for you. I found two scholarly articles from the State History Museum in Columbia. One was brief and dated the week after Autumn died. The other came five months later.”

I leaned forward, cupping the mug between my hands. “What were they about?”

Mom and Dad's heads swung between Bo and me like they were spectators at a tennis match.

"The first one described a crate they received, documenting a potential dig site in Myrtle Beach. The sender didn't leave a name nor a return address. A note was inside saying that the artifacts inside the crate were unearthed during excavation for a building near the ocean."

My heart galloped in a pounding rhythm inside my chest. "Go on."

Bo was into it. He'd told me over the weekend while I was trying to find out who killed Zach Lawson that he thought it was exciting I was involved in murder investigations. Now he was included, playing a role which brought him to life.

"Inside the crate were pottery shards, shell artifacts that were used for tools, ornaments, and jewelry."

"There it is," I said.

"There is what?" Mom asked.

"What they covered up," I answered, "except that some good Samaritan thought that the findings were too important to bury and sent them in for examination."

Bo held up a finger. "That's not all. The museum announced their findings in the article that followed five months later."

"What were they?" Dad asked from the edge of his seat.

"I'd never heard of this before last night," Bo said, "but the spear points were distinctive. They were fluted and used in the Clovis culture."

"I've never heard of them either," Mom said. "How old did they determine the artifacts were?"

Bo answered, "About thirteen-thousand years old."

Mom gasped. Dad leaned back on the couch.

"Wow," I said. "I mean, I've heard the Waccamaw and Winyah were the first ones to inhabit the Grand Strand. I think they were here for thousands of years before European explorers first came through here in the 1500s. What was dug up would have predated them. Amazing."

"Do you think they knew the historical significance when they dug them up?" Dad asked.

"I doubt it," I said. "Whoever was running the site clearing must have alerted their boss who ran it up the ladder until it reached Zach. He would have consulted with his attorney, Rosen, about what to do." I told them about how they tried to bribe officials over a similar situation on St. Grant's Island and how they'd put up a hotel in downtown Myrtle Beach after Autumn's death. "So, here this had happened again. Someone may have contacted Judge Whitley, who runs the Historic Committee, and she may have told them to delay building so archivists could come in and examine the scene in situ."

"And if they had a deadline to meet to open the hotel," Mom theorized, "this might have been an unacceptable setback."

"Bingo," I said. The scene in Whitley's chambers played like a movie in my mind. "Let's picture this. Some construction workers using an excavator dig up a bunch of pottery shards or whatever. They stop work so they can figure out what they found and if it was important enough to halt progress. The foreman makes a call and the next thing we know Rosen, who was not mayor but an attorney at the time, enters the courthouse to speak to Whitley about the situation for his client. She advises him that they need to call someone in, and Rosen presents her a bribe."

Mom gasped. "And Autumn overheard the entire thing."

"Correct," I said. "I remember that week as clear as day. Autumn told me they had a busier docket than usual, which would require her to stay late a couple nights. She did the night before her death and the day of."

"Do you think Rosen knew Autumn was there?" Dad asked.

"It's possible he didn't." I rubbed my jaw. I'd forgotten about the coffee. It was growing cold. I was energized by pure endorphins now. "Autumn's office was next door to Whitley's. You would come to Whitley's door first without having to pass Autumn. There were no cameras in that hallway, but there was by the entrance. It could have caught Rosen coming in."

"What do you think happened?" Bo asked.

I tapped a finger on the armrest. "Let's say Rosen came in to get Whitley to change her mind. Whether by coercion or bribe, Autumn was next door working. She may not have even known Rosen was there. She could have needed to ask Whitley a question and heard them talking through the door."

Dad set his empty mug on the coffee table. "Would their voices have been muffled?"

"Somewhat," I answered. "The walls and doors inside that old courthouse were thin. She may not have heard every word, but she may have been able to make out the gist of it."

"Do you think she confronted Rosen?" Mom said. "I can't see her doing that face-to-face."

"Me neither," I said. "She probably ducked back into her office and waited for Rosen to leave. Autumn and Whitley were close enough that I can imagine Autumn saying something after Rosen left."

"Which means that Whitley was in on it," Mom said. We waited for a further explanation. With mom being a mystery aficionado for her voracious consumption of mystery novels, her vivid imagination envisioned the different strings tying this all together. "The hotel got built, didn't it? We would have heard if someone found traces of people in downtown Myrtle Beach dating back millennia, right?"

Recalling my time as a member of the Downtown Development Committee, I said, "We would have shouted that from the rooftops. It would have been another arrow in our quiver to draw people to Myrtle Beach."

Mom spread out her hand. "Let's say Autumn heard this bribe offer and confronted Whitley about it."

"She would deny it, of course," I said.

"Of course," Mom agreed. "Let's say she did and found a way to explain her closed-door conversation with Rosen in such a way that Autumn conceded that she'd heard wrong, whether she believed Whitley or not."

"And Whitley would have told Rosen about Autumn who would then tell Zach." I said. "Got it. Then they decided they needed to get rid of Autumn before she brought their plans to a halt. That still doesn't explain how she was killed. On the night Autumn died, Whitley told me she brewed Autumn some tea before she left. That's how I figured she was poisoned, but I don't see how it could have been Whitley behind it. If she was, then she confessed to murder."

"Which I don't see anyone in their right mind doing, and I remember her being sharp as a tack when Autumn worked for her." Mom shook her head.

"Exactly. Remember that cast iron teapot I got for Autumn?" I asked.

"I do," Mom answered. "We used to have lovely tea parties using it. Why?"

I rubbed my chin as I tried to reason out loud. "The fire destroyed it. I was hoping to get to it because Autumn had used it the morning she died. I had coffee that day, like normal. I hadn't touched it since her death and was going to have the loose-leaf tea remnants tested for poison. I remember it being a custom blend she got while at work, but I don't know who gave it to her. She could have been drinking it for a while, and it finally got her."

"Which means that whatever tea Whitley gave her might have had nothing to do with her death," Dad added.

"That would be a relief to her if that's true," I said. "All three of them, Autumn,

Banner, and Moody, were singled out. The murderer had to find a way to slip them a poisoned blend without killing unintended victims."

"That's a scary thought," Mom said and turned to Bo. "Is it possible for someone to find out who was working at the Castello delle Onde construction site during the time Autumn died?" Mom asked.

I looked at Bo, who shook his head. There were some tasks he couldn't accomplish via the internet.

"No," I answered, "but I bet law enforcement could. I'll forward all of this to Agent Paulson. I'm sure she has the tools and authorization. Good work, Bo."

"Thanks," he said with a touch of pride.

It felt like we had some forward momentum now. I'd pass along everything Bo found, and my suspicions about Whitley giving Autumn tea the night of her death, to SLED and let them dig into it.

What I had now, concerning the possibility that Rosen had a hand in murdering Autumn, were motive and opportunity. He may have resorted to killing Autumn to keep progress on the Castello delle Onde moving. The promise of money must have been too great for Zach and Rosen to allow Autumn to interfere. If Rosen had met Whitley in chambers the day before Autumn's death, he could have done it again the next day too. There's the opportunity.

Now, to figure out how Rosen would have the means to do it.

As it turned out, learning that came from the unlikeliest of sources.

CHAPTER FORTY-NINE

HAVING THE WARNING THAT I assumed either Rosen or Lucien sent me via text at the forefront of my mind, I didn't want to stay at Mom and Dad's for long, especially since they lived so close to my home that had been firebombed twelve hours ago. That was a phrase I never thought would have entered my life.

Chris had given me the keys to his apartment. I'd been to it a couple times, so I was familiar with where to park in Market Common and the layout of his place.

I drove from my parent's place to his in a trance. This was just what Rosen wanted. For me to be distracted. Where I'd had all my focus on the Autumn investigation, now I had to split it with having to deal with the aftermath of my house burning down and figuring out what I was going to do.

Almost all my worldly possessions had been inside. Items from my childhood like my favorite stuffed animal, a bunny I referred to as "Pinky," and more were gone. Burned to ashes. Photos from my youth, clothes, electronics, all of it. Gone. Some of them were just material possessions, replaceable, but the sentimental items were gone forever.

Trying to focus on the now, I didn't want to stop moving because I was afraid the enormity of it all would send me into a catatonic state. If they resorted to arson, I must be close.

There was a parking spot in front of Gordon Biersch that I slipped the Jeep into. Their covered patio was full of beer sippers and food eaters enjoying a pleasant afternoon. If they only knew what I'd been through today.

I punched in a code on the entryway to The Windsor Private Residences. I'd memorized it from other times I'd been here. After taking the elevator up to the top floor, I made two rights before arriving at the entrance to Chris's apartment. The apartment featured shiny hardwood floors, tall ceilings, a chef's kitchen that featured a huge gas range and hood with granite countertops. There were three bedrooms. I recalled his being on one end of the place with the other two on the opposite side. One was a guest bedroom. The other was an office.

I wasn't sure which was which, so I opened the door on the right first. It was the office. A desk faced a window which overlooked Valor Park and the main thoroughfare running through Market Common. From here, Chris had a view of people strolling, riding bikes, and children playing in the grass amidst water fountains, flowerbeds, and a large lake across Farrow Parkway. It might be the best view in Market Common.

Besides the desk, with the glorious vantage point, the office consisted of a leather couch and accompanying coffee table and a "brag wall" where he had various certificates, an Ivy League degree, and newspaper clippings from where he helped various businesses open.

A new, expensive looking drone sat on a small table in one corner. The box it had come in sat on the floor. An instruction manual and control pad to operate the drone laid beside it.

I closed the door to the office and crossed the hall to what was the guest bedroom. While it was easy to tell that Chris had done most of the decorating in the apartment, it appeared that his fiancée, Erin, had taken the reins in doing the guest bedroom.

The bed had a white duvet with a blue flower pattern. Plush pillows were arranged at the head of the bed. White linen curtains hung from the window. All the furniture matched and was made of walnut. Tasteful paintings with a musical theme hung on the walls. No doubt in honor of Erin's dad, the late Hollywood composer, John Allen Howard. The room had the feel of a ritzy five-star hotel.

A small envelope lay on the bed. It was identical to the one she had handed me when she first walked into Myrtle Beach Reads early one morning with an invitation to attend what turned out to be an ill-fated dinner party at her dad's beachfront estate.

The front of the envelope read "For Clark."

"Hmm," I said to myself, picking it up. I managed to smile. Erin had worked for her dad, assisting him in his day-to-day matters and handling his affairs. They dealt with Hollywood royalty daily, and she knew how to make people feel special.

I flipped the envelope over and ran a finger under the flap. A round Mickey Mouse sticker held it closed. There were two things inside. A hand-written note and a folded check.

The note read:

Dear Clark,
I'm so sorry for what happened to your home. You have my deepest sympathies. I know you've had a rough go of it, and I'd like to help you escape. You have my eternal gratitude after what you did for my family for which I can never repay in full. Please use this check to go somewhere far away from Myrtle

Beach and take a break to get right again.
XOXO,
Erin Howard

Moisture formed at the corners of my eyes. I opened the check and gasped at the amount.

CHAPTER FIFTY

I APPRECIATED CHRIS GIVING me somewhere to crash in the aftermath of my home burning down, but at this moment, I wanted to be around people. To have some connection with the world. I didn't want to be alone right now. The airy spaciousness of the high-ceilinged apartment and lack of sounds made the place seem lonely.

I'd told my parents and Bo that I didn't want to stay at their house for their own protection. If someone wanted to come after me, a late-night home invasion didn't seem out of the question.

However, it occurred to me that if I kept myself in a busy, public space, Rosen's goons might hesitate to come in with figurative, or literal, guns blazing.

I left my overnight bag on the guest bed and left Chris's apartment.

What I needed at this point was to be somewhere that calmed my soul. Somewhere to focus. Although I was safe at Chris's, I wanted to be around people. I left the apartment and headed to my sanctuary, Myrtle Beach Reads.

Being at the bookstore held several comforting positives besides it being my home away from home. It was public, busy, and had security cameras. No one, not even Lucien, would be dumb enough to come into the store and plunge a knife in my gut in broad daylight.

I returned to the Flood Tide Inn and paid cash for another night for which I wouldn't be there. The same two dudes were there, still talking about football. At least they'd changed their clothes since I'd seen them the night before. We talked about the Panthers for a few minutes before I bounded onto the sidewalk in my nice new clothes. I had to say, Mom had a good sense of style. Despite all the madness of the past three days, I had to admit I looked way better than I felt. No, to be honest, I looked good which improved my mood.

The Boardwalk was packed with tourists, and it took me much longer to navigate through the foot traffic than it did last night to reach the store. I stopped off at Grub N' Go Eats and grabbed a burrito along the way. The owner might be a crook and in jail, but they made good food.

The bookstore was busy with book browsers and coffee drinkers. In the middle of an afternoon during one of the busier weeks of the summer season, I'd hoped this would be the case. I settled into a table near the coffee bar. Humphrey might lack book-selling ability, but he made up for it as a barista. While Karen handled the book sales, Humphrey manned the coffee bar. He was a year out of high school and hadn't decided what he wanted to do with his life. He'd sampled some of the coffees I’d had and took an interest. Without telling me, he took home the instruction manual to the Astra espresso machine Erin had bought for me after I solved her father's murder. He learned how to work the machine inside and out. Then, he watched hours of YouTube videos learning the craft of coffee. He'd turned out to be much better than me at making craft brews. It didn't bother me a bit to sit here and let him handle the cappuccinos, espressos, and lattes.

While foot traffic bustled around me, I stared at my laptop screen, trying to figure out what happens after a house burns down. After a disheartening five minutes, I logged off. I'd be able to rebuild, but I might be homeless for up to a year or more depending on how long the haggling between the insurance company and the restoration contractor took. At this point, I couldn't fathom what that might be like or where I would stay after Chris and Erin returned.

As the afternoon wore on, my thoughts kept straying to Gomez and what happened to her or where she might be. She'd seemingly disappeared from the face of the earth. When I waded into the pond to look inside her car, the mere thought of losing her left a cavity inside my soul that was almost as large as the one caused by Autumn's death. Since I'd met Gomez, she'd been the one who had tugged at my heartstrings the most. Even more so than Andrea. I had to admit, part of the reason why I asked Andrea out to begin with came in the aftermath of learning about Gomez's engagement to Lucien.

There was no doubt I found Andrea attractive. Her beauty was undeniable. But now that I knew she came into my life because of Rosen, I couldn't trust her.

Having an awareness of her schedule, the odds were that she was on the other side of the wall separating my store from hers right now. After what happened yesterday at Paradise Hideaway and this morning, I couldn't face her. Not now.

While I sat there lost in thought, the same distinctive voice I'd heard here the other day started speaking. His back was to me, but his voice and accent stood out. His shaggy, curly blond hair also marked him. It was great when tourists came in multiple times during their weekly stays.

It turned out, I was correct. Andrea was next door. Now, she was here. Standing above me. She came in while I was lost in thought.

"Clark, we need to talk," she said, breaking me from my stream of consciousness.

At that moment, the guy at the counter turned and said to Andrea. "Julie?"

Andrea involuntarily swiveled her hips and looked at him. Her face paled and jaw dropped. "No! Get away from me!"

She turned and ran out of the store, bumping into several book browsers along the way.

The guy remained frozen in place. He didn't seem as surprised as she was to see each other. Almost like he expected to see her.

I got to my feet while the guy watched her leave. His jaw worked back and forth as he pondered his next move.

"Excuse me," I said.

He peeled his eyes away from the closing front door and looked at me. When I first saw him, something about him seemed familiar. I couldn't put my finger on it. Now, I could. He and Andrea's daughter bore a striking resemblance.

He'd called Andrea by a different name—Julie—but now that I had learned she'd been lying to me, it wouldn't surprise me in the least if Andrea wasn't her real name.

"Yes?"

"Did you just call her Julie?"

"Uh-huh."

My ears started to turn red. "I thought her name was Andrea."

“That's her middle name. Her first name is Julie,” he said in a way that left no doubt that he was telling the truth.

“What makes you think that?”

He made a move toward the front door in pursuit of Andrea. Before he took his second step, he turned to me and said, “Because she's my wife.”

CHAPTER FIFTY-ONE

THE GUY RAN OUT the door, hot on Andrea's tail, leaving his coffee sitting on the counter.

For a moment, I was too stunned to move. First, I'd learned that Andrea had been lying to me. Now Andrea might not even be Andrea. Well, she was if Andrea was her middle name, but she'd gone by "Julie" long enough that someone recognized her as such. Since the guy bore a resemblance to Libby, it didn't surprise me to say he was Andrea's husband. Her not-so-late husband who "died in a car accident."

Whoever he was, she didn't want to talk to him.

No matter how I regarded Andrea, if this guy wanted to insert himself into her life, then that meant he'd be in Libby's as well. After the shock of what just happened faded, protective instincts propelled me to get up from the table and follow the guy outside. Perhaps, there was a very good reason Andrea went by her middle name and moved far away. He could be dangerous.

The sun shined through the buildings. Puffy white clouds drifted out to sea. Seagulls squawked. Traffic moved on Ocean Boulevard at a steady pace.

To my left, the guy stood in front of the entrance to Coastal Décor, looking through the glass.

"Can I help you?" I asked.

He turned his attention away from the store's interior to face me. His face and body language hinted at an easygoing manner. Outwardly, he seemed...nice. Now, having the notion that he was married to Andrea, his blue eyes and curly blonde hair made Libby the spitting image of her dad. This guy was of average height and had coiled muscles. He wore a Kenny Chesney T-shirt, jeans, and flip-flops. A hint of a tattoo crept from the hem of the sleeve on his left bicep. He had the looks that if you were to see Andrea on his arm out in public, you wouldn't have been surprised.

They were on each other's level on the physical attractiveness side. The tenor of his voice caused him to stand out even more. Andrea had a great voice too. She said she used to sing while she was in college. Hearing this guy who claimed to be her husband caused me to envision them singing country duets in the corner of smoky bars together for rent money.

"Yeah, maybe." He tried the door. It was locked. He pointed at the window. "You know Julie?"

I cocked my head to the side. "I know her as Andrea."

He twisted his lip. "Naw. Like I said, that's her middle name. Wonder why she told you she went by Andrea?"

"Beats me," I confessed. "It seems that there's other things she didn't tell me about her."

He turned to look inside the window, scuffed his flip-flop on the wooden walkway, grinned, and said, "Like that she's married?"

I couldn't take it anymore. He said it a second time, erasing any doubt that I'd misheard. My jaw hung open. I said, "Excuse me," and sat down on the deck, folding my legs in front of me.

He took a step toward me. "Are you okay, sir?"

The guy, Andrea's—scratch that, Julie's—husband looked like he was a decade younger than me. I groaned. "Just needed to sit down. Please. My dad is 'Sir.' Call me Clark."

"Pleased to meet ya," the guy said. "I'm Owen."

I rubbed my hand across my forehead. "She told me you were dead."

The guy tightened his lips and tried to see Andrea inside the store. "Can't blame her for that. I was a good-fer-nothin' so-and-so."

Owen's accent was deep Missourian. Much like Andrea's. I couldn't call her Julie in my head just yet.

"Why would she say that?"

He glanced across the street at the ocean. "Guess she wanted to get as far away from me as possible after what happened."

"She said you died in a car accident late one night."

He looked down and rubbed his flip-flop on the deck. "May as well had. I screwed up big time, drinkin' and drivin' like that."

"What happened?"

He tried the door again with no success. I guessed he was hoping it would magically unlock. Like Andrea, he didn't seem like the elevator went to the top floor. As much as I hated to think that way of her, I had little patience for her at the moment.

He sat down on the deck and leaned his back against the wall. If he came here from Missouri, then he would be at the end of a long journey. Owen looked as weary as I felt. He smelled of cheap body spray.

If I had any questions as to the standing of my relationship with Andrea, finding out that she wasn't Andrea and that she'd lied about her husband's death were the final nails in that coffin. "It's like this," he started. "I had a drinkin' problem since high school. Couldn't help it. Runs in the family. Genes, I guess. Daddy died of cirrhosis when he was in his mid-40s."

"Sorry, man."

He waved me off. "He wasn't no good to me or Mama. I got exposed to it on weekends after high school football games and didn't quit until after the accident."

I snorted. "I played baseball in school. Know exactly how that goes. I remember the first time one of my teammates handed me a flask after practice."

He broke into a smile that could grace country music magazines. "Those were some wild times. Anyway, Julie and I were high school sweethearts and ended up going to college together. Somehow, we made it through without her getting pregnant, but almost the day we got our degrees, she got two blue lines on one of those tests."

"That's how it goes," I said. "Life can be so random."

He squinted. "I used to think everything was predestined. You know, like we didn't have a say in anything that happens to us. I remember thinking when she broke the news to me that this was how it was meant to be, whether I was ready to be a daddy or not."

"What changed your way of thinking?" This conversation, right here, right now, was just what I needed to take my mind off everything. Yes, it signaled the end of my relationship with Andrea, but it was the break my brain desperately needed.

"The car accident," he stated.

"What about it?"

He puckered his lips. "After Libby was born, Andrea stayed home most of the time with her. We liked to go out to a particular bar in the next town over on weekends, but I hadn't gone there in months. We got word that one of our old high school friends was in town and wanted to see us there. Andrea didn't go because she wasn't drinking at that time, and someone needed to stay home with Libby."

"How old was Libby when this happened?"

“Not quite six months old.”

I saw where this was going but didn’t interrupt his narrative.

“I had a few too many to drink,” he said, “but climbed behind the wheel of the truck anyway. It was one in the morning, so there was hardly anyone on the roads. Figured I’d be okay if I took it slow. Which I did.”

“Except?”

“Except that there was this one sharp turn out in the middle of the woods on this old country road where I cut it too close. There was a guy coming home from his shift at a truck stop out on the interstate who inched close to the line. We sideswiped each other. We both went into the trees on opposite sides of the road. Thank goodness I had on my seat belt. The guy's car didn't have airbags. Smacked his head hard enough on the steering wheel that it broke his skull. Died on the spot."

"And they got you for drinking and driving and manslaughter, right?"

He nodded. "Sure did. Second-degree vehicular manslaughter. Served four years at the Boonville Correctional Center. Guy was single. No kids. Lived in a trailer park near us. It was a small town, but somehow, we'd never met."

I didn't know how to respond to that, other than with, "That's a shame."

Owen flinched. "Yeah, it was. I sent letters to his mom to apologize, but she never responded. Not that I blame her."

Neither of us spoke for a few minutes. Tourists walked past our sitting positions on the deck. The aroma of baking waffle cones used to float past here, but with the creamery shut down, that was gone. If Karen was correct in the gossip that she had heard that wonderful smell might soon be replaced by the aromas of a restaurant. I might need bigger pants if I stayed outside the store. I'd miss Teresa's catcalls at I Heart MB Tees. She might have been a crusty, shriveled old woman with a smoker's voice and leopard print tights, but she was always an interesting character to speak to in a Boardwalk full of them.

Owen broke the silence. "She told you I was dead?"

"She did."

"Can't say I blame her. I would have too if I were in her shoes."

At the age Libby was when Owen ran the other man off the road, I doubted she had any memories of him. If Andrea had decided that she was going to tell Libby that her daddy had died in a car accident, then that's all the little girl would know.

"How long have you been out?"

"Three months, eleven days."

"How did you find her?"

"Her mom."

A smirk came to my lips as I looked out on the passing traffic of Ocean Boulevard. "Not surprising."

"What's not surprising?"

I looked over at him. Here we were, two men having a casual conversation, sitting on the deck of a small retail shopping center, oblivious to the swirl of people around us.

I laughed sadly. "That you learned where she lived from her mom. Andrea—Julie, sorry— told me she'd lost contact with her parents."

"Her mom didn't know where she lived, only where she worked."

Now the protective part of me wanted to surface. If this guy was an alcoholic and had spent years locked up with all sorts of despicable people, I didn't know if I wanted this guy around Libby, much less Andrea.

"How long have you been sober?"

Owen looked at stained wood slats overhanging the walkway. "Five years, three months, twenty-eight days." He glanced at his wristwatch. "And fourteen hours, give or take ten minutes."

"That's good," I said and meant it. "I know what you're doing here, but what's your goal?"

He looked me square in the eye. "I just want to see my wife and little girl. Especially Libby. I've felt so bad over not being there for her these early years. I thought of my baby girl not having a daddy every minute of every day in the pokey. About how I'd failed her and Julie as a father. I didn't want to be like my dad. I talked to a preacher while inside almost every day. Got religion while I was there. All I want to do now is to be the best dad and husband I can be. If they'll have me back."

Every word he said touched me right in the middle of my chest. This was love. This was a determination to shed his past and grow up and try to regain what he lost.

I said, "You know Libby doesn't know who you are."

He bit the middle of his lower lip. "I figured so but—look, Clark—I had to try. You know?"

I don't know if it was the sincerity in his voice or the verbal repentance of his wrongs, but I believed him. Libby needed a dad. Andr—Julie needed someone to be by her side, and it wasn't going to be me. Not after her possible involvement in all that I was trying not to think about at this moment. I'd seen enough of her natural side—the non-acting side now that I look back on it—to have developed some feelings for her. I had no future with her, but someone would, and I wanted that someone to have her and Libby's best interests at heart.

"I know," I said and got to my feet, dusting off the back of my shorts.

"What are you doing?" Owen asked from his seat on the deck.

I nodded at the door to Coastal Décor. "I'm going to go talk to her, unless she fled out the back door."

"I hadn't thought of that," he said. "She may have been gone this entire time."

"It's possible. I'll go check."

"How are you going to do that?"

I reached into my pocket. “I have a key.”

CHAPTER FIFTY-TWO

IT TOOK SOME CONVINCING, but Julie agreed to speak to Owen. She asked me to remain present in case he tried anything. I did her one better. I called Battles. He had a family obligation this evening but sent his partner Dame over to preside.

Libby wasn't present. The Silver Girls were watching her. It was for the best as the little girl shouldn't have been present for this extremely awkward meeting.

At first, Julie was reluctant to speak to Owen. I suggested in a firm tone for her to let him say his piece. Although I no longer trusted a word she said, the same wasn't true for me with her. She had no reason to think I would let harm come to her.

Dame came and watched without a word like he was Julie's bodyguard. Which, in this case, he was. I was more of a mediator.

After an hour, Owen convinced Julie that he had changed and wanted nothing more than to be back in her and Libby's lives.

Having my own problems to deal with, I left them to hash things out.

I went back inside my store and back to the table where I had been before Julie saw Owen and ran from the store. I was about to lay my head down on the table when, of all people, that goober Caleb sat down across from me.

He was the last person I wanted to see today. If I would have paid attention, I would have used my feet to hold the chair in place so he couldn't pull it out. I'd seen him on an increasing frequency that I didn't care for. Almost every time I'd seen him, he'd been half sloshed. He always wanted to talk to me about the cases I've investigated, but I kept blowing him off. There was something about him that seemed, I don't know, annoying.

He'd turned up like a bad penny since the Connor West case at the Wicked Tuna down on the 4th Avenue Pier when

I'd found West's Jeep Gladiator in the parking lot. Since then, I'd seen Caleb on the ramp leading to a cruise ship in Charleston, at a fashion gala at the Burroughs and Chapin Art Museum, at 1229 Shine in Market Common, and the other morning at the Swaying Palms Golf Club. I had avoided him like the plague, but it seemed like he was everywhere.

Right now, my defenses were down, and I had nowhere to go. If I really wanted to avoid him, I could run through the store and lock myself in the office in the back. If ever there was a time when I could humor this guy, it was now. Maybe he'd help take my mind off matters. Sometimes a distraction can help that deep recess in my brain come up with a solution to a case.

I looked at him and asked myself, "Why not?"

"Caleb," I said in a flat tone.

"Clark, I heard about your house, and I wanted to come offer my sympathy and see if there was anything I can do to help."

I looked at him with a blank expression. We didn't know each other, but he'd shown up to offer support out of the kindness of his heart. Maybe he wasn't such a bad guy after all. "Thank you. I'm not sure how you can help, but I appreciate you offering."

"Look," he said, "I know we haven't had a chance to talk. I'd love to pick your brain sometime about the cases you've done and about your writing. I read your first book and loved it. I'd put it up there with any Agatha Christie or James Patterson novel."

I wasn't sure I'd go that high with the praise, but he was entitled to his opinion. "Thank you." I said awkwardly. I'm not sure I'd ever get used to the compliments.

"Do you know how the fire started?" he asked.

"They say it was arson." The statement slipped out. I wasn't sure what came over me. Whether it was his kindness or the need to talk about everything that had happened to me over the last three years, I wanted to talk to someone not directly involved. It turned out that Caleb was a big coffee lover too, so I got up and poured both of us a cup.

After getting back in place and taking the first sip from my Mickey Mouse mug, I said, "Here's how it went down."

Then I told him everything, down to the last detail. He didn't say much but listened intently. Up close, his big blue eyes radiated intelligence and kindness, despite his goofy not-quite-Southern accent making me want to give him an IQ point deduction. Perhaps I'd been wrong in my assessment of Caleb.

When our mugs were almost empty, and I was done with my story, Caleb pursed his lips and said, "Do you know about Rosen's grandma?"

The hair on the back of my hands stood on end. "No, I don't."

"His grandma was British, and his grandpa was from up in Wilmington. They met and fell in love when he was stationed near there while in the military. She was originally from Cornwall."

I recalled the scenery and cliffs above the ocean from the show Poldark but wondered where he was going with this. It didn't take him long to get to the point. "It looks beautiful there."

"Agreed." He traced a finger on the table. "Anyway, his grandma comes from a long line of tea blenders."

Goosebumps peppered the skin on my arms. "You don't say."

He lowered his chin. "Yes. I do say. So, Rosen's grandma and grandpa returned to Wilmington but eventually bought a farm near here, outside of Aynor. They have a few kids, then he collapses one day while tilling a potato patch. Leaves her with little. Take a guess at what she did to support her kids and get by?"

It was a lightbulb moment for me. "She opened a tea shop."

"Bingo. Guess what Rosen's first job was?"

"Working in said tea shop."

"What do you think he learned to do while working there?"

I beat a fist on the table. My heart was racing. Everyone in the store blended into the background. It was just Caleb and I. "Learned to blend tea."

He drained the last of his coffee. "Double bingo."

CHAPTER FIFTY-THREE

"How do you know all of this?" I asked Caleb.

"Because my wife, Tasha, owns a bakery down on the MarshWalk and sources her tea from his grandma's business. She's dead, but Rosen's mom still runs the place."

"You don't say."

"I do say."

I stared at him, trying to think about what to do with this new information. I'd already sent the information about the digoxin in Moody's blood to Pendleton and Paulson.

"Is Rosen still involved in the business?" I asked.

"Not that I'm aware of," Caleb responded. "I think he just did it as a teenager before going to college."

Which was decades ago. It was possible Rosen hadn't forgotten how to blend tea. Maybe he hadn't stopped. Rosen had offered me tea yesterday in his office at the same time he asked if I wanted whiskey. He'd probably seen me in the parking lot from his window. I gulped. He wasn't drinking tea but had brewed some although no one but three of us were in the building and he had a drink of his own. Something told me it was prepared just for me. Was that from his poisonous blend stash?

Rosen had to have a source of ingredients, particularly foxgloves and oleanders. I had a good idea of where that might be.

"Two questions," I said. "Do you know how to pilot a drone, and do you know where Rosen lives?"

He squinted at me. "Uh, yes and yes. My wife has catered shindigs at his house. It's not oceanfront, but he lives up on the Dunes."

"Does he have a fence around his property?"

"Yup. A tall, six-foot brick wall."

Tall enough to keep people from seeing what might be growing in his backyard.

I held up three fingers. "Third question. Are you up to go on a mission with me that might be a little dangerous?"

He smiled. "In the words of Darkwing Duck, 'danger is my middle name.'"

***

We left the bookstore together. He'd parked his new Toyota SUV behind the store in the employee parking area, which he wasn't supposed to do. With the sun falling, we hurried back to Chris's apartment in Market Common, grabbed the drone, and sped up to the Dunes.

Caleb had gone with his wife to Rosen's place to deliver food for parties. That was the same excuse he gave to the guard at the gate to get into the neighborhood again. We wound through several streets before coming to one that dead-ended at a large community pool and recreation complex.

He pulled into a spot on the far end of the lot, away from other golf carts and vehicles. Now that I've been in close quarters with Caleb, he smelled of a mixture between smoked meats and Old Spice.

"Why did you park here?" I asked.

"Come on man," he said. "Haven't you ever read any spy novels?"

"Yes, I've read my fair share of Ludlum and Le Carre." If I wasn't so on edge, I'd laugh. The amount of research I had to do to write a book...

Caleb pointed to a house on the other side of the complex. A tall, brick wall surrounded it. "That's Rosen's place. I didn't want to pull up on the street in front of his house and start flying a drone. He or one of his neighbors would have the cops here in an instant."

"Ah, so we park here where the residents are occupied with their fun and act like we're doing some recreational drone flying."

"Bingo," he said.

Caleb seemed to really like that word.

"What do I need to do?"

He unbuckled his seat belt and opened the door. "Keep an eye out for anyone watching us. I can handle the drone."

“I’ll especially be watching for anyone looking at us and talking on a cell phone.”

“That would be our sure sign to beat it.”

According to Caleb, Chris’s drone had the latest technology with a 4K camera and stealth flight. It was lightweight and Caleb had it connected to his phone within seconds. The controller looked like a video game console. It had two antennas, two joysticks, several buttons, and a holder that held his phone in place below it. The screen showed his flight path, coordinates, and a live view from the camera.

Caleb got the drone in the air and started flying it in circles above our heads to get used to the controls and countering the breeze coming off the ocean. No one seemed to be paying any attention to us. A family passed by on bicycles but didn't look our way. The pool was packed, and all the chairs faced the pool, not us.

"Here we go," Caleb said, and shifted his left thumb on the joystick. The drone responded and started floating toward Rosen's property. I flicked my gaze between the recording phone screen and the drone, expecting a shotgun blast to blow it out of the sky, but that didn't happen.

"I've never been in the backyard," Caleb said as the drone came upon the fence. "Only as far as his dining room to deliver pastries. Here we go. Look."

He tilted the phone for me to get a better view of what the drone was seeing. A shimmering, blue swimming pool took up most of the backyard. Off to the side was a small garden. No one was visible.

In one corner of that garden were two different, but now familiar plants among others. One was about four feet tall and had purple flowers with downward-facing, funnel-shaped blooms. The other was taller and lay behind the first plant with stems that splayed outward. It had dark green leaves and lovely, clustered pink flowers blooming at the end of each stem.

The first was foxgloves and the second was oleanders.

If I wanted to craft custom blended tea with a sprinkle of poison, I wouldn't want those plants out in the open.

As Caleb would say, Bingo.

CHAPTER FIFTY-FOUR

With this new evidence in hand, it gave me vindication in knowing that I hadn't been jumping at shadows trying to piece together Autumn's potential murder these past fifteen months. After Caleb and I put the drone in the cargo hold of his Highlander, and climbed in the car, I had Caleb send the video to Pendleton and Paulson.

First, I called Moody's wife, Marge. "When Gomez and I talked to you at your house, you'd told us that your husband had gotten something to drink before going to sleep. Do you think it was herbal tea?"

"Yes, it could've been," she answered. "He drank that to help him sleep."

I squeezed the phone in my hand. "Thank you. That might have been what killed him."

Marge didn't seem like the kind of woman to get worked up about anything, but my comment caused her to raise her voice. "What?"

I explained what Caleb and I discovered and promised her and I would fill her in on the rest soon. "Can you go find the bag or container your husband got the tea from? We might need to have it tested."

"I can do that. Hang on." She took a moment before answering. "Seems like there was a little paper bag of tea leaves he left by the kettle. It's not labeled with a brand name."

It was all I could do to not let out a loud "Whoop!" in the vehicle. After hanging up, I called Paulson. She answered after half a ring. "I got some video from a drone. What am I looking at here?"

"That's mayor Rosen's backyard," I said. "The murder weapon that killed my wife, Ed Banner, and Moody are in the flowerbed."

She understood. "I'm on it."

I spoke to her as Caleb navigated through the neighborhood, back out to Kings Highway. I'd instructed him to return me to the bookstore. He said he'd do that, then he'd have to get home and help his wife get their son to bed.

"Also," I said, reflecting on my confrontation with Rosen at city hall, I told Paulson, "Check his office. You might find a poisonous tea blend there." I relayed to her what Caleb had told me about Rosen's family business.

"We will," she said.

I didn't know what she'd have to do to get a warrant to search the mayor's office, but something told me she could get it.

"Have you found Gomez?" I asked.

"We're still searching," she said.

My heart fell.

When I didn't respond, she said, "Don't lose hope. If she's out there, we'll find her."

"Thank you."

She breathed into the phone. "There's something else."

I pressed the phone harder against my ear. "What is it?"

"We found Lucien's truck."

"But not Lucien?"

"Affirmative. It was left in the parking lot of a boat launch in Conway. There are no cameras there, so we don't know if he got into another vehicle, hopped in a boat, or just walked away."

"Great."

"That's not all. Your neighbor across the street has one of those doorbell cameras. At around 1:33 this morning, he pulled up on the street in front of their house, which triggered the camera to start recording. It shows him getting out of the truck, looking around, then going to the back and preparing firebombs before moving around the truck and out of view. He returned a few seconds later and high-tailed it out of there. We saw the flames through your front windows before the recording clicked off."

In a way, her news was a big relief. "So, if nothing else, you can get him for arson."

"Correct," Paulson said. "But that's not all?"

"More good news?"

"Not exactly." She had missed my sarcasm.

"What is it?"

"It's Rosen."

"What about him?"

"He's disappeared."

***

Caleb dropped me and the drone off at Myrtle Beach Reads ten minutes before closing. The store was empty. Humphrey had already left for the day. Karen counted the money from the register till. Her phone was on the counter, playing a Turkish soap opera.

I smiled at her little addiction. She was so distracted by the video and counting coins that she didn't notice me approaching the counter. "What did I tell you about watching those while on the clock?"

She jolted and put a hand on her chest. "Gracious, Clark. You scared me!"

"Sorry," I said, not meaning it.

A zipper pouch we used to take deposits to the bank sat on the counter next to the phone. Karen had already counted out the excess cash from the till and stuffed it in there after marking it down. The pouch bulged.

"Busy day?" I asked.

"Incredibly. You were here. You saw how many people were in here. Kept Humphrey busy over there at the coffee bar and out of my hair."

I barely noticed the amount of foot traffic during the times I was here earlier. "Yeah. Sorry, I had other things on my mind."

She reached out and grabbed my hand. Hers was warm. "I'm so sorry about what happened to your home, Clark. Forgive me for forgetting about what you've gone through today."

I patted her hand on mine. "Don't mention it. You've been busy and had your mind on other things when I walked in."

Then the power went off in the store, plunging us into darkness. Karen gasped. The video on her phone glowed. I looked at the front of the store and then the back, listening.

"Shut that video off, duck down behind the counter, and call 911," I whispered in an urgent tone to Karen.

The weather was pleasant outside in the fading daylight. Even amid the strongest storms, the power here rarely went out, a credit to the power company. A glance out the front window told me that we might be the only ones without power. Lights still shone in the surrounding businesses.

The bell on the front door chimed at the same time the back door slammed open. I hadn't locked the front door after I'd entered because my rule was not to do that until the exact minute it was time to close. You never knew when a last-minute shopper would come in and want an armful of books. If the posted closing time was seven o'clock, that's how long we stayed open.

The back door was a different matter. It was supposed to have been bolted shut. However, if someone got through the back door at Garden City Reads to spray paint the windows, that same person likely knew how to do the same here. It didn't take long for both men to reveal themselves, and I wasn't in the least bit shocked by either of them.

Despite the lack of surprise, my blood ran cold. Fading sunlight streamed in through the front windows. The outlines of books, tables, and fixtures were still visible in the dimness. I was standing in the middle of the store. The men had already seen me. There was no hiding.

Karen was huddled down behind the counter, speaking in quiet but rushed words to a dispatcher. "I don't know what's going on, but someone just shut off the power and broke in through the back door."

I was sure it was me they wanted to see. They weren't here to buy books.

"We're closed!" I shouted to the newcomers and headed to the front, angling away from Karen's hiding place.

Lucien maneuvered around a shelf coming from the back with a gun in his hand, pointing at me. We were near the front of the store, with Lucien and Rosen standing next to each other in front of me. Lucien had a rectangle of gauze taped to his forehead. The mayor was dressed in a dark jogging outfit and had his back to the street. Anyone passing by wouldn't recognize him.

"That's fine," Rosen said. "You're about to be closed. Permanently."

CHAPTER FIFTY-FIVE

WITH THE POWER SHUT off, that meant that the security cameras were also offline. Therefore, Rosen's presence wouldn't be recorded.

He had other bad news for me. "Don't even think about calling 911. I paid off the dispatcher working tonight. All calls coming from this location will be recorded as pranks. Told her you were having a wild party and wanted to cause trouble for me."

Pain stabbed into my abdomen. Not from an exterior blow, but from my stomach suddenly wanting to expel what it contained.

My eyes didn't leave the gun in Lucien's hand. Rosen himself didn't pose any physical threat to me. He was too smart to brandish a weapon. That's what Lucien was here for.

The store was quiet. Not even the continuous hum of the air conditioning was going.

Rosen and Lucien had to know that with whatever they were doing here, they didn't have much time. I had to keep talking and hope someone would come to help.

Deep down, it was obvious that they weren't here to discuss the situation.

The matter had come to a head and the only way out of trouble for them was to silence me.

But I held a few cards up my sleeve they didn't know about.

"You know SLED and the Sheriff's office is out looking for you two, right?"

"I'm aware of that," Rosen sneered. "We won't be here long, then we're going to slip away where we can't be found. You won't be around to learn if they ever find us."

I cursed myself for not thinking to tell Karen to record this conversation. I wasn't sure how far away a phone microphone could pick up three people talking, but there was a chance to get it on audio. I didn't want to risk glancing back at the counter at Karen and draw attention to her presence.

“I know how you did it,” I said to Rosen, stalling for time.

With a smug set of his jaw, he asked, “Oh, how’s that?”

“You poisoned them with tea.”

Rosen’s mouth formed an evil grin. He was too savvy to come right out and admit to it.

“Oh, I did, did I? Ludicrous.”

“That’s right. You did. I think you bribed Judge Whitley to make a cup of tea using your special blend for Autumn before leaving the courthouse that night. The judge may not have known what was in the tea but figured it out afterward. Then you did the same to Banner and Moody.

Probably because they knew too much or were going to blow your secret."

Rosen snarled. "Oh, what secret was that?"

Lucien held the gun steady. He hadn't spoken yet.

I tried to ignore him as much as possible and said to Rosen, "That you were part of the group who built the Castello delle Onde and dug up some historic artifacts. You didn't want a proper excavation to delay the building's completion date. My guess is that you already had buyers and renters for the various units inside and didn't want to put off getting their money."

"That's a reasonable guess," Rosen said, "but complete nonsense."

I cocked an eyebrow. “Is it? You tried to do the same thing on St. Grant’s. Why wouldn’t you do that here too?”

He didn’t answer. I was surprised he hadn’t told Lucien to shoot me yet. Maybe he was seeing what all I had uncovered so he could try to kick sand to cover his tracks.

I turned to Lucien. “Let me guess. You cut your face up while driving Gina’s car through the woods and ditching in a pond.”

He involuntarily raised his free hand to touch the thick bandage. That’s all I needed to see to know he was the one behind crashing Gomez’s car into the water.

Still trying to keep control of the conversation, if you could call it that, I said to Lucien, "How did you get involved in all of this? Is he bribing you, or were you jealous that your fiancée and I made out?"

Lucien's eyes darted to Rosen and back to me. The gun didn't waver, but his finger tensed on the trigger. Through clenched teeth, he spat out a simple question, "What?"

"Easy. Not yet," Rosen said, holding out a hand toward Lucien like a matador trying to stop a bull from charging. "I didn't have to bribe Lucien for anything. Let's just say I learned about something he'd done when he used to work patrol that would land him in jail for a long, long time if it were discovered, something only he and I know about. Ed Banner knew what Lucien did too, but he's dead."

I wasn't sure what Lucien had done to serve as Rosen's gutless flunky, but it might have been what got Banner killed. What "it" was, I may never know.

At this point, I wasn't confident help would be coming. An idea formed in the base of my brain as I tried to edge over a few inches to the special classic book display at the front of the store.

To Rosen, I said, "Tell me. There's no point in denying what you did. You're going to kill me now. The three of us know this. Why did you do it?"

He grinned. "The same reason anyone does anything. Money."

His admission caused a fire to light deep inside me. This man and his pure greed—greed that would bring him to kill multiple people, especially Autumn—sickened me. I spit on his Italian leather shoes.

Rosen looked down at the spittle spreading out over the front of one of his expensive shoes, his face grimaced, then as his gaze darted back at me, he shifted into a bemused smile. “You’re nothing but a fly in the ointment.” He looked over at Lucien and waved a hand going from the gun to me. “Go ahead. We have a plane to catch.”

“With pleasure,” Lucien said in his best tough-guy voice.

He raised the gun and pointed it at my face. It always sounds so cliché in books and TV shows, but my life literally flashed in front of my eyes, fast memories moving through my mind in milliseconds. Through it all, I mostly saw Autumn—the first time I met her, our first date, our wedding, opening Myrtle Beach Reads together, and the night I learned the news of her death. Then the images shifted to Gomez. Our first awkward meeting when I found Paige Whitaker's body. Her natural beauty caught my attention the first time I saw her in normal clothes at the Bar-B-Cue House in Surfside. That jaw-dropping green dress she wore to the fashion gala at the Burroughs and Chapin Art Museum. The time I rode with her to Charleston in pursuit of Brian and Shelly, and her singing along to 90's rock music on the radio. The soundtrack of my youth. And lastly, the steamy, all-too brief make out session we had in her car on the return trip.

Then, like a dream come to life, the image was real. I did see Gomez.

She was outside the window of the bookstore looking in. Her clothes, the same ones she was wearing the last time I saw her, were tattered and torn. Her face was bruised, and her hair was a mess, but my goodness, her arrival could never be sexier than this moment.

The best news for me? She had a gun in her hand.

CHAPTER FIFTY-SIX

SHE FIRED THE GUN through the window. It shattered.

The bullet missed Lucien and embedded itself in a shelf filled with Lee Child thrillers to my left. He flinched and instinctively turned, firing blindly in the direction from which the bullet came.

Gomez cried out and went down.

Rosen's jaw went slack. With him distracted, I reached over to the book display and grabbed a heavy, thick hardcover of Moby Dick and slammed it across the side of Lucien's head like I was swinging for the fences. He dropped like a sack of potatoes. The blow knocked him out cold.

I held the book in my hands for a moment and faced Rosen. He held his hands up. The door was directly behind him. All he had to do was turn, open it, and dart out the door.

Gomez growled in pain from the walkway.

My stomach dropped hearing her in pain. And yet, it meant she was alive.

Rosen twitched as if he might act.

I only had one method of keeping Rosen in place, and it wasn't with a brick of a book

I reached behind my back and pulled the gun Gomez had given me from my waistband and pointed it at the mayor of Myrtle Beach.

“Don’t move,” I commanded.

He looked down at the gun but didn’t panic. “Oh, what are you going to do? Shoot me? If you do that, then you’re no better than me.”

A motion behind Rosen gave me all the comfort in the world.

“I don’t have to. You’re going down, Rosen. You killed my wife, Banner, and Moody, and got an officer shot. I have proof, made sure many others were told, and you have nowhere to run.”

"Shows what you know." He ignored the gun in my hands. With an all-too-confident smirk, he said, "I'm out of here."

Rosen started to turn to leave, but Battles and Dame crashed through the front door at the same time, freezing the mayor in his tracks.

They both had their guns drawn on him.

"Hold it right there," Battles ordered. "Sid Rosen, I'm placing you under arrest for the murders of Autumn Thomas, Edward Banner, and Phil Moody."

"Among other crimes," Dame added.

Rosen raised his hands in surrender as Battles grabbed his hand, twisted it behind his back, turning him toward me as he grabbed the other wrist to lock him in handcuffs.

The soon-to-be former mayor shook in rage, hiding his embarrassment of having cuffs slapped on him. His grand scheme was in ruins. Still, he had the gall to say to me, “Watch your back, Clark. I have longer arms than you know, and I’ll be out on the street before you know it.”

I stood my ground. “Actually, it’s you who should watch your back. How many of those convicts at the state pen got there under your watch? Besides, you look like you haven’t had a hard day of work in your life. I bet they’ll remind you of that.”

I was done with him and had more important matters to attend to. I handed Dame the gun and rushed over to Gomez.

Her eyes were squeezed shut. She had one hand grasping her left shoulder.

Blood seeped around it and fell on the wood deck.

Sirens rang out in the distance.

I went behind Gomez and cradled her in my arms, giving her a way to elevate her shoulder.

“I’m hit,” she said.

“You’re still alive. You’re going to be okay.”

Gomez held one of my hands over her stomach and the other over her bullet wound. I had her in my arms the same way I did on the dock at the Dunes Marina on Sunday when we had been under gunfire.

She looked over her good shoulder at me with trembling lips. Her face was pale. “I love you.”

I tenderly kissed her forehead. It was cool to the touch. “I love you, too.”

CHAPTER FIFTY-SEVEN

I DIDN'T REALIZE IT at the time, but Officer Dame told me later that I had tears of joy streaming from my eyes at this point. He also laughed and said that I couldn't have fired the gun at anyone. Gomez had handed me an empty gun with the safety on, knowing I didn't have a clue. The safety was still on when I had it pointed at Rosen. Gomez had given it to me for my peace of mind more than anything else.

Lucien was taken away under police supervision to the hospital where he was treated for a concussion. Rosen was hauled to the police station in the back of a squad car. Good riddance to bad rubbish. Apparently, my unbreakable lock fell victim to a drill by Lucien's unsavory skills that bested thieves. I had to replace it that night, paying for an emergency locksmith to do so.

Paulson had already executed a search warrant on Rosen's office at city hall and found a tea blend in a sealed bag in his desk. It was the same type of tea and pouch Marge had found in her kitchen. They had a video doorbell that, when they went back and looked at camera footage from the night of his death, found someone who matched Rosen's size wearing the same jogging outfit he wore when he came to kill me at the bookstore.

During the weeks that followed, Judge Whitley confessed to accepting a bribe to brush the artifacts found during the lot clearing for the Castello delle Onde under the rug. She had shredded the document submitted by the shift supervisor at the construction site. After our meeting in the parking lot, her conscience wouldn't keep her from helping, even if it meant criminal charges would be leveled against her. At the same time, Rosen had given the judge a tea blend to make for Autumn. With the crazy week they were having inside and outside the courtroom, Whitley didn't stop to consider that the blend might have been a foul mixture until after Autumn died at her desk. Whitley would have to live with what she'd done, inadvertently poisoning Autumn. For three years, and it had eaten away at her conscience.

With a plea bargain for a reduced sentence by Zach's murderer, the Feds untangled enough of the trail left behind by the various shell corporations owned by Zach and directed by the ex-mayor to bring charges of racketeering, tax evasion, and several other federal charges against Rosen and Zach's businesses. Behind bars is eventually where Rosen wound up as he awaited sentencing and his trial. With the amount of evidence we had found, he would never see the outside world again. He'd ruined countless lives during his mission to acquire power and wealth. It would never bring back our loved ones, but all who'd suffered at his hand would get the last, bitter laugh.

Unfortunately, it took surgery to repair Gomez's shoulder. The bullet had broken her clavicle. The surgeon said she might not ever regain her full range of motion in that arm. She'd have to go through weeks of rehabilitation. The flipside of that was, she'd get an early retirement from the police department with paid healthcare and a full pension. She told me that, after what happened before Lucien shot her, she would have quit anyway. Now? They're going to pay her not to work.

Speaking of Lucien, he was likely going to spend years in jail too. While he didn't murder anyone, he'd been an accomplice and committed other crimes as well, several charges of obstruction of justice. I'd always disliked the man, but now even more so because of what he had done to Gomez. After she had left me at the motel the other night, she'd gone home to confront Lucien, but he'd overpowered her and tied her up, leaving her locked in the attic above their townhome. They lived in an end unit, and the place next door was vacant. Lucien had placed a gag in her mouth so no one could hear her scream. He'd tied her to a chair with ropes. Gomez had eventually been able to work herself loose and escape. The rope burns on her wrists would leave scars.

After she'd gotten out of the attic, she'd called Battles and told him to grab Dame and meet her at the bookstore. She'd placed another tracking device of her own on the gas tank of my Jeep when I hadn't been looking, unaware that Lucien had placed another in one of the wheel wells. It was for my protection, she said.

I couldn't complain.

In between all that, I attended Phil Moody's funeral at a lovely church off Grissom Parkway. The pews were packed with mourners who came out to pay their respects. I sat in the third row with Gina. She wore a sling on the arm where the bullet struck to the event and a tasteful black dress. Moody's numerous family members were all in attendance. I recognized many of them from when Gina and I had gone to his house to speak to Marge.

As I offered Gina a tissue, and looked down at my shoes, I reflected on the late detective and what he'd done in setting the whole endgame in motion. I'll never be able to express my gratitude to the man. I didn't learn until after his death that he was involved in Rosen's dealings, but the fact Moody wanted to turn on the man pulling the strings and died trying to help me is something astounding that I'll be eternally grateful for.

Through all the tears around me, I smiled. Then chuckled. Gina glared at me, no doubt wondering what in the world I could be laughing at on this solemn occasion. If we were going to be together, she'd have to accept that sometimes...I marched to the beat of a different drummer.

I didn't care. With the smile engraved on my face, I did my best to impersonate Moody, met her eyes, shrugged, and grunted.

CHAPTER FIFTY-EIGHT

I remained by Gomez's bedside for the week she was in the hospital. They couldn't have pried me away. I gave two tell-all interviews. One to Taylor Maresca at WMBF, and another with Greg Rowles on Carolina AM, but that was all I wanted to do with the media. My third media contact, Erica Sullivan, had moved onto bigger and better things in Atlanta.

I called my agent and told her I wouldn't have my book done in time. I had a great excuse, but now that this chapter in my life had ended, I had many great stories to tell. The publisher was sympathetic, knowing that what happened had stirred up national attention. Now that my name was out there, and it was known that I was a mystery author too, they figured that my next book would be a veritable printing press for money.

No pressure there.

The insurance company and everyone involved with the reconstruction of my house worked together to get the project started. Since my neighborhood doesn't have cookie-cutter houses like many of the communities that popped up in the Grand Strand in recent years, I was able to hire a custom home builder for the job. I picked a floor plan similar to the old house, but with a more modern exterior. It would be a fresh start, but still remind me of the house where Autumn and I used to live. Of course, there could be someone else sharing the house with me eventually...

The builder said it would take upwards of six months to complete.

Andrea/Julie and I had the "breakup" conversation that wasn't necessary at that point. She and Owen had hashed it out. She told me Owen truly was a great dad to Libby during her first six months of her life. Owen had been a good, hard-working husband too. He convinced her that he was the same man, just more mature. He hadn't had a drop of alcohol since the night of the accident. He'd had training as an electrician while in prison and hoped to find work as an apprentice. With the housing boom happening in the Grand Strand, that shouldn't be a problem. I might even be able to help him with some of my connections.

Bo's house sold in California, netting him a nice nest egg and offering him the chance at a new life. He decided to try offering his computer skills to private detectives. I was sure he would do well.

Officers Dame and Battles applied and were promoted to detective on the MBPD. Two other experienced detectives filled the gaping holes left by Moody's death and Gomez's exit. My cop friends would start at the bottom, but I was confident they'd make a good team.

It turned out that our suspicions of Chief Miller were unfounded. We learned after an Internal Affairs inquiry that, while some of the early decisions she made in her new role were questionable, they weren't influenced by Rosen or other parties. She was still adapting her management style to her new larger role after coming from the Loris police department.

During the long days in the hospital, Gomez and I discussed what we each wanted to do next. There was no way she'd go back to the home she shared with Lucien. I had no home to go to yet. She didn't have a job, and I was fortunate enough to have quality employees to run both of my bookstores. For the trauma Karen suffered while being in the store during the shootout, I gave her a week's paid vacation and two tickets for her and her husband to Cancun. Garden City Reads finally opened on schedule over Labor Day weekend to much fanfare. Winona was already doing a wonderful job as the store manager. That fact didn't surprise me.

Gina and I decided to go on a long trip together, just the two of us.

After all that had happened, we both needed a vacation.

We stayed in Chris's apartment during Gomez's rehab. We weren't going anywhere until that was completed. After two weeks, her physical therapist said Gomez should get her full range of motion back in her shoulder. It might take a while to get there. That was fine. We hoped Gomez wasn't going to have to pull a gun on a suspect in a hurry ever again. Knowing the way my life had gone over the past year, I somehow doubted we'd be so lucky.

Gomez and I had spent a good number of evenings with my parents. Both of hers had passed away a while back. She had a younger sister, a single mom with a young son, still living in New Jersey. They came and stayed a week before heading home for the start of the school year.

During Gomez's recovery, I contacted Antonio Bianchi on St. Grant's Island. I told him what had happened here in Myrtle Beach and how the investigation ended up involving a bribery scandal from before he'd moved there.

He said he lived on a bay in a nice house with four bedrooms right on the water and invited me to come visit anytime.

We took him up on his offer, starting the day after the last session of Gomez's physical therapy.

***

Poetically, my new life began on the first day of Autumn. My wife, Autumn, would always hold a piece of my heart that would never be replaced or repaired. But it comforted me to know that, not only had her killer been caught, but I had also helped bring him to justice.

This morning before dawn, Bo had dropped Gomez and I off at the Myrtle Beach International Airport where we hopped on a short flight to Atlanta and, after a three-hour layover, got a connecting flight to Guadeloupe. Gomez and I held hands the entire time.

After disembarking from the small plane at our next-to-last destination, we headed for the nearby harbor. We stood on the bow of a water taxi, taking us from the picture-perfect island to the smaller St. Grant's. I'd never seen such blue waters and beautiful beaches. The sun was scorching, but the serenity of the islands caused me to ignore the sweat dripping down my back.

St. Grant's came into view after twenty minutes in the waters of the Caribbean. A peak from a long dormant volcano poked above the horizon. The summit was covered in lush greenery. Before long, seagulls circled in the air above our boat. Dolphins swam alongside, jumping out of and back in the water, as though they were escorting Gomez and me to our new lives together. Her hand squeezed mine in anticipation.

Our boat entered the harbor of a small fishing village. The shoreline curved away in both directions as far as the eye could see. Tall palm trees, pregnant with coconuts, covered the island. Colorful tropical birds made their homes here. Their calls were music to my ears. It was a birdwatcher's paradise.

A variety of boats floated on the tide, near land. Some were fishing trawlers. Others were sailboats used for recreation. Huts and other wooden structures made up the town. We were below the imaginary line where hurricanes traveled. The last one that hit St. Grants happened during the 1960s.

At long last, our boat approached a dock where several people waited for a return trip back to Guadeloupe.

Farther down the dock, I spotted Antonio shouting and waving his arms at us. A young woman with tan skin and dark hair wearing a thin blue sundress stood beside him, likewise with a smile on her face.

The boat bumped against the dock. A deckhand hopped onto the deck and tied a rope to a metal cleat to hold it in place. The captain came out after killing the engines and extended a wide plank of wood, connecting the boat to the dock.

I grabbed our bags and smiled at Gomez.

She placed a hand on my hip and kissed me. "I love you."

"Love you too."

Those words had been repeated many times to each other over the last few weeks, but we couldn't help it. It was beyond true. We'd gone through the fire with each other in a way most couples never do. I would never wish what happened to us on anyone.

I hefted a bag over my shoulder as the captain helped Gomez cross from the water taxi to land. I followed her down the dock to where Antonio and his companion stood.

His dark, curly hair had grown unruly since his days as a high-powered insurance salesman. He'd grown a beard and lost weight too. He sported a tan that indicated an outdoor way of life. From all outward appearances, island life had treated him well.

We embraced each other before he introduced us to his fiancé, Dominique. She and I shook hands. Gomez gave her a light hug.

“Welcome to St. Grant’s,” Antonio said. “We’re so glad to have you.”

“Thank you,” I said. “This place is more beautiful than you described.”

He beamed. “Words can’t do it justice, my friend.” To Gomez, he said, “It’s nice seeing you again now that you’re not investigating me as a murder suspect. I’m so glad you’re okay.”

Gomez laughed, which she'd done more of in recent weeks. "Appreciate it. I'm glad I'm okay too."

There was an awkward moment where no one had anything to say or had made a move to leave the dock. One thing that had struck me about the island was the tropical fragrances wafting through the air. The place smelled wonderful.

Just then, my nose picked up a distinct heavenly aroma.

"What do you want to do now?" Antonio said.

He, Dominique, and Gomez all looked at me for an answer.

At the end of the dock was an open-air Tiki hut topped with a thatch roof. It had to be the center of the aroma my nose had picked up.

I drew a deep breath and smiled. “Let’s go get some coffee.”

EPILOGUE

RAIN SPLATTERED ON THE sidewalk as the former prisoner stepped through the prison's front gate. A shrub-lined walkway, leading to an expansive parking lot, lay in front of him. This was his first moment of freedom in over thirty years. The ratty denim jacket he wore was already soaked, as was the green canvas duffle bag containing all his worldly possessions. The rain caused dark hair to stick to his face, forcing him to brush it aside with his fingers.

The East Jersey State Prison was in Rahway, but most people referred to it as "Rahway Prison." Barbed wire spiraled across a twenty-foot-tall chain-link fence that extended for a hundred yards in both directions behind him. From above, the prison looked like four multi-story red-brick wings radiating diagonally from a dome at the center. If an architect combined the grandeur of a state capital building with the drab stylings of an inner-city high school, it would resemble the Rahway Prison.

The now ex-con took a deep breath, taking in his first smells of freedom. It smelled of car exhaust and wet pavement.

Shock didn't begin to describe the emotions he'd felt when he received news from the warden of someone wanting him to file a habeas corpus petition to challenge the legal basis for his detention. Before that, he had no clue it was even a possibility. He'd already resigned himself to the fate that he would die inside the prison walls. Then an attorney had showed up with a thick file on the inmate's original case from three decades ago. He said an interested party requested his law firm to investigate the evidence surrounding the inmate's conviction.

The prisoner had agreed to let them reopen the case. He had nothing to lose. After months of court proceedings, it had been determined that the investigating detective had wrongfully obtained evidence through an illegal search. A search that had discovered the murder weapon.

Most of the players who had been involved in the case were dead or close to it and had little memory of the proceedings. The judge ruled in the inmate's favor and granted him his release.

However, the inmate remained in the dark about how or why this mysterious benefactor took an interest in his case, much less who the person was.

The prospect of getting out of prison had its perks but also scared him. He had no family. A reentry program at the prison prepared him for life outside the prison walls. Doctors gave him a clean bill of health. Therapists checked to make sure he was mentally prepared for freedom. An apartment was leased to him, and a bank account was created all through the help of his benefactor.

He looked around. A white Mercedes SUV idled at the end of the path. Rain fell in sheets. The rear door facing him opened as he approached, exposing an empty leather seat. The front passenger side window cracked open enough for the newly freed man to see the person inside.

The former prisoner cocked his head. "Didn't expect to see you out here."

Tendrils of gray cigar smoke escaped the Mercedes's interior and disappeared in the rain. With a strained voice, the passenger said, "A simple 'Thank you' would suffice."

Drawing closer, the ex-con hoisted the canvas bag over his shoulder, sending drops of water flying. "You're responsible for getting me out?"

The other man leveled his gaze. "I wouldn't be sitting here in this wretched rainstorm if I didn't have a score to settle."

The prisoner scuffed a foot on the pavement. "I suppose not." Then, "Thank you."

"Don't mention it," the passenger said. "Get in. You're letting my seats get wet. We've got work to do."

Silently, the man tossed his duffle bag into the car floor and climbed inside. The Mercedes sped away.

During the thirty-plus years he'd spent in a jail cell, not a day went by without him pondering how he would kill the detective who had put him away. Thoughts of revenge consumed him. He'd kept the anger under control and didn't let it show.

Now he could.

If the detective who put him away were still alive, he'd find him and kill him. If not, then the cop's family would suffer. Maybe they all would anyway. He hated the detective that much.

The snake detective's name was Severino Gomez.

To Be Continued...

ACKNOWLEDGEMENTS

Writing is by itself a lonely endeavor, but that doesn't mean that an author does everything themself. I'd like to thank Dr. Stephanie Rose for being my go-to for medical and murdery advice. Retired police officer Mike Dame always available to answer any procedural questions. If he doesn't know the answer to a specific, he has a plethora of contacts who can get me answers within minutes. Thank you all.

Brian Schmitt of the Myrtle Beach Downtown Redevelopment Corporation was a huge resource in laying out the vision of the changes coming to revitalize that area. This book was written with some of those future updates to streets and buildings already implemented.

The Michelle Shumpert described at City Hall is indeed the real Chief Financial Officer of Myrtle Beach. I thank her for the tour and hospitality during my unexpected visit to her offices. Preservation Consultant, Janie Campbell, helped me sort out what happens when artifacts are discovered.

As always, I want to thank my editor, Lisa Borne Graves, and my beta reading team of Angela Barnhardt, Darren Bourn, Rob Ledger, Haley Mellert, Karen Polhemus (aka: Courthouse Karen), Jatana Royster, and my mom.

All mistakes are mine.

All books in the series are available on Amazon, Barnes and Noble, Books-a-Million, and wherever books are sold.

Don’t see them in your local store or library? Ask the bookseller or librarian to order them for you.

Learn more on his website at calebwygal.com.

ABOUT THE AUTHOR

Caleb is a member of the International Thriller Writers, Mystery Writers of America, and Southeastern Writers Association, the author of eleven novels, woodworker, occasional golfer, reacher of things on high shelves, beach walker, shark tooth finder, and munchkin wrangler.

His two Lucas Caine Adventure novels, Blackbeard's Lost Treasure and The Search for the Fountain of Youth, were both Semi-Finalists for the Clive Cussler Adventure Awards Competition.

He is currently at work on the next book in the Myrtle Beach Mystery Series.

He lives in Myrtle Beach with his wife and son (the munchkin).

Milton Keynes UK
Ingram Content Group UK Ltd.
UKHW041418270924
1887UKWH00028B/66

9 798330 410095